DEADLY
MEMORIES

A Novel

S. D. O'Donnell

WINDSTORM BOOKS

Deadly Memories
by S. D. O'Donnell

WindStorm Books
P.O. Box 7438
Broomfield, CO
80021

For more information about this book, visit www. sdodonnell.com

Edition ISBNs

Trade Paperback ISBN 978-0-9884556-0-3

E-book ISBN 978-0-9884556-1-0

Cover Design by Pete Garceau
Book Design by Christopher Fisher

For my father
You've been gone awhile but are still always with me

DEADLY
MEMORIES

Prologue

SHE HUDDLED ON DAMP EARTH, knees to her chest, back pressed against something rough and wet, comforted by the smallness of her retreat. A thin cold film of moisture enveloped her skin. Why? When had that happened?

Honking geese broke the silence, reminded her that a bigger world still thrived, outside.

Dew. That's what the film of moisture was.

She didn't want the night to end, wanted to stay in the quiet, alone in the darkness, the smallness. She heard splashes, a duck's quack, piercing yips that passed and faded into the distance.

Each sound scraped against her nerves.

Wet drops traced down her checks. Fat drops. Not dew. She heard a sob and realized it was hers.

Someone called out, "Hello?"

She gasped.

"Are you okay?"

She needed a new place to hide, one where morning couldn't reach her. Without moving, without thinking, she escaped to a safer, even smaller place.

CHAPTER 1

SAUL BECKER SURFED THE WASTELAND of early morning television, one of his more successful tactics for overcoming insomnia. When that didn't work, he sat for hours in the dark, thoughts tumbling through his head like clothes in the dryer.

He'd finally achieved a kind of mental numbness he would have happily called sleep when a shrill noise brought him out of his chair. He yanked a pistol from the end table drawer before the phone rang a second time. Feeling like an idiot, he glanced at the clock as he picked up the receiver. It was seven thirty.

"What?" he said, his voice like gravel.

It was his elderly neighbor, Mrs. Blackstone. Her voice sounded an octave higher than normal as she rattled off something he didn't quite follow.

"Say again?"

He slid his custom Colt Series 70 M1911A2 back into the drawer.

"Get down here," she said. "There's a lady crying inside the tree."

***

Saul took a moment to stretch in the cool August morning before jogging down to the lake behind his townhome. He could see the Rocky Mountains on the western horizon, the early morning air north of Denver still clear enough to make the foothills seem closer than they really were.

He worked hard to stay in shape, proud to still be lean and muscled as he edged over forty. He had fair skin, sky-blue eyes, and sandy hair with hints of red. Add his freckles, and he looked a stereotypical Irishman.

The townhomes were built on top of a hill and he kept his stride short as he ran down the trail to the lake. When he got close, he saw Mrs. Blackstone pacing beside a huge cotton-wood tree. Two patrol cops watched from fifty feet away. They jerked around at the sound of his approach, hands moving toward the service pistols at their waists. Saul braked to a walk, holding his hands up, palms out.

When he was close enough to identify who they were, presuming they could do the same, he lowered his hands and called out a greeting.

"Roan. Mathews. Been a while."

Roan's height made Saul's 6'4" look short and Roan was built to intimidate. Mathews was barely 5' 10" and looked more like a geek than a cop, right down to the thick glasses sitting on the bottom of his nose.

"Becker." Roan rubbed a hand across the stubble on his chin. His palm didn't hide a slight frown. "What're you doing here?"

"That's my neighbor." Saul nodded at the white-haired woman next to the tree, who interrupted her pacing to dab at her eyes with the edge of a thick shawl. "She called me, I told her to call you."

"So we've got you to thank for this end-of-shift call," Roan said.

"Thank the woman she found. You seen her yet?"

Mathews rolled his eyes. "We were just wondering if your neighbor isn't quite right in her head. Maybe what we really need here is the loony toon squad."

"Why?" Saul said.

A yawn cut off Roan's snicker. "She pointed to the tree and yelled, 'She's in there.' What would you think?"

"That the woman is inside the tree."

Saul sprinted down the path and circled around to the side of the tree where Mrs. Blackstone waited.

"Finally." She gestured at the tree. "Go see if she's okay."

Several years prior a lightning-induced fire had burned through about five feet of the trunk's interior from the ground up, creating a hollow that still smelled of stale smoke, and a black-rimmed hole that allowed entrance.

Saul ducked inside and squatted for a minute to let his eyes adjust to the shadows. A woman sat with her legs pulled up, her arms wrapped around them, and her face buried between her knees.

She didn't move when Saul said hello. She didn't move when he tugged gently on her arm.

"Well?" Roan's voice sounded muffled. "What's in there?"

"I told you already," Mrs. Blackstone said. "It's a woman. She was crying." Saul heard impatience in her answer.

"Not crying anymore." Saul backed out of the tree. "Don't think she's all there mentally."

"You couldn't have brought her out with you?" Mathews said.

Saul shrugged. "I gave her a tug. She didn't want to come."

"Aw, shit." Roan pressed his hand against the rough bark as he bent over, looking as if he had folded himself in half. He emitted a low whistle. "This is your job, Mathews. I won't fit."

Mathews took his turn to look inside.

"If I do this myself," he said as he crawled into the tree, "you owe me big time."

From outside, they heard Mathew's grunts, interspersed with a string of curses.

"Do something," Mrs. Blackstone said, with a light push on Saul's shoulder.

"You know I don't do this for a living anymore."

"Hey!" Mathews yelled. "Need some help here."

He'd maneuvered the woman to the opening. Saul took her elbow and held her head down with his other hand until she cleared the entrance. Once she was standing, he kept his grip until he was certain she wouldn't bolt.

She was close to 5' 11", underfed, no older than her mid-thirties. Her shoulder-length pale blond hair resembled fine silk, though it was stringy and matted. Sapphire eyes with specks of gold blinked in an uneven pattern. Lines of dirt streaked across a perfect face. Even dirty and disheveled, she belonged in a class of gorgeous Saul had only seen on a movie screen.

She wore faded jeans, a dingy gray T-shirt, and a purple hoodie. No socks or shoes.

"I don't see anything else in there," Mathews said, flexing his back when he was out of the tree. "She seems okay except for being nonresponsive. What do you think, Roan? Call an ambulance or take her back and call Social Services?"

"We call an ambulance—one of us has to sit with her at the hospital."

"One of us is gonna have to sit with her anyway."

"Hanging out at the station beats the hospital."

Roan placed his hand on the woman's arm and took a few steps. She moved with him.

"Hold on," Mrs. Blackstone said. "She's barefoot."

Roan glanced up the trail.

"Short of throwing her over my shoulder, I don't think we have any choice here." He shortened his stride to match the woman's but began walking faster as they neared the parking lot. The woman stumbled.

Saul sprinted forward to catch her. The maneuver left her lax body tightly wound in his arms and he felt a memory playing hide-and-seek. It vanished before he could place it.

Within minutes of reaching their vehicle, Roan, Mathews, and the woman were gone. Saul and Mrs. Blackstone retreated up the hill to their homes.

They lived in a group of townhomes known as The Courtyard. Saul paused at the edge of the real estate's namesake, a square yard in the middle of the U-shaped complex, hoping the sunlight would burn away the memory that had threatened him as he caught the stumbling woman.

Instead of burning away, it ripped open. Every muscle from his face to his feet clenched in a surge of rage and grief.

The woman in the park had felt like Martha.

Closing his eyes, he shoved all recall of her back into the off-limit corners of his mind.

He opened his eyes to Mrs. Blackstone watching him.

"Tea," Mrs. Blackstone said. It wasn't a question.

When they reached her door, they found her potted plants scattered across the ground. Some of the pots were broken.

"Well, look at the mess our raccoons have made," Mrs. Blackstone said.

Saul bent to pick up a pot.

"Leave them be." She slapped his hand away. "I'll take care of it myself in a bit."

A faint pattern in the scattered dirt looked almost like a smiley face. He startled, then shrugged. The wind must have swirled through the yard and used the dirt as canvas. He followed his neighbor inside, where he was greeted by the faint aroma of potpourri.

He waited on the sofa while she brewed one of her custom tea blends. She served his in a thick-walled mug, then sat in an armchair across from him. Her hands shook visibly and her china cup rattled against the saucer when she lowered it.

"I wonder what happened to her." She sighed. "Poor thing. And so lovely too, wasn't she?"

Saul grunted in agreement, happy that his neighbor's equilibrium seemed to improve with each sip of tea. He put his empty mug in the sink and made it as far as the door before she spoke again.

"Saul?"

He knew that tone.

"I just can't stop worrying about her. Would you go down to the station and make sure she's okay?"

He didn't think she really understood what she was asking, but then he wasn't sure it would stop her if she did. He rubbed an open palm over his stomach as it hardened into a knot and wished he'd just let the damn phone keep ringing.

CHAPTER 2

SIGHTS AND SOUNDS, ALL FAMILIAR, washed over Saul as he paused inside the door to the station that had served as his second home for ten years. A small, wiry sergeant at the front counter broke into a huge smile when he spotted Saul. Coming out from behind the desk, he grabbed Saul's hand, pumping it enthusiastically.

"Becker! Great to see you, really great. You here to see Leonard? He's out on a call."

Sergeant Hendrix slapped Saul's back and led him around the desk.

"I'm looking for the Jane Doe found in the park by my place this morning. Roan and Mathews brought her in?"

"You mean the la-la lady? She's sitting by Roan's desk in the bullpen. Hasn't moved since he plopped her there."

"He still around?"

"Yeah, he drew the babysitting gig."

"Okay if I show myself back?"

Sarge nodded and returned to his paperwork, wide smile slipping back into a well-worn scowl.

***

Saul found the woman sitting straight-backed in a hard wooden chair next to Roan's desk. Roan pounded on his keyboard, muttering to himself.

"Name? Got nothing for me? Okay, plain Jane Doe it is."

"That's a new one," Saul said. "Plain Jane Doe. I like it. You just now starting the paperwork?"

"No rush. Social Services is moving slow." Roan stifled a yawn. "I should've at least tried going into the tree. Now Matthews is home in bed, sleeping, and I'm…" He nodded his head toward the visitor's chair.

The woman licked her lips and swallowed, a motion Saul interpreted as thirst. He fetched a cup of water and a spoon from the break area while Roan continued unleashing his frustrations on the keyboard.

Dropping to one knee at her side, Saul held the cup up to her vacant eyes.

"I brought you some water."

No reaction.

He touched the tip of the cup to her mouth. Still no response.

He dipped the plastic spoon in the cup, then placed it between her lips. When she didn't drink, he tilted the spoon. Water dripped from her closed lips down her chin.

Roan glanced over at them.

"Giving her a bath?"

Saul pulled up the edge of his shirttail and dabbed the water from her chin.

"Come on, Plain Jane. I know you're thirsty."

This time when he tried to give it to her, she opened her mouth and took a few sips before pressing her lips together. He felt someone move up behind him.

"You come down here after all this time and don't even bother to say hello?"

The calm, even voice held an undercurrent, like a gentle wave washing atop a violent riptide.

Saul turned to face Chuck Leonard, his partner for the last five years of his career as a detective. They were exactly the same height, but Chuck had dark hair, soulful chocolate eyes with thick lashes, and a broad smile—not that his smile was showing.

Chuck had reluctantly given him space to work out his demons after Saul left the force. They hadn't spoken in almost a year.

"Hard to say hello to somebody who isn't here," Saul said. "So now that you are, hello."

Chuck shook his head. "I assume you're not here to re-up and get me out of partner purgatory?"

"This woman was found in that hollow tree at the lake. My neighbor asked me to check on her."

"Well, here's your early warning order," Chuck said. "You being here negates my promise to stay away. I expect you to start answering your door and returning phone calls. At least when it's me on the other end."

He waited until Saul grunted in agreement, then nodded toward Saul's old desk.

"New guy," he said and finally smiled.

The cop who walked to the desk holding a mug of coffee was young and had a face that looked like he might need a razor twice a week at most. His hair was a fraction too long for regulations, and his clean but wrinkly shirt wouldn't stay tucked in.

When he sat down, the chair whooshed all the way to the lowest height setting, sending hot coffee into the air like a geyser. Laughter scattered around the room as the kid opened a desk drawer and pulled out a roll of paper towels.

"Your handiwork?" Saul said.

"Temporary partner," Chuck said. "Breaking him in kind of thing. Hey, I need coffee—you want any?"

Saul shook his head.

Roan picked up his mug.

"Since you're here, I'm sure you won't mind taking watch while I join the detective," he said and followed Chuck to the coffee pot.

Saul perched at the end of Roan's desk and took a slow look around. The constant noise, phones ringing, people talking, some laughter, merged into a single, dull pitch. The relentless hum of a lawn mower seeped in from outside and mingled with the buzz. Except for a few new faces, nothing seemed to have changed in the year and a half of his absence.

He jumped when he heard a female voice beside him.

"Don't call me that."

"What?" Saul said.

The woman's posture remained unchanged, her stare still blank, but she spoke again.

"I'm not Plain Jane."

Her voice was soft, not much more than a whisper, but anger was there.

Saul rolled Roan's chair over and sat so he could look directly into her eyes.

"Who are you, then?" he said.

Less than a second after he spoke, he saw a flash of intense emotion—fear?—and she was gone again. Just like that.

He waved a hand in front of her face.

"What the hell are you doing?" Roan said from behind him.

"Did you see that?" Saul stood so Roan could reclaim his chair.

"What?"

"She spoke to me."

Chuck and Roan both glanced at the shell of a woman, then back at Saul.

"She said her name wasn't Jane."

"She happen to let you in on what it is?" Roan said.

"No. Just that she wasn't a plain Jane."

"What does that mean?"

"I don't know. Maybe she spells her name with a Y. You know, J-a-y-n-e."

Roan shrugged and sat down at his desk.

"Crazy subject talked to crazy ex-detective then returned to her mental Disneyland," he said aloud as he typed.

"Piss off, Roan," Saul said.

"How long are you sticking around?" Chuck said.

"I guess until she gets picked up."

Roan leaned his head into a cupped palm, eyelids losing the fight to stay open.

"You finished with that paperwork?" Chuck said, tapping Roan's shoulder.

"Yeah."

"Go home, then. I'll handle Social Services when they show up."

"You sure? Could be a while."

"Saul can baby-sit," Chuck said. "Give us a chance to catch up."

Roan took a quick swig of his coffee and unfurled himself. A brisk walk had him halfway across the room before he remembered to shout back his thanks. Saul relocated to the chair, trying not to stare at the woman. Her face had the smoothest texture he'd ever seen.

"Why did you say you're here?" Chuck said.

Saul realized he was watching the woman a little too intently.

"My neighbor's peace of mind," he said.

"Uh-huh," Chuck said, then yelled to the fresh-faced kid, waving him over.

"Former partner Saul, meet new guy Danny."

Danny held his hand out to Saul.

"Heard a lot about you."

"Yeah, I'll bet," Saul said, completing the handshake.

A uniformed man walked by and did a double take when he saw who was there.

"Hey, Becker, looking good. Glad to see you finally made it in to visit."

"He wouldn't bother with a visit, Walters." Chuck clapped Saul a little too hard on the back. "He's here on business."

"Why don't you stop by the joint after our shift? Stiles would love the brag time. He finally finished first in the target and combat pistol courses since you weren't here to beat him." Walters glanced at the clock. "Gotta run. Big day down at the lake—first Jane Doe here, now someone's found mutilated squirrels."

"Mutilated how?" Saul said.

"That's what I'm on my way to find out." Walters continued toward the door with a backhanded wave.

"Do you still shoot?" Danny asked.

"Does he still shoot?" Chuck said. "Saul not only still shoots every day, he still runs every day. Why, he probably runs to the firing range."

Saul grimaced. He did in fact start each morning by running five miles to the firing range, taking target practice, then running back home.

"Hey, that was a good idea," Chuck said. "Your coming by the bar tonight."

Saul shrugged.

"I wasn't just suggesting," Chuck said.

The commander, new since Saul's exodus, stuck his head out of his office and called to Chuck, who looked at the computer screen on Roan's desk.

"Would you mind printing that report for me and closing out the system?"

"Sure," Saul said. But before he printed, he made a few extra keystrokes.

The caseworker from Social Services arrived with a pair of size nine sneakers. After she'd put them on her new ward, she glanced at the paperwork.

"Jayne with a Y?"

"Don't ask," Saul said.

CHAPTER 3

SAUL PUSHED THROUGH A WALL of warm air as he headed into the dim interior of The Lucky Bar and Grill. He spotted Chuck in the back corner, sitting at the same old table with mostly the same old faces. The last time Saul sat there, he'd decided to amputate his life and see what grew back.

He watched a waitress dance through the gaps in the crowds, her motions so smooth they looked choreographed. As he moved toward the back of the room, a woman came out of the restroom and stopped short to stare at him. He didn't recognize her and when she just stood there, he continued toward Chuck.

He'd taken a few steps when someone grabbed his elbow.

He yanked his arm back, his elbow knocking into a guy's beer, and spun around. He stopped his other arm mid-punch when he registered that it was the woman who had been staring.

Saul muttered an apology to the beer drinker, dropped his arms to his side, and flexed his fingers.

"What the hell?" he said.

She was a petite blond in her late twenties, dressed in gray slacks and jacket, with a stuffed, multi-pocketed bag slung across her shoulder.

"Sorry," she said. "Didn't mean to startle you. Won't be doing that again anytime soon."

"What do you want?"

"You're Saul Becker, aren't you?"

"What of it?"

She pulled a wire-bound pad and a pen from her bag, then clicked the top of her pen in and out several times.

"I'm Lorel Martin," she said, "from *The Denver Post*. I was just leaving to find you. A guy back there said you might be willing to help me with a story I'm working on."

The bartender caught Saul's eye and waved a towel in the air. When he had Saul's attention, he tossed it.

Saul nodded his thanks and mopped at his beer-soaked sleeve.

"What story would that be?"

"I'm putting together a 'help us ID this woman' story about the Jane Doe found in the park today." She made a show of consulting her notebook. "You're the one who actually found her, right?"

"No."

"But you were there?"

He nodded.

"And you're the same Saul Becker who worked the Martha Kennedy case."

His hand tightened into a fist, squeezing the towel so hard his fingers shook.

"What's that got to do with anything?"

She smiled and shrugged one shoulder.

"It's an interesting angle if I put you in the story too."

He pulled the towel across his palm and slapped it against his thigh, wishing he could choke her with it. Two years had passed since the press used him as fodder for their emotional-shredding machine, but once a target, always a target, he supposed.

"Your name would catch people's attention," she said. "Maybe someone who knows this woman will read the article because of that. Someone who wouldn't read it otherwise."

He slapped the towel against his thigh again.

"Come on, don't you want to help?" Lorel said.

"Help the woman? Or help you?"

Saul turned his back on her and gave five dollars to the man whose beer he had spilled. He heard a pen scribbling, turned around, and grabbed the pad from her hands. She'd written, "Any history with this one?"

"You're unbelievable," he said, tossing the notebook back at her.

He hated dealing with the press when they smelled blood.

"Any comments then?" When he didn't answer, she said, "Story will be in tomorrow's paper either way."

He waited until the door closed behind her before tossing the towel back to the bartender.

At Chuck's table, Saul glanced around the group.

"You guys sicced a reporter on me?"

"Oh hell no," Chuck said. "She said we did?"

Saul moved an empty glass to the middle of the table and sat next to Chuck.

"Yeah."

"She was sniffing around about the la-la lady," Chuck said. "We talked to her some but never sent her after you."

"She was sniffing around all right," Walters said, tossing a wadded-up napkin at Chuck. "For your phone number."

Chuck blocked the napkin, which bounced into Danny's face.

"Never hurts to keep a good relationship with the press, a lesson Saul here never learned. Bet a month's salary Lorel Martin got to see Black-Eyed Saul."

Danny said, "What's a black-eyed Saul?"

"It's something Chuck made up—"

Several people at the table spoke at the same time.

"Oh, no it's not."

"Saul doesn't like to believe it," Chuck said, "but sometimes he gets so pissed his pupils widen all the way over his irises. At which time, his eyes look black. And when that happens, he is one scary-looking motherfucker."

"Not just scary-looking," someone said from the other end of the table.

"Enough already." Saul held his finger up to signal the waitress. "What's the status on your so-called la-la lady?"

"Jennings caught the case, not me. Hey, Ben," he yelled across the table. "Saul wants to know about your Jane Doe."

"You mean my Jayne-with-a-Y Doe?"

Chuck grinned as Saul's cheeks reddened. "Yeah, her."

"No one in the neighborhood recognizes her," Ben said. "No bus driver's seen her, no taxi let her out at the park. Her fingerprints don't match any records, including NCIC, and there are no missing persons reported who match her description. If she doesn't wake up on her own and tell us who she is, I predict she'll fade into the system and that'll be that. Oh, the doc said she has the start of bruises on her arm in the shape of a hand. Looks like someone grabbed her and she struggled."

"Hey, you picking up the tab tonight?" Walters poked Danny's arm and nodded at Saul. "He's rich, you know."

Danny looked like he wondered what joke he'd missed. Saul reached over to the candle in the middle of the table and extinguished the flame between his thumb and forefinger.

"I inherited some money," he said. "I'm hardly rich."

"He owns property," Walters said. "What's it called? The Courthouse?"

"The Courtyard." Saul waved at the waitress again and this time she came over. "Hennessey XO for me. And whatever these vagabonds order. This round's on me." The guys let loose with their enthusiastic thanks. Saul waved them off. "What was happening with the squirrels at the park?"

"Creepy stuff, to be honest," Walters said. "They were still warm to the touch. Their heads were bashed in."

"Any claw or teeth marks?" Saul said. "You know there are raccoons and coyotes in the area."

"Raccoons don't slice stomachs open with a sharp instrument and then pull the guts out. No blood in the area, so the lake was just a dumping spot."

"Where at the lake?"

"Next to that burnt-out tree."

Saul glanced down at the goose bumps rising on his arm and rubbed it.

"So, Danny," he said. "What's your story?"

"Story?" Danny said.

"You know, why you joined the force. Every cop has a story."

Danny fidgeted and took a long swallow of beer.

"My dad was a drug dealer," he said. "I grew up around a bunch of pissed off people with loaded guns and all the drugs I wanted. My older brother ODed when he was fourteen and my baby sister's an addict. I knew by the time I was a teen that I wanted to join up for the opposite side of the war."

"Your dad still dealing?"

"Nah. He was shot to death about five years ago."

Saul was impressed. The kid had a lot going on underneath that baby face.

"Enough serious shit," Chuck said. "I asked Saul down here to have some fun. Let's play pool."

***

After a couple of games, Saul used the smell of his beer-soaked shirt as an excuse to leave. Chuck walked with him to his truck.

"And you're really leaving why?" Chuck said.

"Plenty of daylight left. I have trees to plant."

"You'd rather be working than hanging out at the bar?"

"Yep."

Chuck laughed.

"Some things never change," he said.

CHAPTER 4

SAUL WAS WORKING THE NEXT MORNING when the teenager who delivered the paper rapped his knuckles against the sliding glass door to the downstairs bedroom. Saul used that space as his office and slept in a loft bedroom cut into the two-story cathedral ceiling.

"Good picture of you," the kid said, handing the paper over. "Front page, section B."

MYSTERY WOMAN FOUND was followed by a smaller headline: KENNEDY CASE DETECTIVE RESURFACES. Above the headlines was a picture of Jayne Doe taken at the station and one of Saul in uniform. The article said the ace detective, whose personal involvement with a victim led to his leaving the force, was potentially involved with another victim. The piece continued on page six, where few readers would bother to go. That was where Lorel finally got around to saying the woman was catatonic and no one knew her identity.

So much for the help-ID-this-woman angle.

***

A week later, he was in his office fielding inquiries about a new vacancy in The Courtyard. He'd just replaced the phone in its cradle when it rang again.

"Is this Mr. Saul Becker?"

"It is. You interested in the townhome?"

"What? No, this is Dr. Frank from the Metro Mental Health Hospital. I have a patient I'd like to talk to you about, if you have a minute."

He knew of only one patient who might be in such a facility with any connection to him.

"This about the Jayne Doe?"

"It is, the Jayne-with-a-Y Doe. I understand you were there when she was found and that she spoke to you."

"Only once. Very briefly."

"She's been here over a week and is still nonresponsive. You're the last person she spoke to…"

Saul pictured a slight, elderly man with glasses and a pointed gray beard. A psychiatrist who didn't relate to the world around him much better than his patients.

"What is it I can do for you, doctor?"

"I'd like to hear any impressions you might have formed about her. For example, what was she like when she spoke?"

"Let's see… I called her Jane Doe a few seconds before she spoke and it seemed to make her mad. She said don't call her that and added that she wasn't a plain Jane. That's kind of where the Y-thing came from."

"Hmm. Was anyone else around when she spoke?"

"Just me."

"I see." The doctor cleared his throat. "Mr. Becker, she's catatonic. The condition could be attributed to anything from schizophrenia to a head injury. I can't confidently treat her without a history and I can't get that without talking to someone who knows her. And I can't find anyone who knows her without her help."

"Sounds like you're stuck in a catch-22," Saul said.

"Well, I do have one idea. It's why I called. I'm hoping you'd be willing to come by the hospital and visit her."

"Why?" he said, more harshly than he'd intended.

"I admit I'm grasping at straws here, but it seems to me if she responded to you once, it isn't outside the realm of possibility that she might do it again."

Saul wanted to say no, didn't want to get involved. But hey, she was catatonic—how involved could he get? And if he saw her and she came out of it, he'd have done his part. No further involvement required.

Surely it couldn't hurt to see her just once.

The hospital grounds took up several blocks of a neighborhood east of downtown Denver. The brick buildings had faded and huge old trees slouched toward the ground. There were no barriers across the road but Saul stopped at the gatehouse anyway and got out of the car. As he neared the open door, he saw the young guard on the phone.

"Mom, please." He glanced over at Saul. "I have to go... No. No. Don't say that... Mom, I'm hanging up now... I'm not angry, but I have to go."

After he hung up he turned to Saul.

"I'm really sorry."

"I have caller ID on my phone at work," Saul said. "That way when my mom calls, I don't have to answer it."

The guard's smile held a touch of anxiety.

"Sometimes I think she needs to be a patient here," he said. "How can I help you?"

"I'm here to see Dr. Frank."

"Oh, well, you don't have to stop here."

"Then why have a guard house?"

"A long time ago they had a real guard here. Now you check in at the receptionist desk. I'm just here to monitor deliveries and give out directions. Do you know where you're going?"

"Building three."

The kid pulled out a photocopied map of the campus and circled where Saul should go. It wasn't far.

The parking lot sat between two groves of large cotton-woods and aspens. Sparse sunlight pierced the leafy canopy, the filtered radiance muted and weak.

The building's foyer had high ceilings and a polished wooden floor that creaked as Saul walked. The receptionist belted out a greeting.

"You Mr. Becker? Come sign in, please."

He was clipping on his visitor's badge when a door banged.

"There's the doctor now," she said.

Dr. Frank was black, a six-foot-tall potential linebacker, clean shaven and not much older than Saul.

No glasses, no pointy beard.

"Mr. Becker? I'm Dr. Frank." He extended his hand. "Thanks for coming."

Saul switched a bundle of flowers wrapped in newspaper to his left hand and shook Dr. Frank's.

"My neighbor sent them," he said, nodding at the flowers. "For Jayne."

"Wish I thought she'd notice them."

Dr. Frank punched the buttons on the wall control. The heavy metal doors swung open and they proceeded down a long hall, its solid white interrupted only by the indentation of heavy doors with slim glass windows.

"I want you to know I have no expectations for this visit,"

Dr. Frank said. "Jayne is in decent physical condition, outside of some dehydration and a little malnourishment, both of which we're addressing. Yet she responds to nothing."

"That's how we found her."

"Except that once, between then and now, she spoke. To you. Why is a mystery, but rest assured there was a trigger involved. The sound of your voice, the emotions you emit. Something. If you spend time with her, maybe we can recreate the breakthrough."

They stopped beside a door near the nurse's station.

"This is her room," Dr. Frank said.

Glancing in, Saul could see Jayne, propped upright in bed, staring at nothing, eyes unfocused. Something was tied to the railing on each side of her bed. He pressed closer.

"What the… She's got restraints on?"

"Just on her wrists," Dr. Frank said. "We've left her legs free."

Something about the shackles seriously gnawed at Saul's comfort zone.

"It's not something I like to do and I never do it lightly," Dr. Frank said. "She's become severely agitated on several occasions and pulled out her IV. It's how she gets nutrition, how we keep her hydrated. It staying in place right now is more important than her being allowed full movement."

A perfectly reasonable explanation that didn't make him feel any better.

"Let's get this thing started." Saul reached for the door but stopped when Dr. Frank didn't follow.

"You said she spoke when you were alone with her," Dr. Frank said, "so I'm not coming in. Cindy here, the nurse on duty, will check in on you from time to time. Stay as long or as short a time as feels comfortable. Cindy can show you my office when you're done."

"What do I do?"

"Anything similar to what happened at the station. Or try talking to her."

That was all the instruction he got.

The window in Jayne's room faced a garden surrounded by hospital walls. Full, mature trees edged a circular lawn, somewhat green but mixed with brown tufts common in a semi-arid region, when the owner didn't want to pay to water it more than once a week. Flowerbeds added a splash of color. Because the window shades were open, it was bright in the room even though the overhead lights were off.

He waved his hand in front of Jayne's eyes. No response. He picked up an empty plastic cup from the nightstand and tossed it on the floor. Nothing. He closed the window shades. Waited in the dark. Opened them. More nothing.

Finally he pulled up a chair and sat next to the bed, facing the door. *Try talking to her.* It was as good a plan as any.

"What should we talk about?"

He tried not to stare at the restraints. He hated being controlled. He hated seeing others controlled, and with that thought, he realized it wasn't just Jayne's restraints pissing him off.

"I lied to the kid at the gate," he said.

Saul couldn't imagine why he had spoken such a confession but after all, he was really just talking to himself. And what else did he have to talk about?

"I overheard him on the phone with his mother and I could tell she was really overbearing. I lied and told him I used caller ID to avoid my mom's calls. Truth is, she was a lifelong alcoholic and died of cirrhosis when she was forty-eight. I guess I wanted him to know there are ways to handle people like her. I wish someone had told me that when it mattered."

Cindy's face appeared briefly in the doorway and broke whatever spell had caused him to get so personal. He crossed the room and watched a hummingbird explore the feeders hung throughout the yard.

This was crazy. He'd never talked about his mother, not even in his department-mandated therapy.

He heard rustling and turned back to see Jayne pulling halfheartedly at her restraints. She licked her lips and swallowed. Like at the station. She'd spoken after he gave her water.

He ran the motor on the bed until she was more upright and she stopped yanking her wrists. He offered her a cup of water. She was nonresponsive when he pressed it to her lips.

She'd seemed angry when she spoke at the station. Maybe something about that had been the trigger.

"I didn't mean to insult you when I called you a plain Jane," he said.

Frustration built when she swallowed again. She was thirsty. He knew it. Why wouldn't she drink?

"I'm trying to help," he said. "Please. Let me give you some water."

Her eyes stayed fixed but she opened her lips and took a small sip. He thought she might take another, but she turned her head away when Cindy came into the room, a multipurpose machine-on-wheels clattering behind her.

"Sorry to disturb you," Cindy said as she wrapped a blood pressure cuff around Jayne's arm. "I need to take her vitals."

He watched for any signal that Jayne knew he was there, that she'd known what she was doing when she drank the water, but her eyes were unfocused and she barely even blinked.

"No problem. I need to go anyway." He lowered Jayne's bed to its original position, then leaned down to speak close to her ear. "Sorry I couldn't help."

"These are beautiful flowers," Cindy said.

Saul had put them on the night stand. They were still wrapped in the paper.

"My neighbor grows them. I don't have a vase though."

"I've got a castoff out at my desk," she said and made a quick trip out of the room to retrieve it.

Saul waited until she returned before asking how to get to Dr. Frank's office.

He took a last glance at Jayne as he left the room. She'd resumed the rhythmic tugging at her restraints.

She felt cool, crisp fabric underneath her and over her bare legs. She heard humming but couldn't place the song. Did that come from her head or the woman who'd just moved into her line of sight? The woman thumped on a tube with her forefinger, looked at it, then thumped some more.

She closed her eyes. Her arms were spread out and when she tried to move them, she couldn't.

She heard rustling, then receding footsteps and a soft click. She was alone.

She forced her eyes back open. She didn't want to fall sleep.

A sliver of light reflected off something. She had to watch it for a while before the image and a name came together in her mind.

Flower vase.

She kept yanking on her wrists until she remembered. They were tied to something. They weren't uncomfortable and suddenly she didn't care. It wasn't worth the effort.

She couldn't fight it any longer. She fell asleep, content.

Until the dreams came.

***

"How'd it go?" Dr. Frank said.

Saul shrugged.

"Nothing much happened," he said, "except she took some water from me."

"Interesting. What made you think to try that?"

"She spoke not long after I gave her some at the station."

The phone started ringing. Dr. Frank pushed a button and it stopped. "Anything else?"

"She keeps yanking on the restraints."

Dr. Frank rubbed his hand across his chin, stopped with his thumb and forefinger touching the tip.

"It could be she's registering the restraints at some level of consciousness and wants them off," he said. "More likely it's just stereotypy. That's when a person performs a repeated, sense-less motor activity—it happens in catatonic states. She didn't speak though? Or in any way seem to regain consciousness?"

"No."

Dr. Frank rapped his knuckles against his desk as he stood.

"It was worth a try. I'll walk you out."

They headed down the hallway, back toward the long cor-ridor to the main entrance, pausing in front of the closed door to Jayne's room. They could see that her eyes were shut, her breathing shallow. Her hands lay still.

"Our tests have pretty much ruled out a physical cause for Jayne's catatonia," Dr. Frank said, "so I feel strongly the root cause is psychological—"

Jayne started twisting under the sheets like she was on fire.

Dr. Frank jerked the door open, called to Cindy, and rushed to the bed.

Jayne's thrashing legs kicked the covers off, and her back arched off the mattress. Dr. Frank grabbed her legs and pinned them against the bed while Cindy held down her chest.

"IM Ativan. Four milligrams," Dr. Frank said.

Cindy ran out of the room and Saul took over holding Jayne still. If she did this often, he could understand the restraints.

Cindy returned, carrying a liquid-filled syringe she deftly emptied into Jayne's hip muscle. Moments later, Jayne stilled but her eyes stayed open, staring at the ceiling.

"What causes that?" Saul asked as he and Dr. Frank returned to the hall.

"I can only guess at this point, but it seems to me she struggles when asleep. I've had to keep her medicated to prevent these episodes. I didn't give her the meds today, just to see what would happen. I was hoping she'd be past this stage—she'll have a harder time becoming responsive if we have to keep her medicated."

Jayne still tossed slightly, first in one direction, then the other. A few low moans punctuated her movements. Her eyelids fluttered as if they were fighting to stay open. Eventually, they stilled, and Saul assumed she was asleep.

"More than you bargained for, I'd say." Dr. Frank held out his hand. "Thanks for giving it a try."

CHAPTER 5

AN ACCIDENT STRETCHED SAUL'S thirty-minute drive home into two hours, most of which was spent at a standstill in the stifling air of sunbaked asphalt and idling engines. Too much time to think about Jayne. Too much time for anger and dissatisfaction to take hold. He didn't even know from what.

The first thing he saw as he crossed the footbridge into the courtyard was Mrs. Blackstone, watering the potted plants around her doorway and keeping an eye on the bridge, like a spider from the corner of its web. She waved when she saw him.

"Hey," she called when he didn't respond.

He gave her a quick wave back, entered his home, and closed the door. He ignored the light tapping on his door but when it turned into heavy pounding, he figured he'd better do something.

"I have a bell you know," he said as he opened the door.

"It isn't nearly as satisfying as the pounding," Mrs. Blackstone said.

"What do you want?"

He expected a retort, but she seemed stricken by his curt response.

"I need... I mean, I wanted to ask..."

Seeing his feisty friend flustered, Saul felt twinges of guilt. She seemed to realize her frailty was showing and pulled herself upright.

"I wondered how it went."

"Didn't do any good, far as I could see."

"Well, tell me about it."

"Tomorrow," he said, shutting the door.

He expected her to renew the pounding but she left him alone. In the back of his mind, he knew that was odd, but he was too tired to care.

Saul was on his porch step, cooling down from his morning run, when Mrs. Blackstone came out of her apartment. She ignored him, shawl wrapped tightly around her torso, as she walked to the mailboxes and slipped a letter into the drop box. Her shoulders relaxed when Saul waved at her.

"Speaking to me this morning, are you?" she said, walking over.

"I have to. Apologizing to you is at the top of my list today."

Mrs. Blackstone leaned over for a look at the legal pad on his lap. The first item was "Apologize to Mrs. Blackstone."

"Well?" she said. "Let's hear it."

"I'd been stuck in a traffic jam. I was tired. I didn't want to talk—to anybody—but I'm sorry I was a jerk about it."

"Thank you."

That was the sum of her response so Saul said, "And I got the feeling there was something you wanted to talk about."

"Oh. It was nothing. I mean, I found one of my plants tipped over again."

He cocked his head to the side, studied her, then shook his head.

"Nope. Not buying it."

Her lips tightened.

"What do you mean? Of course I really found the plant pushed over."

"I mean, there was something else on your mind."

She blushed.

"Okay, fine," she said. "Meg needs your help."

Meg lived two doors down from Saul. She worked as a travel ER and ICU nurse and was often out of town. She'd returned two days ago after being gone for six weeks.

"Is she back for a while?"

"She's going out again tomorrow. To New Orleans. She says nobody wants to take an assignment in New Orleans during hurricane season, but they pay really well and she needs the money because someone got access to her bank account and cleared it out."

"And how can I help?"

"I told her you used to be a detective and maybe she should talk to you."

"Tell her to go to the Westglenn police. Ask for Detective Chuck Leonard. Tell him I sent her. He'll help her sort it out."

Mrs. Blackstone pursed her lips.

"And tell her she doesn't need to pay rent until her finances get straightened out."

Mrs. Blackstone had the look on her face that meant she had a lecture saved up for him.

"So just the one plant this time?" he said.

Later that afternoon, Saul yelled out "Maintenance!" as he rang the doorbell for the townhome next to his.

Julie Nelson had a lanky build and long, dark hair that she kept pinned at the back of her neck in a ponytail. She worked as a software engineer and loved to cook. She had rented the place for the five-burner stove and the double-walled oven. Saul had purchased them from a defunct restaurant supply store because they were cheap. The arrangement worked out for both of them. Julie got professional-grade equipment at no extra charge. Saul got lots of free, professional-grade food.

Julie answered the door and showed him to the kitchen. The sink was full of brackish water.

"I hate to tell you this but it plugged up after my nephew visited. I think he stuffed a Happy Meal toy into it."

"That's an easy fix then, if it didn't get past the trap."

"Do what you need to. I'm on my way out. We're working nights while we switch over to a new billing system."

Saul followed her to the door, locked it behind her, and started to work.

Saul had an easy time finding the plastic walking hamburger, round and perfectly sized for getting stuck in pipes. He had a harder time getting it out. Eventually brute strength with a piece of rebar cracked the toy enough to break it up.

He lay on his back, head and shoulders crammed into the cabinet below the sink. As he fumbled to get a good angle, he scraped his elbow against the rough siding. He pushed out from the cabinet and cradled his elbow in his hand. It felt sticky. He brought it up to his face for inspection.

The metallic smell of blood reminded him of Martha, but he jerked himself back. What the hell. He'd gone long months barely thinking of her until Jayne showed up.

At least he hadn't started dreaming of her again.

For over a year after her murder, Martha had walked

through his dreams, leaving trails of blood in shallow, red-black pools.

The only way to avoid her had been to avoid sleep to every extent possible. Easier for him than some because of his chronic insomnia but even he eventually got too tired for sheer willpower to keep him awake. He'd drink caffeine in any form available, regardless of the hour. He'd exercise anytime he got drowsy. He drove himself hard at work. He started taking pills. Anything to keep awake.

Saul's eyes slipped shut as he lay on the cool tiles. He hadn't slept at all the night before, and when he realized he was dropping off, he twisted in a drowsy panic. Thinking of Martha as he fell asleep would be asking for those dreams to come back. He struggled with the exhaustion and pushed himself upright.

An image of Jayne struggling in bed popped into his mind and in a flash he understood.

She didn't fight *while* she was asleep.

She fought against sleep itself.

She was watching pinholes in the ceiling panels when a voice started talking. She'd heard it before, inside her head.

"I know something about nightmares," the voice told her. "Truth is, the more you struggle, the stronger their hold becomes. Ghosts don't leave you alone until you stop fighting them."

She'd thought the voice was wise. Obviously she'd been wrong.

"Here's the thing," it said. "The terrors aren't real. When you stop struggling, nothing happens."

What did the voice know of terror?

"I used to be a cop."

It stopped then and when it picked up, she could tell the voice did know.

"A woman I tried to help? She... was murdered. After her death, she visited me for a long time in my dreams. Every time I fell asleep."

She strained to hear the voice, which got lower and lower.

"I'd do anything to stay awake, and if I fell asleep I'd force myself back for as long as I could. I recognized that in you. But one night, I was too tired to fight. I told her to go ahead and haunt me. When I didn't struggle, her visits got shorter, less bloody, and one day she stopped coming. Looking back on it, I think my struggle is what kept the nightmares alive."

She felt a light touch on her arm.

"I just wanted you to know there's hope. The dreams aren't real. You'll be okay if you let go."

The hand left her arm and she heard the soft swish that meant the door had opened, followed by the second swish indicating it had closed.

That was when she realized the voice was outside her; it didn't come from her head.

Chapter 6

After the talk about nightmares, Saul continued to see Jayne. Each visit began with the ritual of lifting the bed to a slight angle. Then he'd offer her water. Sometimes she took it but not always. He'd open the blinds, pull the chair up to her bed, and start talking.

He'd begin with chitchat, as if they were friends catching up over a drink, only one of the friends stared into space while the other one talked. Eventually he'd move on to personal things. He let his secrets rise organically and kept nothing back, except Martha. Maybe he'd get there someday.

He told her his mother had gotten pregnant with him at Woodstock and didn't actually know who the father was. Her family, Catholic and prominent in Denver society, had wanted her to go into seclusion and give him up for adoption. They cut her off when she refused, which on the surface seemed noble, but he still struggled to understand why she'd kept him. She never seemed to like him, much less love him. She hit him a lot, until he grew big enough to hit her back. One day he whaled on her and kept at it until her boyfriend pulled him off.

He'd been twelve at the time and already knew the only way he'd ever be safe was to count on himself.

At the end of each visit with Jayne, he'd make one last offer of water, then lower the bed. He'd thank Jayne for listening and say he hoped she'd sleep well. And she had been sleeping well. Somehow, in spite of everything, he knew he'd gotten through to her about the nightmares.

Then he'd go home, feeling lighter in heart but troubled in mind. Jayne was becoming a habit, an addictive one.

She had to wonder, was she even alive?

When her eyes were closed, she saw black. When they were open, she saw white.

No thirst. No hunger. No pain.

Was this heaven?

No. Heaven wouldn't have the nightmares.

But hell wouldn't have the voice.

Saul ran his hand through the warm, wet hair at the back of his neck. Jayne's room seemed hotter than usual.

"I'm ready to tell you about Martha."

He crossed his arms. Jayne's eyes were open. They stared at the ceiling, rarely blinking.

"You know, I dreamed about you last night. You were awake and your eyes... God, they were beautiful. We laughed a lot. The weird thing is, it all seemed so normal. I think part of me sees you that way every time I come here."

He pressed his fingers against his nose. That confession wasn't an impassioned retelling of things that clung to his soul like leeches. It was a simple truth, as stark and clinical as the room.

And much more frightening.

"So, about Martha Kennedy. A doctor informed us she had a patient with injuries consistent with abuse. Of course, Martha claimed they were caused by an accident. We gave her the business card for our Victim Advocate and thought that would be it unless she ended up in a hospital or worse. You can't help someone who won't help themselves."

He had seen the pattern a million times. Abuse is as obvious as neon lights to everyone but the victim.

"About a month later, she surprised us when she came to see the VA. Turned out her husband had been psychologically and emotionally abusive for years, minor physical abuse until he threw her against a sliding-glass door—that was the incident the doctor alerted us to. Since then the violence had intensified and he'd threatened to kill her. She absolutely believed he'd do it. We got her to a safe house and she became the poster child for abused women taking control of their lives. Her husband was beyond furious. I got a few anonymous death threats but was never able to prove they came from him."

He took a deep breath and let it out slowly.

"So she followed all the rules, put her life back together, and stayed safe. Until she let her guard down—enough for her husband to kidnap her from a grocery store parking lot."

His throat had gone dry, so he poured himself a cup of water and drank it slowly. He considered not telling the rest of the story. It wasn't like she'd know if he held back.

"Martha's husband was a self-taught entrepreneur. Because he was so smart, he thought everyone else was stupid. But I found her and rescued her. I'd broken a few big cases not long before that, so the press already knew my name. They made a big deal about the cop who outsmarted the genius. It was all bullshit to me because I never caught the bad guy. We counseled Martha to leave town, start over where he couldn't find her. And she did."

He got up and walked over to the window. He stared out at the yard for a while and when he resumed talking kept his back to Jayne.

"There's some background here I should probably mention. Martha was frightened and fragile and desperately needed someone to call in the middle of the night. Someone to be strong for her. She picked me and I didn't turn her away. The department therapist calls me a rescuer. Guess it's true. Anyway, everything looked like it would turn out okay. She disappeared for a year; I assumed she was safe. Then she shows up on my doorstep one night. Shocked the shit out of me. Says she's doing great but she missed me. I got a call from work while she was there, had to go in. I told her to lock the door and stay put. I told her not to open it for anybody."

He turned to face Jayne but stayed where he was.

"Like I said, you can't help people who won't help themselves. Her husband followed her there, or maybe he was watching my place to see if she'd show up. I don't know. What matters is that he was there and she opened the door to him. He called me from my own phone and told me I'd better come home."

Had Jayne made a sound? No, she was still staring into space. He was imagining things.

"He told me he timed his call so I could be there when... you couldn't recognize her face, she'd been beaten so badly. Stabbed too, ten times. I held her, just like I held you at the park, but she didn't last long enough to be rescued."

His face was slick with sweat. He went into the bathroom to splash water on it. His hands gripped the sides of the sink, face lowered so he didn't have to look at himself. When he returned, Jayne's eyes had closed. He lowered the bed.

"That's the story, I guess, except for the aftermath. The press crucified me for failing to protect her. Internal Affairs got involved. In the end they let me keep my job, but it was never the same. I'm done with the rescue business. The only thing I want people to rely on me for now is to fix their plumbing."

There was one more confession he could make. He'd been lying about it for so long he wasn't even sure he could speak the truth.

"The thing everyone wanted to know, especially Internal Affairs, was how close we really were. I've maintained all this time that we were only friends."

He wiped his palms on his jeans.

"That's a lie."

CHAPTER 7

SAUL STOPPED AT THE GAZEBO at the edge of the courtyard and slid his backpack to the ground. The backpack was a handmade, custom design that allowed him to jog comfortably with a pistol strapped to his back. He pulled a water bottle out of the mesh side-sleeve and sat, facing the western horizon. The sun, out of sight behind the peaks, shot a few golden rays up through pink clouds.

"I take it this was a two-run day?"

Mrs. Blackstone, cup of tea in hand, entered the gazebo and sat opposite him.

"I was feeling a little hyped this afternoon. The run helped."

"If you have time, I'd like to talk to you about that problem I mentioned a while back," she said.

"You mean the one I asked about and you completely clammed up on?"

"Well, I didn't want to burden you," she said, pulling her shawl up around her. "I would have anyway, of course, but I found someone else to help."

He would have quizzed her more but a shout of "Yo" interrupted them. He turned to see Chuck crossing the yard.

"Checking up on me now?" Saul said.

Chuck climbed the gazebo steps and leaned against the entrance, shaking his head.

"It's not always about you, Becker." Then to Saul's surprise, he added, "How are you this evening, Mrs. B?"

"She hates being called that."

"Oh, I already told the detective he can," she said.

"You two know each other? When did that happen?"

"A few days ago." Mrs. Blackstone looked smug. "He's the help I just mentioned."

"It's that serious?" Saul stood up. "What's going on?"

Chuck moved into the gazebo, sat next to Mrs. Blackstone, and patted her knee.

"Nothing we can't take care of, right?" Then he laughed. "I'm sorry, Mrs. B," he said. "I'm not laughing at your situation. It's just that Saul's always so serious. It's good to see him thrown off his game from time to time."

"It's all right, Detective Leonard," she said. "I understand the urge."

"One of you had better spill it," Saul said.

"Some of us here have been robbed," Mrs. Blackstone said.

A burglar was hitting his property and no one had told him?

"Now calm down," Mrs. Blackstone said. "I've only known the extent of this thing for a few days."

He realized his fists were clenched, took a deep breath, and forced them to relax.

"Their cash cards and pin numbers have been stolen," Chuck said.

"Remember I told you Meg's account was cleaned out?" Mrs. Blackstone said. "That's why she's on the road again so soon. Then I discovered my account had some suspicious withdrawals, and when I talked with other people here, it turned out the same thing happened to several of us."

"Why didn't you talk to me before you went to the police?" Saul said. "I'd have gone with you."

Mrs. Blackstone adjusted her shawl with a slow and exaggerated precision before answering him. The gesture was her less-than-subtle sign of annoyance.

"To begin with," she said, "I didn't go to them. They came to me. And you *told* me this nice detective would sort everything out, remember? And while we're getting all persnickety with each other, why didn't you tell me you thought my broken pots were an act of vandalism?"

"What the hell are you talking about?" Saul said.

She apparently got her shawl into the perfect configuration, stopped fidgeting, and lifted her chin.

"Before I'd decided what to do about the thefts, Detective Leonard showed up on my doorstep asking about the vandalism complaint. I said as far as I knew raccoons had broken my flower pots, but since he was already here, I told him about the missing money."

"Again, what the hell are you talking about?"

"What part of this are you not understanding, young man?"

She'd only called him "young man" three times since he'd known her, and it was not a good sign.

"The part about filing a complaint," he said.

She formed a soft "oh" with her lips and Chuck stepped in to explain.

"We got a complaint about her flowers pots. I wouldn't normally work such a low priority, but since it was here at your place... to be honest, I thought you were jerking my chain."

"First of all, Chuck, you know I would never file a frivolous report, even as a joke." He kept his voice low to prevent himself from shouting. "And second, there aren't enough new people down there to take a report and think it was me doing it. They all know what I look like."

"The complaint was filed online."

"Online?"

"It's a new thing. You can file non-emergency complaints through a form on the department's web page."

"It wasn't me," Saul said.

"No shit?" Chuck shook his head. "Well, I'll see if we can figure out where the complaint was submitted. In the mean-time," he said, again patting Mrs. Blackstone's knee, "I've got news for you. Sit down and stop pacing, Saul. You're making me antsy."

"You'll let me know who put in that bogus report?"

Chuck rolled his eyes. "I'll think about it. What I'm here for right now is to tell Mrs. B how the thefts were carried out. It happened down the street, at The Corner Store. We found a skimmer and a hidden microcamera at the ATM there. Latest and greatest technology on the skimmer. You could barely tell it was there, even if you were looking. Camera too."

"That's good news, right?" Mrs. Blackstone said.

"Means it won't be happening anymore, at least not there. Doesn't mean we'll ever catch who did it. No prints. No secu-rity shots of the person installing it."

"Inside help?" Saul said.

"Could be," Chuck said. "Just as likely, a perp really smart about technology."

"No video on anybody retrieving the numbers then."

"The thing uses wireless transmission. That's all I've got for now." He slapped his thighs and stood. "And with that, I need to move on. I'll keep you and the others informed, Mrs. B."

They left as a group, walking back through the courtyard. Dusk had settled and the solar lights lining the walkway glowed yellow. They could smell someone's dinner cooking, barbeque on a backyard grill.

"Hey," Saul said, breaking the silence. "Why does he get to call you Mrs. B?"

"Because he's such an accommodating gentleman." She quickened her pace and pulled ahead of them.

Chuck grinned. "She thinks I'm accommodating. And a gentleman."

"She's wrong a lot," Saul said.

Chuck gave a quick punch to Saul's upper arm.

"Look at you," he said. "You remembered how to make a joke."

CHAPTER 8

SAUL SIGNED IN AT THE DESK, waved in the direction of the nurses' station, and made his way to Jayne's room. He stopped at the door and stared through the glass window.

"This is new," he said.

"What's up?" Cindy made her way over and peered into the room, then immediately hurried back to the station and paged Dr. Frank.

Jayne stood at the window overlooking the garden, rigid, one arm at waist level, the other clutching her IV pole. The thumb on her free hand kept touching the tip of each finger, starting at the little finger and working up, then pausing at the index finger before repeating the sequence.

When Dr. Frank arrived, he interrupted the finger motion by holding her hands in his. He led her back to the bed, where she crawled to the middle of the mattress and drew her legs up to her chest, hugging them.

Dr. Frank beckoned Saul.

"Were you here when this started?"

"No. Is it good news?"

"She's displaying stereotypy—don't know if I'd categorize it as good news. She's still catatonic."

Saul glanced at Jayne. "But she moved on her own. That has to mean something."

"There might be some progressive activity associated with a return from catatonia," Dr. Frank said. "I've also seen it happen almost instantly. It's good in one sense. I can describe it as enough progress to keep her here for another week before she gets moved to a long-term care facility."

Dr. Frank joined Cindy just outside the open door to begin issuing new orders.

Jayne got out of bed and went back to the window, fingers playing against each other again. After a moment she flexed her hand and splayed her fingers on a pane, leaning toward the glass until her nose touched, staring out into the garden.

Her eyes seemed to have a bit of focus. Saul felt certain she was looking for something but when he tried to make eye contact, the vacant glaze returned.

"I've got to tell you, Jayne," Saul said a week later, "bad things are going to happen if you don't snap out of it."

She had continued to move on her own, most often to stand in front of the window. He usually found her there, looking out, when he arrived. Today she was in bed.

She took a small sip of water when he offered it. After she drank he set the cup on her tray table. He didn't follow his routine. Today was not the usual visit.

He placed his hand over hers. The width of his palm could have covered hers twice, but their fingers were close to the same length. He felt warmth in the listless hand. Jayne was in there somewhere. Unlike Martha, she had the option to come back.

He leaned over and spoke directly to her vacant eyes.

"Jayne. You need to listen. This is serious. They're moving you tomorrow. Too far for me to visit. I need you to come back."

He stood at the side of the bed, arms folded against his chest, for what seemed like hours. He admired the lines of her perfect face, imagined a sparkle in her gold-speckled eyes. He felt a sense of impending loss, which made no sense. He didn't even know her.

"This is goodbye then."

He reached inside the railing to lower the bed.

But Jayne's mouth was moving. She licked her lips and rolled her tongue, then reached for the cup of water on the tray in front of her.

While Saul followed her movements, open-mouthed, she took a sip, waited, took a few more.

"Don't," she said in a low, dry voice, grabbing his wrist, still poised above the controls.

"Don't lower the bed?"

"Don't go."

CHAPTER 9

IT SEEMED A SUDDEN THING to everyone but Jayne. She may have been hidden and comforted by a white mist but she was always aware. She heard sounds as if they were playing on a radio in another room. Sometimes it was just background noise, but sometimes she listened to the program.

Occasionally she could identify shapes, usually points of color with blurred edges. Sometimes pieces slipped together and she knew what she was looking at, like a blanket with a dozen mountain ranges outlined in its folds, or a tube leading from her hand to a bag of liquid.

She never questioned why she was in that white world, only knew with a passionate certainty that anywhere else would not be right for her.

She took comfort in the warm voice that visited, but he frightened her when he pressed on the wall between them. He wanted to push it down, but she resisted. Then he said she would be taken away. He was her friend and she didn't want him left alone with all of his pain.

Terror like a strong hot wind pushed against her, held her in place. She felt burning fingers grab, try to pull her deeper into the mist, almost succeeding.

But they didn't. She fought her way back.

She did it for him.

Saul stared at Jayne in her bed. She stared back. Really stared, eyes connecting with his.

"Saul."

A short-lived dizziness seized him when he realized what she'd said.

"You know my name?"

She scowled, then looked around the stark room.

"Where am I?" Her voice cracked with the effort of speech.

"A mental health hospital. In Denver."

"How did I get here?"

"My neighbor found you in a park near our home."

"We live together."

Why would she think that?

"I meant my neighbor's home, and mine. I'm getting the doctor."

But Dr. Frank was already at the door.

"Saul. I'm glad you're still here. I wanted to thank you—"

"Look at her," Saul said.

Dr. Frank looked at Jayne, then back at Saul.

"It just happened," Saul said.

The doctor walked to Jayne's side.

"Well, hello there." He put his fingers on the pulse in her wrist, then asked, "Do you mind?" as he pulled a pencil light from his pocket. At her shrug, he checked her pupils.

"How do you feel?"

She shrugged again, her attention glued to Saul. He felt an overwhelming urge to run and never look back.

"Should I go?" he said, moving toward the door in answer to his own question.

"No!" Jayne looked at Dr. Frank. "He can't go."

"What do you mean?" Dr. Frank said.

"I came back for him."

Both men spoke at the same time.

"For me?" from Saul.

"For him?" from the doctor.

Saul tried to ask why but his mouth was too dry.

"It's all right. Saul will be back, won't you?" Dr. Frank said.

Saul stood, frozen. Finally, he nodded.

"Today?" Jayne said.

She sounded as panicked as he felt.

"Yeah," he said and fled the room.

Saul's reaction wasn't even close to what she'd expected. It felt lonelier without him in the room than it ever had in her private world. She missed her void, felt a hole in her heart, like a mother might feel if a child were ripped from her arms and spirited away.

The doctor sat in the chair by her bed, demanding that she interact.

"What did you mean when you said you came back for Saul?" he asked.

His presence was an intrusion; his question annoyed her.

"I didn't want to leave him," she said, not even trying to keep the unspoken *duh* out of her answer.

"And why would you think you were leaving him?"

"He said you were moving me. Is that not true?"

"It's true. We were preparing to move you."

"Well then," she said.

The doctor changed the subject.

"Tell me about yourself."

This brought a new surprise. She could not think of one thing about herself outside of the world she'd recently departed.

"Do you know your name?" he said.

She could, at least, answer that.

"Jane."

"What's your last name?"

"I don't know."

"But you're sure your name is Jane?"

"That's what Saul calls me."

"Ah. We call you Jayne—spelled with a Y, by the way—but we don't actually know your real name."

He was watching, trying to gauge her reaction. She felt like a large body of water separated them and she was trying to cross in a boat without oars.

"Do you recall why we use a Y in your name?" he asked.

"Because that's how I spell it?" Her head hurt, a dull throb behind her eyes. "I recognize your voice but I don't know who you are."

"I'm Dr. Frank. I've been treating you since you came here, close to four weeks ago. Do you remember anything at all?"

"Being here." She closed her eyes. "Saul."

"Saul," Dr. Frank said.

There was something hidden in that simple repetition of his name.

"I'll tell you what little we know about you," he said. "You were found in a park by Saul's neighbor. She called Saul and the police. They took you to the station and Social Services brought you here. At the time, you were catatonic. Do you know what that means?"

Having just spent weeks inside herself while listening to life continue on the outside, she knew far better than he ever would what it meant to be catatonic.

"Yes," she said.

"You've been catatonic until now, except for once. You

spoke at the police station." He paused, searching her face. "Do you remember that?"

She shook her head.

"You spoke to Saul."

"Because he's my friend," she said. If she were going to talk, it would be to him.

Once more, a puzzled look crossed the doctor's face. It was beginning to irritate her.

"I can't help feeling I'm missing something important," she said.

"You're right, Jayne. There is something, but I'm very concerned it might be more than you can handle."

"Tell me," she said.

In a slow, calm voice, he tried.

"You appear to have amnesia, so you wouldn't know. You had never met Saul before you were found in the park. You spoke to him though, at the station. You were being called Jane Doe and you told him you didn't like such a plain name. That's why he added the Y to the spelling. And then I asked him to visit you here. To see if you would respond to him again."

"I don't understand," she said.

Dr. Frank tapped his fingers on the clipboard in his lap. He kept talking but she tuned him out. She knew he was trying to make a point but it eluded her. It pinged against the walls of her mind like a frenzied handball.

"Jayne?" The doctor stood up. "Jayne? Stay with us. You need to stay with us, okay?"

The ball of confusion slammed to a stop and she finally understood, really understood, what he meant.

"My God!" she said, her hand moving to cover her mouth.

It didn't seem to be the reaction he'd hoped for.

A hysterical giggle formed but she held it in. She'd ripped

herself from her cocoon because she thought Saul needed her. Only to discover they had never even met.

Nothing mattered but rectifying her mistake. She reached for her home in the white world—and felt as though she'd been kicked in the gut.

The door was gone.

"How is she?"

Dr. Frank tapped his lips, watching Jayne's door for a moment before answering Saul.

"She's not catatonic but that doesn't help much. She has amnesia."

"She doesn't remember anything?"

"Not really."

That's not how it seemed to Saul.

"When I told her you'd never met before she was found in the park, she seemed shocked. I'm not sure what's going on in her head right now but she wants to talk with you in the garden."

"She already knew my name. How did that happen?"

"Most likely she heard one of us call you that."

"That's... possible?" Saul said.

"Possible? Yes, of course."

A simple answer but one that shattered any stability he'd previously felt about his involvement with Jayne like glass in a gale force wind.

The nurse pushed the garden door outward and a surprisingly cool breeze lifted a strand of Jayne's hair. Denied entrance to her internal solitude, Jayne had used the last of her strength to insist on meeting Saul and had chosen the yard seen from her window as the place to do it.

She dreaded seeing him, felt a searing combination of shame and anger at the thought, but she had to know. Why had he said he needed her to come back to him? He owed her an answer and she wanted to look him in the eye when he explained it.

He was already there, waiting. As he turned around, she straightened her shoulders and adjusted the robe the nurse had given her. He looked at her with a fierce intensity—and the kindest gaze she'd ever experienced.

Saul turned at the clink of the heavy metal door as it locked back in place. There she was. He approached but had no idea what to say.

Jayne broke the awkward silence.

"Can we sit?" She pointed to a bench.

They sat at opposite ends but facing each other. She rubbed her forehead.

"You tricked me," she said.

The directness surprised him.

"I didn't mean to."

"I don't care, you still did. Who are you?"

"Saul Becker."

"Not what I meant," she said. "Who are you, as in why are you here?"

"Good question," he said. A spark of anger flashed in her eyes.

He could give her the bare facts, answer the literal question, but he sensed that nothing short of the naked truth would satisfy her.

"I didn't want you to be alone," he said.

That was as naked as he could get.

She nodded, more to herself than to him.

"Because you know what it's like to be alone."

Her certainty unnerved him.

"I didn't say that."

She ignored his protest and said, "Why did you tell me all those things about yourself?"

Saul felt like someone was sitting on his chest. He struggled for an answer.

Because he thought she couldn't hear him? Because it felt good?

"Maybe because I don't know you."

That was the best he could do.

She snorted. "I know you pretty damn well."

"I didn't mean—"

"It doesn't matter," she said. "You may not get this, but I was happy where I was. I came out because I thought we were close somehow. Close enough that getting here to help you was worth the price. It was stupid of me, I admit, but now I can't get back."

"You've tried?"

"I've tried."

He'd never considered how she might feel about his visits. Why would he, when he thought she'd never know about them?

"I want to understand what happened between us while I've been here," she said.

His thoughts raced. Nothing happened. He visited because Dr. Frank asked him to. Then he visited because he liked the release of talking about his past. But how could he admit to that?

"Dr. Frank knew you talked to me at the station and had hopes we could recreate the breakthrough. I had to do something while I was here, so I talked. I didn't know you could hear me."

"And if you had, would you have done anything different?"

Absolutely. But he couldn't say that out loud. It felt like a lie.

"I... can't explain it. I liked talking to you."

The sun had moved beyond the courtyard, their bench covered by shadows. She shivered and wrapped her arms around herself in a hug.

"I liked hearing you talk," she said, "but I thought we knew each other."

"And if you'd known we didn't, would you have done anything different?"

She rolled her eyes. "Yeah. I'd still be catatonic."

"Then I'm glad I did it."

She jumped off the bench.

"What? How can you say that?"

"You might as well be dead as live like that. Whatever happens now, it's got to be an improvement."

"It wasn't your decision to make."

"I didn't. You did."

"Because I thought you needed me."

"Or maybe part of you knew it was time to snap out of it. Maybe that's why you can't get back."

She got as far as the door before she hesitated, then came back and sat down again.

"You'd like that, wouldn't you?" she said.

"Like what?"

"For me to leave and let you go back to your isolated life. Let you pretend like I don't even exist."

"And how is that any different than what you want to do?"

He'd said it in anger, but his words felt like a splash of ice water on his face.

"Huh." She closed her eyes and began rubbing her forehead again. "You know what? I'm tired and my head hurts. I want you to come back and finish this conversation in the morning. Can you handle that?"

The edgy attraction that had pulled him to her time and

again was still there. In fact, the connection had actually strengthened with his new understanding. The difference between what he'd been doing for the last two years and Jayne's catatonia was just a matter of degree.

"I can handle it if you can," he said.

CHAPTER 10

SAUL FOUND MRS. BLACKSTONE in the gazebo with Julie.

"Hey, Saul," Julie said. "We're talking about holding a party in the courtyard—you know, for all the tenants."

"Like a block party?"

"Only better," Julie said. "No traffic. That okay with you?"

"I guess."

"I'll take that as a yes," she said. "I'll post a list of possible dates next to the mailboxes, get some feedback, and advertise a final date. Jimmy said he'd post a music request sheet there too. He wants to DJ the party." Jimmy was a college student who lived next door to Julie.

"What kind of music does he have?" Mrs. Blackstone said.

"Ask him and he'll say he can find anything on the Internet."

After Julie left, Saul filled Mrs. Blackstone in on Jayne's awakening.

"You need to apologize," she said.

"For what?"

"I think she was right. You wanted to get her so mad she'd tell you never to come back."

"What is this, beat-up-on-Saul day?"

"Something drew you to her—don't pretend it didn't. And it seems something has drawn Jayne to you. So why don't you let your guard down just a tad and see what develops?"

"You like her so much, you can go in my place tomorrow."

"I'd like to meet her, but not tomorrow. I have to take my car in to have the tire fixed."

"What's wrong with your tire?"

"I didn't tell you? I got a flat today. Fortunately, I was just down the block and a nice young man came along to help." She held her hand up between them. "Don't even say it, Saul. I had my pepper spray ready. And I refuse to be unfriendly just because the world's gone crazy. Anyway, I'm fine, but I've got one of those baby tires on my car now."

Saul was leaning against the frame of the gazebo. He pushed off, preparing to leave.

"Oh," Mrs. Blackstone said. "Did he ever get ahold of you?"

"Who?"

"The man who changed my tire."

Saul was thoroughly confused. "Why would he?"

"He was here to look at the open townhome. Said he'd called but no one answered so he came over to check it out."

"Haven't heard from anyone today. What was his name?"

"Bill. He must be interested. He'd done some homework on you."

"Oh?"

She nodded. "Knew you were the owner and you used to work for the police department."

That was odd.

"When he mentioned it, was he just making conversation or did it seem as if he was prying? Like fishing for more information?"

"My goodness, Saul. Must everything in life be suspect? It's not like he was waiting close by, just hoping my tire would blow out. He wouldn't even take money for helping me! He said, 'What kind of world would we be living in if a man can't help just because it's the right thing to do?'" She drew her shawl tightly around her arms as she stood. "It was a breath of fresh air to meet someone who still seems to care about people."

That evening, while Saul worked out in his basement gym, he could feel something nagging him, struggling to surface. It was the kind of thing you had to let go of before you could remember.

So he spent the early morning hours in his usual position, letting random ideas shoot from both his subconscious and conscious mind, like fastballs out of a berserk pitching machine.

One such notion concerned his empty townhome. He hadn't found a suitable tenant and in fact, had not spent much effort to do so. Unless the mystery man called again and proved to be acceptable, he decided he was happy to just let the place sit empty for a while.

And there it was—the thought he'd been trying to get to, indirectly, all night.

He never put his name in for-lease ads but he did have it on his phone message. So if Bill knew his name, he had to have called. Mrs. Blackstone even said he called. He knew there were no unheard messages on the office phone but there should still be a record in the missed call history log. It would have Bill's number and give Saul a way to follow up on him.

He went to his office and checked through the log for the previous several days. There wasn't a single number he didn't recognize.

CHAPTER 11

AFTER SAUL LEFT, JAYNE SLIPPED into a dreamless sleep. When she woke, the darkness outside the window seemed just a shade lighter than nighttime. She guessed it might be around four or five in the morning, but there was no clock in her room on which to verify.

Sitting on the edge of the bed, she realized she couldn't picture her own face. She felt it with her fingers and couldn't visualize any features. In the dark bathroom, she stared at the shadow of her head in the mirror and tried to fill in the details.

She was... kind of mousy. Unremarkable.

She flipped on the light and flinched when she saw a vibrant blond, with a face she had to admit *was* remarkable, even stunning. She touched her cheek and the reflection copied the gesture.

Yep. It really was her.

She suddenly realized she was starving and rummaged through the drawers, looking for her clothing or the robe she'd been given the day before. She found neither but was so hungry she was willing to risk the embarrassment of leaving her room in the hospital gown. At least it was fastened with snaps, not ties, so her ass didn't hang out.

There was a nursing station not far from her door and a stern, dark-haired woman looked up, startled, when Jayne come out.

"Hi," the nurse said. "I'm Eve. I heard you'd returned to consciousness but you were asleep when I came on duty. How are you feeling?"

"Starving. Where's my robe? Or my clothes?"

"Sorry, psych patients aren't allowed to have them without supervision." Eve pulled out her records, flipping through the pages. "I'll ask the doc about your clothes but he does say you can eat. You should probably go with something light since you've been on intravenous food for a month. Unfortunately, it's a few hours before breakfast. Let's see what we have in the fridge."

Eve lead her to the staff room, a rectangular space that housed a kitchen and smelled like burnt popcorn. All the cabinets had locks on them.

Eve rummaged through the refrigerator shelves and pulled out some Jell-O and a container of chicken broth. She unlocked a drawer and gave Jayne a plastic spoon, then unlocked another cabinet and grabbed a handful of crackers.

"I need to get back to the desk," Eve said, relocking the cabinets. "You can warm the broth up and eat in here if you want, or come sit with me."

Jayne put the soup in the microwave for a minute, then took a sip to test its warmth. Before she could stop, she'd slurped it all down, tipping the cup up to drain the last drop.

She grabbed a hefty handful of crackers and the pink Jell-O, then went to sit next to Eve at the desk.

"Finished the soup already?"

"I told you I was hungry."

The cool texture of the Jell-O soothed her dry throat and filled some of the empty spots in her stomach. She had to fight an urge to lick the plastic cup clean. She threw it into the trash to eliminate temptation, moving on to the stack of crackers.

"How long before breakfast?"

Eve laughed. "A while yet. I did add you to the list."

"Did you ask for double servings of everything?"

"You'll fill up faster than you think. It's been a month since you had real food."

"Maybe longer," she said. "Since I don't remember the last time I ate."

Eve didn't respond for a moment, and the quiet became so deep you could hear the crunch of Jayne's crackers.

"It must be strange. Not knowing who you are." Eve hesitated before continuing. "I don't mean to offend, but you don't seem upset about it."

"Not offended," Jayne said and spent some time thinking. "You're right. I'm not upset."

"How could that be?" Eve seemed earnest, wanting to understand how such a thing was possible. "Someone must be out there, hunting for you everywhere. Doesn't that worry you?"

Jayne tossed the remainder of the crackers into the trash.

"You were right," she said. "I'm already full. I'm going back to my room."

Once there, she sat on the edge of her bed and waited for her heart to slow. She didn't know why, but the thought of someone hunting her had scared her to death.

After an early morning shower, Jayne surrendered to an impulse to hide in bed, curled in a tight ball with the covers drawn over her head. She had no expectation of actually falling back asleep, didn't even realize she had until she heard a deep, male voice saying hello just outside her door. A female, probably a nurse, responded.

With those extra moments, Jayne bolted out of bed and into the bathroom. She was relieved to find clothes stacked on the cabinet. Jeans and T-shirt. Probably what she'd been wearing when they brought her here. She sniffed them. They smelled like laundry detergent.

There was a knock on her room door.

"It's Saul."

A sudden onslaught of nerves made her fingers tremble and she closed them into a tight ball.

"Stop," she said, speaking to her fists. She cracked the bathroom door and yelled, "Come in! I'll be there in a sec."

After she dressed, she tested out a smile on her mirror-self, straightened her shoulders, and made her entrance.

Saul started to say something but stopped before any words came out. Apparently it was up to her to get the conversational ball rolling.

"It occurs to me," she said, "that I never said thank you. I do understand you've been trying to help. So, thanks. You know, for making the effort."

She twisted her hair into a knot off her neck, then let it fall back down in a gesture that felt familiar. A small, perky woman in pink scrubs stuck her head in around the doorframe. Jayne recognized her from the previous day. Her name was Cindy.

"Sorry to interrupt," Cindy said. "You doing okay? Need anything?"

"We're fine," Jayne said. Her stomach rumbled so she added, "But I'm… did I miss breakfast?"

"Afraid so. There's probably a tray with your name on it around here somewhere, but I wouldn't recommend it. The food isn't all that great when it's fresh. I sure wouldn't want to eat it cold."

"Is there some other option?" Saul said.

"The campus cafeteria is in the basement of this building. You'd have to pay for the food, though."

"No problem," Saul said. "I've got money."

Resentment rippled through her.

"I don't need your money," she said.

The words felt foolish as soon as they were out of her mouth. She chewed her bottom lip to help temper the strong emotion.

"I mean," she said, in an attempt to divert Saul from how serious she'd been, "I'm willing to wait on lunch."

She could tell she hadn't fooled him. What she sensed was his cop face settled in, sifting through the details of the moment, analyzing the trigger, wanting very much to keep digging until he understood.

"Leave it alone," she said.

He startled.

"Sure. If that's what you want."

"The truth is," she said, "I'm very hungry. Can I get you to make the offer again? I promise this time I'll just say yes."

Saul nursed a glass of iced tea, keeping a watch on the room behind Jayne as she ate.

"So, about that conversation you wanted to finish?" he said when she was done.

She took the time to stack her dishes on the plastic tray and wipe the crumbs on the table into her palm. She brushed off her hands over the tray.

"I'm not mad anymore," she said.

Their table was beside a window. She watched a butterfly rise and fall as it flapped its wings, making flight look like a struggle.

"I was talking with my neighbor last night," Saul said, "the one who found you. She says it's obvious something drew me to you, since I kept spending time down here. She also says it's obvious something drew you to me, since you came back when you thought I needed you. She can be a nosy pain in the ass sometimes, but she isn't half bad when it comes to advice."

"And that is?"

"That we should let our guard down and see what happens between us."

"What do you think of that?"

"I'm afraid you think I'm creepy for coming here, telling you what I did."

She shook her head. "I'm afraid you'll think I'm creepy for coming back to help you. Like maybe I'll turn into a homicidal stalker."

He almost laughed.

"I'm going to trust my instincts here and not worry about you being homicidal."

"Okay. I'll trust my instincts and not worry about you being obsessive." She extended her hand to him. "Friends, then. At least for today."

She turned to look as a noisy crowd entered the room. The sudden flood of strangers frightened her and she whipped her head back around to face Saul.

He studied the group. Most of them wore hospital IDs around their necks. No one struck him as out of place.

"What is it?" he said.

"The crowd just spooked me. I… remembered being afraid this morning. Of someone hunting for me."

She expected him to laugh or tease her for being irrational. Instead, his expression turned even more serious. He believed her completely. The idea made her hands start shaking again.

"You know something, don't you?" she said. "What is it you know?"

"Just that trusting your instincts never steers you wrong."

***

Later that afternoon, Jayne told Dr. Frank about her reaction to Saul's offer of money.

"I was furious when he said he had money. It seemed so condescending, and…" She searched for the right word. "Arrogant, maybe? Like his having money made him better than me, gave him power over me. I felt too inept to make my own choice."

"Interesting wording," Dr. Frank said. "Saul had power. You were inept."

"It wasn't Saul that I felt had the power. It was his money."

Dr. Frank rubbed his cheek while watching her with his study-a-bug-under-a-magnifier look.

"I'm wondering, can you give me a description of who you are?" At her hesitation, he added, "What you're like, I mean."

"How could I possibly answer that without any memories?"

"Can you give me a description of how you want to be, then? What would make you happiest to discover about yourself?"

The walls in Dr. Frank's office were home to framed diplomas and awards, plus one large framed print of a wolf peering out from behind a tree with only one eye visible. She loved the picture.

"I'd like to be like him," she said, pointing at the wolf. "Watching, holding back, waiting to make his next move on his own terms and only when he's ready."

"Sounds like someone accustomed to taking care of herself. I wonder if you projected a general resentment onto Saul and his money. Maybe we all seem a little arrogant to you right now for thinking we know what's best. It would be a normal reaction."

"Maybe," she said. "To be honest, it gives me a headache trying to figure out what's going on in a brain that won't let me in."

"Therapy can be frustrating for people who *have* memories,

so I understand how that frustration is magnified for you. Still, we can only go with what we have so here's what I think. You're a strong-willed woman who's accustomed to being in control of her life."

"I guess," she said, "but I don't see how I can do anything about it. I *am* in a mental institution, after all. That tends to make the caretakers bossy."

"It won't be for much longer. When you're ready, there are several halfway houses that will help you get on your feet. Worst-case scenario, of course. Best case is you recover your memory soon and go home."

"I like it here."

"What do you think about testing the waters, just for an afternoon? Saul mentioned he has a neighbor who wants to meet you, the lady who discovered you at the park. Do you think you'd be up for meeting someone new, spending a few hours out of the hospital?"

She smiled. "I think I'd like that."

"You aren't ready yet," he said, "but we'll work on getting you there."

A seed of anger began to germinate. Dr. Frank had it right. She didn't like being told what to do. It was time for her wolf to come out from behind the tree.

"No. I'm ready now. I'll tell Saul myself next time I see him."

CHAPTER 12

JAYNE WOKE EARLY THE MORNING of her outing with Saul and paced by the nurses' station while she waited. He stopped midstride when he came around the corner.

"You're stunning," he said.

Cindy had given her some makeup and a short-sleeved tailored cotton shirt, purple with black pinstripes. She ran her hands down the front of the shirt, smoothing it out. Talk about her looks made her uncomfortable.

"Where's Mrs. Blackstone?"

"Waiting in the car, pretending that because she's over eighty she shouldn't have to walk this far just to turn around and go back to where she started."

"Makes sense to me," she said.

"Well then, I suspect the two of you will get along great."

A few steps beyond the front door, Jayne suddenly couldn't breathe. She held her palms together, touching her lips as if in prayer, until an order to inhale suddenly reached her brain. The resulting gasp was audible.

"Maybe we should go back," Saul said.

"No. Just give me a minute."

Very slowly she refilled her lungs. Then, just as slowly, she released the breath. Four counts in. Hold. Four counts out. Repeating the rhythm until her nerves calmed.

"You know yoga breathing techniques?" Saul said.

"I don't know, do I?" She spotted a small, white-haired figure standing by a tree. "Is that Mrs. Blackstone?"

"That's her and her car. I only have a pickup, so she's driving."

Jayne approached her, a bit hesitantly.

"I'm glad to meet you, Mrs. Blackstone. I'd like to thank you for helping me."

"Don't mention it. I'm so glad to see you're okay—except for the memory thing, of course. And let's hope that's temporary."

Saul helped them both into their seats. Once buckled in, he said, "Any idea what you want to do?"

"It's a beautiful day and I'm tired of indoors," Jayne said. "Can we do something outside?"

The day was cool, with a touch of fall.

Mrs. Blackstone recommended the zoo.

They stopped inside the entrance, at a dry fenced yard with a few scraggly trees and a family of anteaters massed in the shade. Their den smelled like old hay and musk. Jayne watched Saul out of the corner of her eye as he studied a map.

"Lions or monkeys?" he said.

Her head brushed against Saul's chest as she leaned over to see the map. She could feel the definition of well-worked muscles. Glancing up, she saw something flicker in his face and blushed as she moved back.

"How about wolves?" she said.

"The Wolf Pack Woods is to the right."

"To the right, then."

He took a few steps down the path but paused when she didn't follow. She blushed again, that time because he'd caught her staring at him.

"Everything okay?" he said.

She'd been thinking about her attraction to him. Sure, he was handsome, but looks weren't the biggest appeal. He had a powerful presence, always fully in the moment, intensely aware of everyone and everything. There was no way she was willing to voice those thoughts so she just smiled.

He smiled back.

"Oh my God!" she said. "You need to do that more often."

"Do what?"

"Smile. You have a great smile."

He almost, but not quite, showed the smile again before turning down the path.

The wolf pack was a natural habitat exhibit but none of the animals were in sight. While they waited to catch a glimpse of the wildlife, Jayne read aloud from the display.

"Wolves are social animals that live in packs consisting of seven to eight related members. There is a highly complex social order in the pack and every member has a place within the dominance hierarchy." She sighed. "I wish I was that secure about my place in life. I don't even have a den to sleep in."

"Saul mentioned that you'll need a home soon," Mrs. Blackstone said. "I think you should come and stay in my extra room."

Jayne spread her fingers out over her heart. Before she could thank Mrs. Blackstone, her new friend had begun an apology.

"Oh, I'm sorry," she said. "I can be such a meddlesome so-and-so. I don't mean to pressure you."

"No, I'm grateful." Jayne lowered her hand. "I think I'd like that. Obviously, I can't pay you. At least for now."

"Good, because I wouldn't accept payment," Mrs. Blackstone said. Pleased with herself, she insisted on treating them to celebratory ice cream.

Saul didn't comment one way or the other on the offer of a room. Jayne was certain silence meant he was thinking. Did he not want her living at his property? Would she change her mind if he did? She thought not. She already loved Mrs. Blackstone and had been dreading the idea of living in a half-way house with strangers. He'd just have to adjust.

As they left the Wolf Pack Woods and moved onto the main path, Saul turned abruptly, scanning the crowd. She followed his gaze and saw nothing but a few groups of casual visitors. None of them paid her any attention as they passed. She moved in closer to Saul.

"What is it?" she said.

He wiped off his frown and looked at her.

"Nothing," he said with a shrug.

Jayne and Mrs. Blackstone sat next to the carousel as they waited for Saul to bring them ice cream. They watched excited children hand over tokens and race forward to choose an animal, followed by older children jostling for the best seats.

"I like the monkey," Mrs. Blackstone said, pointing to a replica of a chimpanzee stretched out horizontally, holding a perfectly peeled banana in front of its mouth. The carousel twirled and the monkey perpetually chased its treat.

A blond woman in dress slacks with a bulging multipock-eted bag slung across her shoulder stopped beside them.

"Is this seat taken?"

She pointed to the open third of their bench.

"No, not at all," Mrs. Blackstone said, moving her own purse into her lap to make more room. "Are you enjoying the zoo today?"

"I'm hoping to." She pulled out a cell phone and began messing around with the keys.

From Jayne's perspective, she never actually accomplished anything. She wasn't calling anyone because she never put the phone to her ear and she didn't seem to be texting. About the time Jayne realized the woman must be maneuvering through a set of menus, the lady raised the phone toward her ear but never spoke into it. The phone was pointed directly at Jayne.

"We should go check on Saul," Jayne said, standing up and turning her back on what she suspected was a camera.

"No need," Mrs. Blackstone said. "Here he comes now."

All three turned toward Saul, carrying a cardboard tray with ice cream cones shoved precariously into the depressions. His lips were thinned in a grimace, eyes narrowed.

"Busted," the stranger said, snapping her phone shut.

Saul handed the tray to Mrs. Blackstone.

"Lorel Martin. What are you doing here?" he said, putting himself between Jayne and the woman.

"Hi, Saul. How are you?"

"Don't say anything," he said over his shoulder to Jayne and Mrs. Blackstone. "She's a reporter."

"You make it sound like I'm the enemy," she said. "I'm just looking to help."

"You mean like in your last story?"

"My editor thought it was great."

"How long have you been following us?" he said.

"Only since the wolves."

Exactly when Saul had seemed briefly unsettled.

"You changed the focus of the story from Jayne to me," he

said. "You had to know that reduced the chances of its helping someone identify her."

"Are you sure you just didn't like the attention?"

"I don't like the attention. It was unwarranted years ago and it still is."

Saul took a step toward Lorel. She took a step back.

"My original story wasn't as… aggressive." She shrugged. "My editor told me to spice it up."

"So you did."

"It's my job."

"Forget it," Saul said. "This conversation is over."

He'd already taken several steps away from Lorel when she called out, "Hey. At least tell me who she is."

He studied her a minute before speaking. "How did you know we were here?"

Lorel readjusted the bag on her shoulder and considered his question.

"I got an anonymous tip that the detective in my story and his lady friend were at the zoo today."

"Man or woman?" Saul said.

A slight hesitation. "Man."

"It had to be someone from the hospital," Mrs. Blackstone said. "No one else even knew we were going out today."

"What time did the call come in?" Saul said.

"You should try reporting. You're real polished at asking questions." His scowl deepened. "Oh fine. About an hour ago."

Jayne grabbed his arm and dug her fingers into his flesh.

"Don't let her put me in the paper," she said.

His lips curled into a grin but it was nothing like the smile she'd enjoyed earlier. The reporter didn't seem to like being on the receiving end of it.

"I'm sure you won't back off just because it's the right thing to do," he said, "so how about this? You pass on what isn't really much of a story—we're visiting the zoo together, big deal—and we'll give you an exclusive on something a lot better when the time comes."

Lorel crossed her arms, fingers tapping against her elbows.

"So what's the real story? And when can I have it?"

"You can have it when my friend is ready, but I'll give you a taste, as long as what I'm about to tell you is off the record until I say so. Got it?" He continued when she nodded. "Mrs. Blackstone was wrong. The call couldn't have come from someone at the hospital because we didn't decide where we were going until we were in the car. Which means someone followed us, then called you. Someone's playing a game, with all of us as the patsies."

Lorel turned to Jayne. "Who is it?"

"How would I know?" she said. "I have amnesia."

Lorel's face lit up, the headlines apparent in her eyes.

"For now, nothing," Saul said. "When she's ready for it to be told, it's all yours."

Lorel bit her lower lip.

"At least give me a name."

"I go by Jayne."

"Really? That's the best you can do?" she said. "Okay, no story tomorrow, but any of you cross me and I will crucify *him*."

She flung her arm out, finger pointing at Saul.

"What else is new?" he said.

The Lucky Bar and Grill still held its afternoon ambience: quiet, laid back, a place for the local professional crowd to gather for off-site meetings or drinks on the way home. Nothing like later in the evening, when the men-in-blue took over and the hard-core drinkers scattered to venues where the law wasn't watching so closely.

Saul sat at a booth facing the front door, drinking a glass of tonic water with lime, disquieted by the fact he had been oblivious to being followed to the zoo.

Chuck spotted him easily in the light crowd and slid into the seat across from him. He mouthed "the usual" to the bartender.

"You look like you want to bite somebody," he said.

The waitress brought a shot of Jameson to the table and set it in front of Chuck.

"About time you got this guy coming back in here," she said with a nod toward Saul. "Where's the rest of the crowd?"

"Be here later, I'm sure. Thanks, Sheryl."

"Anytime," she said, giving Chuck a much more intimate smile than she'd given Saul.

"I see you haven't lost your touch with the ladies over the last year."

"It's a fact. They love me." Chuck watched her glide back to the bar then said, "Let me guess. You asked me here to inquire about the property damage report."

"No, but as long as you brought it up..."

"Turns out it was filed from a computer at a public library. So basically, we'll never know who did it or why."

"Someone's messing with me." Saul took a sip of his drink.

Chuck gave him a minute then said, "You want to explain that?"

Saul leaned back, draping his arm over the back of the booth.

"Hear me out before you decide I'm nuts, okay?" He waited until Chuck gave him an actual nod. "Mrs. Blackstone's plants have been pushed over two more times. The last incident, a neighbor saw someone on her porch but the guy ran off before he could get a good look at him. Then, a few weeks after we found Jayne, a man appeared out of nowhere to help Mrs. Blackstone with a flat tire."

"Same guy?"

"No way to know. He told her he was there to check out my rental. Asked some questions about me but he already knew my name, that I owned The Courtyard, and that I'd worked for the department."

"So?"

"I never say I'm the owner and I don't put my name in the ad," Saul said. "To get that, he had to call the number and listen to the recording. He even said he'd called, but there's nothing in my missed calls log that I don't recognize. So I started watching the missed call log. Suddenly I'm getting a string of calls coming in from the same number— the pay phone outside The Corner Store."

"The one with the ATM skimmer?"

"Yeah."

"How many calls?"

"Four or five a day. At first, if I answered he'd just hang up. Now he stays on the line but doesn't say anything. If I'm not there, he leaves a message. No words, just breathing."

"Did the guy ever call back about the rental?"

"No."

"Who do you think it is? Someone you put away?"

"I'm not so sure it's about me. What if it's about Jayne?"

"That's a big what if."

Saul held up his hand. "Go with me on this. Jayne has a recurring fear that she can't explain, but she says it feels like someone is hunting her."

"Paranoia?"

"Something scared her into that tree. Into catatonia. Caused her amnesia."

"Fair enough. Still…"

"I took her to the zoo today. That reporter from the *Post* showed up. She got an anonymous tip we were there."

"Hospital staff?"

"They knew we were going out, didn't know where."

"Zoo staff?"

"Mrs. Blackstone paid for the tickets while we waited in the car. The person who took our tickets was female. The caller was male."

Chuck shook his head.

"Seems more likely to be from your past. Where's the Jayne connection?"

Saul knew he was missing a piece of the puzzle. It was why he'd wanted to talk with Chuck in the first place.

"I keep going back to that first day, when Mrs. Blackstone found Jayne in the tree. I think she crawled in there to hide, which means someone really was after her. And maybe that person was close by when Mrs. Blackstone called the cops. Remember, Mathews and Roan were already heading in. Their response time would have been minutes. So maybe this person was forced to watch from the periphery as Jayne was taken out of his reach."

"But why all the phone calls, the petty vandalism? If he's out there, all that does is tip you off, and that doesn't make sense."

Saul's focus drifted toward a group at the table next to their booth. Their interaction had seemed a bit stiff, as if they didn't know each other well. His analysis was confirmed when they prepared to leave and went through the social dance of exchanging business cards. He overheard one say, "Tell Don I'll call soon."

"Shit," he said.

Chuck turned around to see what Saul had been looking at. "Shit what?"

"You're right," Saul said.

"Good for me. Right about what?"

"It all tips me off that he's out there and that's exactly what he wants."

"Why?"

"He's leaving his business card, and he has a message he wants me to pass on to Jayne."

"Saying what?"

"That he's in town and he'll be in touch."

CHAPTER 13

SINCE GOING TO THE ZOO, Jayne had found the confinement of hospital life more and more irritating. She was grateful when Dr. Frank agreed to hold their daily session outside.

"Saul's driving me nuts," she said.

"I've noticed, but doesn't the work you're doing with him make you feel safer?"

"I suppose, but he doesn't have to be such a dictator."

Saul had insisted on giving her self-defense training while they waited on her release. He reminded her—time and again—that she needed to trust her instincts, trust the fear she had of someone hunting her, and act accordingly.

"But do you feel safer because of the training?" Dr. Frank said.

"Safer would be not feeling like someone was after me," she said. "But I guess I'm less afraid."

"Good," Dr. Frank said. "As far as finding your memory goes, getting out into the world and establishing a routine is the best thing you can do. Struggling, or trying to force the memories out, is the worst thing. I'm confident you'll get there eventually, with time and rest."

"How will it happen? Is there a big bang and suddenly I know everything?"

"Some people have an 'aha!' moment where they remember everything at once. Or your past might reveal itself in pieces as you regain your emotional strength."

Normally, Dr. Frank would have no more contact with a patient after they left the hospital, but he considered her a special case. It wasn't worth bringing in a psychotherapist to take over her care because she had nothing to work from and no one who knew her to help. Jayne agreed to call him once a week and let him know how things progressed. If it ever became appropriate, he would direct her to further care.

It was time for her to leave the hospital.

Low clouds swirled in from the southeast and stalled against the western horizon, a common Colorado weather condition known as upslope. Given some heat and a little more push, the system would dissipate, leaving blue skies and pleasant temperatures. If not, they'd see either rain or an early snow.

Saul watched the environmental skirmish from the gazebo. He'd come out just before dawn to observe the pattern of shadows around The Courtyard. He watched for places that stayed in darkness longer, places a person could hide. He identified two new locations for motion sensor lights.

When the sun began to filter through the clouds, he headed inside, in no hurry until he heard the phone ringing. He sprinted to his office and grabbed the handset.

"Hello?"

Silence, except for the faint sound of breathing. The call originated at the pay phone at The Corner Store.

Saul gently set the receiver down but didn't hang up. He grabbed his car keys and ran.

Ice crystals covered his truck windows, light enough that he didn't bother scraping them off. The store was only a two-minute drive, but when he pulled up, there was no one in sight. Inside the store, a stick-thin kid slouched on top of a stool behind the counter, watching a small television. His back was to the pay phone.

Saul poured himself a cup of coffee and set it on the counter.

"Just this," he said.

"Ninety-nine cents," the kid said without even looking up at him.

Saul reached into his pocket for his wallet.

"Anyone use the pay phone outside in the last fifteen minutes?" he asked.

The kid shrugged.

"Anyone been inside the store in the last fifteen minutes?"

"Don't think so."

"Are you the only one here?"

The kid finally turned his attention from the television to Saul, glancing nervously outside and back.

"I don't have access to the safe," he said, taking a step away from the register.

Saul tossed a dollar bill on the counter and glanced up at the camera as he left.

He wondered if Chuck was getting copies of the security tapes, to keep an eye on the ATM. Still, if the kid was right, it wouldn't help. The caller had never entered the store.

Jayne fell in love with The Courtyard. A semicircle of trees sheltered the townhomes from the city traffic. An arched wooden bridge was the only break in the tree line, connecting the parking lot and the courtyard itself. A small brook ran under the bridge; its source traced back to the lake.

Mrs. Blackstone's home was a single story. It was cozy, every inch filled but not crowded. After showing Jayne her small but serviceable room, Mrs. Blackstone made tea. They took it with them to the gazebo.

"That's a nice lake," Jayne said, from the vantage point of the hilltop where the gazebo sat.

"I walk around it for exercise every morning," Mrs. Blackstone said. "That's how I ran across you. You can join me, if you like."

"Saul would love that, wouldn't he?"

"You don't need his permission, Jayne."

Her mouth turned dry and she took a sip of tea.

"No. I'm with Saul on this. Right now, the lake feels too exposed."

"I'm sure you know best." Mrs. Blackstone leaned into the railing behind her seat. "I think it's beautiful here, don't you? All the trees and wildlife. Coyotes. Birds. Squirrels—"

She shuddered.

"Something wrong?" Jayne said.

"I saw some mutilated squirrels down at the lake once. It was horrible. Oh, and we have big, fat raccoons. They may be cute but they make a holy mess if you don't make sure the trash lids are on tight."

It was hard for Jayne to imagine that this respite was in the middle of a city.

"This must be a nice place to call home," she said.

"It's your home too now. For as long as you want."

"I guess. I mean, I'm thankful I'm here." She took another sip of the tea. "But doesn't a place need memories to be called home?"

"Maybe, but they don't have to be big ones. Or old ones. You're making some now. Sitting out here with me."

Yes, the feel of the sun on her face. The soothing ambience of the landscape. The fragrant steam rising from her cup.

"This tea smells great," she said. "What's in it?"

"A special mixture I made just for you. Rose hips, because they have an uplifting effect on the nervous system, and rosemary, because it's considered an herbal remedy for memory loss."

Jayne stared toward the distant peaks, sharp against the pure blue sky. "Long's Peak is wonderfully clear today."

Mrs. Blackstone sat up straight. "The names of the peaks aren't something a stranger would know. You must be from around here."

Without any conscious thought Jayne said, "No. I came here from somewhere else."

"You know that for certain?"

Jayne lowered the cup to her lap, frowning.

"It's just a feeling."

"Sounds like a memory to me," Mrs. Blackstone said. "Keep drinking my rosemary. Before you know it, we'll find them all."

CHAPTER 14

THE MORNING AFTER HE BROUGHT Jayne home, Saul sat at his desk and looked through the sliding glass doors. His office would have been roomier if his desk were against a wall, but that would obstruct his view to the outside. He preferred a clear line of sight to more space.

A large flock of geese, necks stretched over their backs and beaks tucked into tightly folded wings, posed like sculptures on the lawn. As he watched, movement in his peripheral vision snapped his focus closer.

Jayne's breath formed clouds of condensation. She tried to open the door, which didn't budge until Saul activated the lock's remote control from a panel mounted under his desk. He waved her in as the alarm buzzed.

"Thought you might already be at work," she said.

All the surfaces, including every chair except his, were covered in books and papers. He cleared a stack from the visitor's chair, glanced around, and left the room to drop the pile on the dinette, since he could find no other place to put it.

Jayne wrapped her feet around the legs of the chair. She wore the hoodie she had on when she was found but still rubbed her arms.

"You cold?" Saul asked when he returned with two mugs of coffee. He rolled his chair next to hers so the desk wasn't between them.

She eagerly accepted the coffee.

"It's barely October," she said. "What happened to fall?"

"Fall here means just about anything. Heat waves. Snow. Wind."

"And today?"

"Today I'm thinking we'll get freezing rain. Good news is, tomorrow it could be sunny and warm."

He followed Jayne's gaze around the paper explosion.

"I know. It's a mess," he said. "I've been thinking about hiring someone to help me get it under control."

"I could help," Jayne said just as the phone rang.

"The Courtyard. Becker here." He listened for a moment. "Just a sec."

He rummaged through his mess to find a pen, then rummaged some more to find blank paper. Not finding any, he grabbed a piece from his computer printer.

"East or west?" He jotted notes on the paper as he talked. "Yeah, I know the place. Two o'clock work for you?"

"Okay," she said as he hung up, pointing to the printer sheet he'd written on. "I'm not asking, I'm telling. I'm going to organize this mess for you."

He needed the help, no doubt. And it would allow her to make some money of her own. That seemed important to her.

"You're hired. How about starting tomorrow?"

"Why not now?"

"I need to go now and I'll be out most of the day. I don't want to leave you alone."

Jayne pushed back into her chair, laid her palms out on her knees.

"Stop," she said.

"What?"

"Stop treating me like I'm made from spun glass."

When he didn't react to her declaration, she came close to him and looked straight in his eyes.

"What could possibly happen to me while I'm locked up in your fortress? I'll close the drapes; I won't open the door to anyone."

"But—"

"*I'm not Martha!*"

He looked at her for a long moment then said, "Wait here." He left and returned with a package in his hands. "I got this for you." He passed her the box. There was an express stamp on it.

Inside she found a small, bright red device about the size and shape of a cell phone.

"It's a taser," Saul said. "I'd be much happier about leaving if you promise to keep it clipped to your waist."

She pulled it out, felt how light it was, and turned it over.

"This turns it on." Saul took it from her. "The probe shoots as far as 15 feet at a speed of 135 feet per second. It has a laser aiming system. See here? You only have to make sure the red light is on the target and shoot. It doesn't even matter where it hits. It won't do any permanent damage but it will completely incapacitate."

She took it out of his hand and clipped it to her waistband.

"I promise to keep it close," she said. "Now go away and let me work."

"A few more things," he said, and took her through the house, pointing out the drawers that had loaded weapons stored in them. Then he showed her where his security controls were, both in front and back.

"Got it. They work just like the one at Mrs. Blackstone's," she said.

He hesitated only briefly when it came time to share his access codes.

After he left, she took a moment to peruse the front of the house. All the walls had solid mahogany bookshelves rising all the way to the top of the cathedral ceiling. Most of the shelves were full.

She settled into the task at hand. By the time Saul returned several hours later, she had every inch of space on the main floor—as well as a half-dozen of the steps going into the loft—covered in small, sorted piles.

"I thought you were going to make this better," Saul said.

She crawled along the floor and dropped some items in their appropriate pile.

"That's the plan."

She stretched her legs to work out the kinks then held her hands up to Saul.

He reached down to help her off the floor. Their fingers interlocked as he pulled, and when she was upright they stood close together a moment longer than necessary. Then he shook his head as if a fly had buzzed by his face and pulled away.

"I love that you live in a library," she said to break the tension between them.

"Yeah?" He shrugged. "I used some of my inheritance to do this. I don't even think about it anymore."

"Do you loan out books?"

"Nobody touches these books but me," he said forcefully, then shrugged. "And Mrs. Blackstone. She helps herself."

"Can I be an exception too? I enjoyed the books you brought me at the hospital."

"I guess if I can trust you with my papers, I can trust you with my books. Downstairs is nonfiction. Fiction is in the loft, where I sleep. Just don't take anything without telling me first. I'd know if something was missing from a shelf."

He glanced at his watch, walked to the closet by the entrance, and pulled out a navy blue top that looked soft and thick.

"Fleece. It's warm. You may need it later. Are you sure—"

"Don't even go there," she said.

Midafternoon, Jayne was eating a sandwich at the dinette when she noticed a Time-Life series called *American Landscapes* on a nearby bookshelf, organized by region. She'd been familiar with Long's Peak—maybe some of these pictures would prompt further memories.

She split the afternoon between filing and flipping through the books. Nothing from either the east or the west coast rang any bells. She moved on to the Gulf Coast, where she spent several minutes mesmerized by a picture entitled "Full Moon in the Marshes." It showed a narrow road, barely one lane, passing through a calm marsh, seeming to float over the water and through the half-dead trees and brushes.

She felt drawn to the road but it didn't pull out any memories, just a faint stirring of an emotion she couldn't pin down.

Hours later a sudden wind rattled the tree branches outside Saul's office door, seeming to shush the world with a high-pitched whistle. Jayne dropped the folders she was carrying.

She picked them up, hugging the papers to her chest as she stood. She dumped the whole mess in an empty file cabinet drawer and banged it shut, hoping her own noise would chase away the nagging discomfort that had surfaced with the on-slaught of wind.

Standing at the sliding doors, one hand caressing the taser clipped to her waist, she opened the curtains. A plastic bag inflated with wind danced across the lawn. Darkness took up full residence, outside as well as inside. She put her hand against the light switch on the wall but that nagging discomfort had turned into an instinct that screamed at her to stay in darkness.

Something banged against the front of the house and she jumped, almost dizzy with fear, her pulse racing as she turned to face the front door. Her hands brushed against the glass of the door behind her and she felt the chill through her touch.

Saul's apartment was probably the safest place a person could be, short of living with armed guards and a police dog. She was just nervous because she was alone in the dark, with the wind banging things around.

After a few moments, her pulse slowed. She turned back around and pulled the office drapes shut.

A scraping noise started at the front of the house.

Just a loose trash can lid caught between the front wall and the rose bushes. No one was watching her. No one was out there.

The noise stopped. The lid must have shaken loose and continued on its windblown way.

Her fear eased, though she left the lights off as she moved from the office to the dining room. She froze when a soft knock began. It was coming from the front door.

Rat-a-tat-tat. Rat-a-tat-tat.

Her pulse ratcheted back up.

The sound migrated to the front window, then turned into a scraping sound along the screen. She couldn't see through the drawn shades to identify the source.

When the scraping stopped, she crept across the living

room to the window and pulled the drapes back just enough to see through. Lights illuminated the courtyard. No one, or thing, was visible. She opened the drapes fully.

"Don't be such a scaredy cat," she whispered into the dark and convinced herself she'd be safe over the short distance to Mrs. Blackstone's.

She pulled the taser off her belt and practiced aiming the glowing red dot. Then she put on the jacket Saul had left for her, gripped the apartment key in her free hand, and opened the door. Knowing she only had moments before an alarm started blasting, she closed the safety net behind her faster than she wanted to.

A survey of the courtyard confirmed she was alone. She made herself walk briskly instead of breaking into a full run. She didn't want to arrive breathless. She didn't want to explain that her nerves had been more rattled by the wind than the windows.

As she reached the porch, she heard Mrs. Blackstone singing inside and the sound calmed her. Smiling, she put her key in the lock. The wind died momentarily, creating a vacuum of silence.

Rat-a-tat-tat.

The noise came from inside Meg's place, all the way across the courtyard.

Meg was in New Orleans.

Jayne's hand froze in midair, then she turned to stare at the darkened window of Meg's apartment.

By the time the wind started up again, Jayne was inside Mrs. Blackstone's with the door locked behind her.

Saul reached for the hand mike before remembering his stakeout was taking place in a civilian vehicle. He'd spent several hours parked in a motel lot across the street from The Corner Store, sitting in the dark and cold, observing the pay phones.

On the seat beside him lay an artist's rendition of the Tire Man, as Saul thought of him. He'd taken Mrs. Blackstone to a sketch artist he'd worked with professionally. Her concern that somebody wanted to hurt Jayne didn't help an already foggy memory, and Saul could tell she was reluctant to describe such a "nice man." She didn't think the end result looked much like him. Saul thought it was a place to start and better than nothing.

He'd shown it to the clerk at the motel across the street, but he couldn't identify the man. Saul waited for someone who matched the description to show up at the store. Just as he accepted the futility of his stakeout, a brand new, blood-red Camaro pulled into the lot, the bass from the speakers thumping out an angry rap to the whole neighborhood. The driver steered into the shadows by the phone booth so he could reach the receiver without leaving the car.

Saul couldn't see the driver in the darkness, but the license plate was illuminated. He had reached for the nonexistent mike, to get a make on the car from the plate number.

Curious more than hopeful, he drove across the street, passing the car as he parked. The music had stopped. The driver-side window was rolled down. When the phone rang, the driver stretched his arm out and answered. The driver's arm was sleeveless, covered in tattoos, and unmistakably black. The Tire Man was white.

Saul got out of his car and headed to the front of the store. The wind had picked up but he still heard the passenger door click open behind him.

He pivoted and was already facing the car before the door slammed shut.

"Hey, motherfucker," the car's passenger yelled, pointing a finger at Saul as he advanced. "Yeah, you're who I'm talking to."

He was much shorter than Saul, with muscles bulging in a black T-shirt with "Bad Ass" printed on the front in neon orange lettering.

"What can I do for you?" Saul said.

He kept eye contact and spoke calmly, hoping to diffuse the situation before the driver finished his phone call.

The kid blinked. Still belligerent he said, "What you watching us for?"

"I don't want any trouble," Saul said, moving one leg back, setting his balance forward, ready to move into a defensive position if necessary.

He took a split second to glance inside the store, hoping to catch the attendant's eye.

"That guy's one of our customers." The kid laughed. "He won't bother us and he sure won't call no damn police for you."

"Like I said, I don't want any trouble," Saul said. "And I don't think you want any trouble either."

The Camaro's driver door opened. Saul only looked that way after the kid did. A gangly man wearing a black tank top despite the cold evening draped his tattooed arms over the open door.

"Hey, brother," he said in a lazy drawl. "Don't you know better than to diss on a cop?"

Saul nodded to the driver, relaxing slightly.

"Tee," he said. "Been a while."

The kid sauntered back to the car. "Sorry, Tee. I didn't know."

"Get in." Tee closed the car door and walked over to Saul. "You messing with my man, there?"

"Other way around. He thought I was watching you."

"Were you?"

"Just looking for someone. Long as you're here," Saul said, showing him the sketch, "you seen this guy?"

"No," Tee said. "Hadn't heard you were back on the job."

"I'm not. It's personal."

"Poor bastard." With a short nod, he returned to his car and his recruit.

Screeching tires had him out of the parking lot and halfway down the block in a matter of seconds.

He returned to an empty home, seriously questioning his objectivity and instincts, especially when it concerned Jayne. Still, if someone was watching Saul, he knew Saul was also watching him.

Out of habit, he moved into his office and checked his phone.

He had a message: faint sound of breathing.

The call had been made from the pay phone outside The Corner Store during his short drive home.

CHAPTER 15

SERGEANT HENDRIX LOOKED UP from a property form, handed a pen to a barely dressed girl, and shook his head at Saul.

"You never call, you never write, then once you start, we can't get rid of you."

"Nice to see you too," Saul said.

The girl flashed him a measuring look, then signed her name, grabbed her possessions, and sauntered out the door.

"Looking for Chuck," Saul said. "He in yet?"

"Just got here," Hendrix said. "Go on back."

Saul inhaled the musk of too many people in one place then heard Chuck's booming voice and followed it back.

"You've got to stop teasing me," he said when he noticed Saul. "You come in here like you've never been gone and I start hoping I'll get a grown-up partner some day. No offense," he said to Danny, sitting at the next desk.

"Fuck you," Danny said.

Chuck laughed. His eyes passed over the folder Saul had tucked under one arm.

"What do you have there?"

Saul placed a drawing on Chuck's desk.

"An artist sketch of the man who helped Mrs. Blackstone with her tire. Recognize him?"

"No." Chuck passed it to Danny. "You?"

"Nah. Who is it again?"

"A guy that has Saul here nervous. We don't really know."

"Want me to make copies and pass them around?" Danny said.

"Hold off on that." Chuck stood up, grabbing his jacket from the back of his chair. "I'm taking Saul down the block for breakfast."

"I don't have the—"

"You're coming. We need to talk."

They sat at a booth in The Café, a twenty-table joint with cheap prices and an old diner ambiance that came from the fact it really was an old diner that hadn't been updated since it opened in 1959. Cracked lime-green plastic chair covers, once-green linoleum floors, and thick white crockery attested to the diner's age and authenticity. A block from police headquarters, it appealed to local law enforcement, who kept the place in business at a time when most mom-and-pop shops had long since been replaced by chain eateries. Pictures of cops, new and old, dead and alive, dotted the walls.

A middle-aged woman with silver streaks weaving in and out of her rich red hair filled two cups with hot black coffee and disappeared. Chuck raised his arms, locking his hands behind his head.

"So," he said. "What's up with you?"

"What do you mean?"

"Come on." Chuck lowered his arms, crossed them on the

table, and leaned forward. "We partnered too many years for you to bullshit me. What the hell are you up to?"

"I still say, what the hell do you mean?"

"Okay then," Chuck said. "Let me tell you what I'm seeing. I see the man who made it his career for almost two years to avoid all human attachments, suddenly obsessed with a beautiful mental patient. You move her into your neighbor's place when she leaves the hospital, then get dragged into her paranoid delusions and start obsessing about a guy who helped an old lady change her tire."

"It isn't like that."

"Fine. Explain what it *is* like. Because I've got to say, you're acting strange, even for you."

"You believed me at the bar the other day."

"I believed what you were thinking wasn't outside the realm of possibility. But unless you've got some new information you haven't shared, it's a long jump from there to getting an artist sketch done of this guy and passing it around."

"I hoped the sketch might be someone I'd recognize."

"And it wasn't."

"Correct. Once I had it, I didn't see any reason not to show it around a few places."

"Asking us to make and distribute copies isn't a casual showing."

"I didn't ask, Danny offered," Saul said, tapping his fingers on the tabletop. "You aren't buying that Jayne has a stalker, or you don't buy that the Tire Man is the stalker?"

"It bothers me that you have a tag name for a guy who's most likely just a good Samaritan."

They were quiet for a few seconds. Flaming meat sizzled and whooshed on the griddle. A bell clanged and a cook called out, "Orders up."

"You remember Meg?" Saul said.

"Your tenant?"

"Yeah. Jayne was on her way across the yard last night when she heard some noise inside Meg's place."

"Meg's still in New Orleans?"

"She is. Based on Jayne's description of the sounds, I'm thinking a raccoon got in. I do a walk around the outside, no torn screens or busted windows, but I go in to clean up for her if something did get in there."

"And?"

"I found a nice little nest. Not raccoons."

Chuck pulled himself out of a comfortable slump.

"So what was it?"

"Fast food wrappers. Half-eaten bags of chips and cookies stashed on the floor. Used towels in the bathroom. Meg confirms none of it is hers."

"Thought you had alarm systems in those places. A master control in your office."

"Tenants make up their own minds on whether to use the alarm system so I don't bother monitoring the master control. Meg thinks she turned hers on before she left but admits she was still shaken up about the theft and might have forgotten."

"Obviously, then she didn't."

"Maybe."

"Teenagers. Vagrants. You remember how fast word travels when a house is known to be vacant."

"You think I could have a teenager or a squatter next door and not know it? Plus Meg's gone a lot and never had a problem before. Nothing was stolen."

"There's not enough there for me to send someone over for prints. We have too much of a backlog as it is. I guess I could come over and take a look at things, if you want."

"No." Saul fiddled with the sugar packets, lining them up

in the container until they all faced the same direction. "I'll keep an eye on the place myself. I've turned on the full system monitor now. Anyone tries to get in, I'll know."

"I still don't see anything tying this to Jayne. Or your Tire Man."

"How long were we partners?" Saul said.

"Over five years."

"And in those five years, what did you always say you valued most about me?"

Chuck sighed. "Your instincts."

Saul's eyes locked with Chuck's.

"I'll agree with you every step of the way that my relationship with Jayne, whatever it is, is crazy. I've decided to just accept it for what it is. But the stalker? That's my professional instinct at work. Someone is out there, watching. Trust me."

Jayne sat in the gazebo and lifted her face to the sunshine, eyes closed. She heard a creak on the wooden steps beside her.

"A sun worshiper, are you?" Mrs. Blackstone said.

The sight of the thin, white-haired woman warmed Jayne as much as the sun.

"I'm thinking yes," she said. "I needed a break from filing. Almost done anyway."

They both turned at the sound of footsteps coming up the walk. It was Leslie, who lived in the townhome next to them. Jayne had never been introduced but had seen her several times, always with a shopping bag full of books and papers so heavy she canted sideways as she walked. She was a teacher and deep lines already etched her young face, as if dealing with high school kids had worn her down.

She waved and entered the gazebo with a hesitant smile. She waited for Mrs. Blackstone to extend an offer before sitting.

"I was wondering if you could give me a ride to the grocery store," she said.

"What happened to your car?" Mrs. Blackstone said.

"It broke down yesterday."

"But I just saw it in the parking lot."

"I had it towed."

"Here?" Jayne said. "Instead of to a mechanic?"

"My husband thought that was best," Leslie said. "It always costs so much just to find out what went wrong, then there's parts and labor. We're going to have to save up."

"What's wrong with it?" Jayne said.

"I was driving along and the engine just stopped."

Jayne asked what kind of sounds the car was making, the year, make, and model, how many miles it had on it.

"It happens all the time with that model," she said. "The alternator goes out around fifty thousand miles. Almost like clockwork."

Mrs. Blackstone looked astonished. Jayne tried to reassure her.

"It's an easy fix," she said. "I could do it myself if I had the tools."

Mrs. Blackstone drove Leslie and Jayne to the auto parts store, Leslie bought the part, and Mrs. Blackstone bought the tools. By sunset, Leslie had a working car.

"I wish we knew where you learned how to do that," Mrs. Blackstone said as she and Jayne enjoyed bowls of ice cream in the living room after supper.

"My dad worked on cars," Jayne said softly. "He taught me."

"My goodness," Mrs. Blackstone said. "You remember your father?"

Jayne closed her eyes. She smelled motor oil, pumice stone soap, pipe tobacco. She rubbed her fingers together and remembered the feel of calluses on his fingertips from years of playing guitar. He sang old country songs in a deep, gravelly voice.

She slid her fingers up her face and found tears on her cheeks, dropped her hand and stared at the moisture. Her hands clutched her chest as she was abruptly linked to more emotion than she knew how to contain. Mrs. Blackstone moved closer and put an arm around her.

"What is it?"

Jayne's throat was so tight she all but choked on the words. "My dad. He's… dead."

She curled up on the sofa, Mrs. Blackstone's arm still around her. She sobbed until her ribs ached and her head throbbed.

Mrs. Blackstone called Saul, who came over and called Dr. Frank. The only other thing Jayne remembered from the rest of that evening was the soft, paper-thin skin of Mrs. Blackstone's hand against her own.

She woke up still on the sofa but leaning on Saul's chest. Mrs. Blackstone was brewing tea.

"Hey," he said when he saw she was awake. His fingers brushed across her neck as he pulled back a strand of hair.

She reached a hand up to touch his heart. She could feel it pounding against her face. He responded by putting his arm around her.

"Talk to me," she said.

"About what?"

"I don't know. Anything. Why do you look so Irish with a name like Becker?"

"My mom's grandparents were born in Ireland. Her original name was Shanahan. When they disowned her, she used a Ouija board to pick Becker as a new last name."

"It must have been hard to lose her so young."

"It was a relief."

She flinched and knew he felt it.

"I'm sorry," he said. "It's different for you. I'm sure your father loved you."

"You don't think your mother loved you?"

"No."

"How can you say that?"

"Knowing her for thirty years." His hold on her tightened. "She could barely speak at the end, but she called me over to her hospital bed. I had to lean down so I could hear her whisper. She said, 'This is your fault. You should have stopped me from drinking.'"

"That's horrible."

"That was my mother."

"But she left you money. Isn't that a form of love?"

"She didn't leave me anything. The money is from a grandmother I barely knew."

"I miss him so much. I don't even know to describe it."

"At least I was saved that pain," Saul said.

How sad it must be to think that way about a deceased parent.

"I wouldn't trade a single second with my father," she said. "Not even to lessen the pain."

She sat up and he put a little distance between them.

"I only remember little things," she said. "His hands were large, strong enough to crush a rock. I wanted so much to have his hand hold mine one more time. I wanted it even more than I wanted to talk with him again... I remember trying to force one of his hands to hold mine when he was in the casket. It felt like cold rubber."

"You remember anything that would help us figure out who you are?"

"No."

"What his name was?"

"Dad?" she said, scrunching up her face. "Maybe… Dean?"

Her face went white the instant she said the name.

"NO!"

Saul turned her shoulders so she faced him.

"What is it?"

"Dean isn't my father's name," she said. "Dean is the name of the man who killed him."

CHAPTER 16

SEVERAL DAYS LATER, JAYNE TOOK her first walk around the lake. She and Saul argued—she wanted to go alone, he wanted to follow her. Of course, Saul won the argument. She felt shrouds of memory dancing at the corner of her eye but somehow knew they would never expose themselves with Saul there.

The next day she escaped without him, leaving Mrs. Blackstone to deliver the news. In deference to his fears (and hers), she clipped the taser to her belt.

Sunlight illuminated the area near the burnt-out tree. She crawled inside and felt the earth beneath her, the tree around her, a natural communion with solitude and shadow. Relaxed, with a clear mind, small memories beginning to reveal themselves like invisible ink exposed to heat.

She crawled out of the tree and more memories flushed over her, hot like a fever.

Dr. Frank had said her mind would reveal its secrets when it was ready. It must be time. She released a question, carefully, like putting a panicked fish back into the water.

Who am I?

No answer.

Did I know who I was when I entered the tree?

Yes. She had known.

An ambulance raced down the street. Its siren morphed into ringing bells, the sound so real she felt the vibrations. Looking up, she expected to see a stone church with a tall bell tower.

"Jayne!"

Saul came up behind her, slightly breathless, and she knew he'd run full speed all the way there.

"I remember," she said.

That stopped the rant she knew he was geared up for.

"Who you are?" he said.

"No. I remember things that happened here, like hiding in the tree. I wasn't catatonic when I went in. That happened while I hid there."

A gust of wind drifted across the water, surrounding her in a damp cold.

"Then there's this beautiful old stone church I can see, surrounded by skyscrapers. One of the skyscrapers is made from mirrors and wraps around it like a blanket—no, like a wall. I wonder what it means."

She could see it all clearly, even though it made no sense.

"You're talking about the Holy Ghost Catholic Church," Saul said. He sounded excited.

"My vision reminds you of something?"

"It's not a vision. That building really exists."

By 1980 downtown property in Denver had become so valuable that the Catholic Church sold everything but their buildings. A forty-story glass skyscraper was built in a semicircle around the old stone Holy Ghost sanctuary. The new building was made of a dark-green glass that reflected the building in its mirror-like exterior.

At midmorning, the drive downtown took only twenty minutes using the HOV lane. They had to park several blocks away and walk. Jayne's pace increased as the skyscraper came into sight.

She stopped in front of the church, mesmerized by the marble carvings in the wall beside the polished wooden doors. Saul tried not to interfere with her experience but pulled her aside when the doors opened and a stream of midmorning worshipers filed past them. The parish had fewer than a hundred members, but several thousand people visited the church every week.

"I know this place," Jayne said. "I'm sure of it."

A middle-aged priest with a mass of curly salt-and-pepper hair blinked at the sunlight as he emerged from the dim interior of the building's foyer. He kicked up the doorstop, sent them a friendly nod, and began to close the door. Then he looked at them again, let the heavy door close behind him, and walked stiffly down the steps, holding the railing as he moved.

"Ceecee, is that you?" He wrapped her in a bear hug, then pulled back to inspect her. "You look great. You look… well, I'm at a loss."

"You know me?" Jayne whispered once he let her go.

He stepped back and frowned.

"Of course, we've been worried about you."

"Why?" Saul said.

"She disappeared around the time a violent street gang was harassing the homeless in this area. I heard they were particularly interested in a beauty that ate here."

Jayne's hands began to shake.

"Oh dear," the priest said. "Please, come sit down."

Jayne and the priest sat on a bench in the concrete garden that ran by the side of the church and around the office building. Saul leaned against a planter box opposite them.

"Who are you?" she said when her hands had steadied.

"You know me. I'm Father Ted. I run the outreach program here."

Jayne shook her head.

"I worked with you when you were homeless. We gave you food, let you in to get warm."

"I was homeless?"

The priest ran his hands through his hair. "What's going on here?"

"Are you sure you have the right person?" Saul said. "And what name did you use?"

"Ceecee, for Cecelia. And yes, I'm sure. She was so striking, although I have to say her beauty shines forth now in a way it never did then."

"When was the last time you saw her?" Saul asked.

"It's been, let me think… It's been almost two months since you disappeared. We feared you'd become another victim of the violence. Perhaps run off by the ruffians or worse."

"Jayne, are you remembering anything here?" Saul said.

"No. I know this place, but…"

A look of comprehension smoothed the lines of confusion around Father Ted's eyes. To his credit, he simply nodded his head and offered more history.

"You just stopped coming to the food lines. No one ever saw you again. But you always were a recluse."

"When did she first show up here?" Saul asked.

"Sometime in… February? I remember it was winter because we gave her a coat and sleeping bag."

"Where did she sleep?" Saul said.

"She never stayed in the same place long. I got the

impression she was afraid of being found. She often wore a hoodie, closed around her head until you couldn't see her face. She picked up her food and ate by herself. She left if someone tried to start a conversation." He turned to Jayne. "You did talk to me some."

"What about?"

"Nothing major at first. You were interested in the mountains. I taught you the names of the peaks. Later, you opened up enough to tell me about your stint in a rehab clinic before you hit the streets here. You said it was too much. Too hard—that's the phrase you used. It must have helped though. I never saw you drink."

On the walk back to the truck, Jayne tried to draw Saul into conversation. He talked in monosyllables, and once back in the truck he concentrated on driving as if they were in the middle of rush hour. They weren't.

She tried again.

"Are you angry?" she said.

"Jayne..."

"Don't Jayne me. We need to talk about this."

"Not now."

He glanced her way, his face hard and closed off.

"I know what the priest said," she continued, "but I can feel when things are right. I don't have a problem with alcohol."

"Or maybe you're in denial," he said. "It's a big part of the illness. I should know."

They stewed in an uncomfortable silence the rest of the way home. When they got there, he unlocked her door from the side control.

"I've got some things to do."

"No you don't." She made no move to get out of the truck.

He growled under his breath but it sounded more exasperated than angry.

"I need time," he said. "I haven't been clear about much over the years but I've always been clear about one thing: I'd never get involved with an addict."

"Are we involved?"

He took a quick glance at her waist, his eyes falling on the taser.

"Pull that out for your walk back to the apartment, okay?"

"Fine." She slammed the door as hard as she could and crossed the bridge without looking back.

"I don't have an alcohol problem, Dr. Frank," Jayne said. "If I did, I'd know. And I don't know—I mean, I do know I don't have a problem."

Dr. Frank had asked her to come in when she told him about what had happened. Mrs. Blackstone drove because Saul was nowhere to be found.

"But you believe other things Father Ted said are true?"

"Maybe. I don't think my name is Cecelia either."

"Do you think it's possible," Dr. Frank said, "that being an alcoholic is part of what you're hiding from?"

"No."

"Because you've remembered enough to know it's not true?"

"Because it feels wrong."

"I think you may be too emotional right now to make that judgment. You need to calm yourself. Perhaps that will help you connect with the truth."

"How do you suggest I do that?"

"Lean back and close your eyes. Follow your yoga breathing pattern."

She did until the quiet of the room was absolute except for the sound of her breath, and even that soon blended into the rhythm of silence.

I don't drink, I don't drink, I don't drink.

She was supposed to be calming her mind. She tried to hush her interior monologue but the words repeated themselves, this time as part of a conversation.

"Come on, Anne. A shot for the road?"

"I told you, I don't drink."

It felt very, very real.

She opened her eyes.

"Well," she said, "I think I've confirmed that I don't have a drinking problem."

She shook her head to clear her thoughts.

"Although," she added, "if that memory's accurate, my name's not Cecelia. It's Anne."

When they returned from the hospital, Saul was waiting outside Mrs. Blackstone's.

Jayne stopped in the middle of the courtyard.

"Can we talk?" he said.

"I'll start water for tea." Mrs. Blackstone was gone before Jayne could stop her.

"I needed some time," he said, taking a short step in her direction. "That's not an excuse. It's an explanation."

"I'm not your mother."

"I know, but can you understand this is a big deal to me? I needed to adjust and I have. Just because you had a problem doesn't mean you haven't faced it. Father Ted said he never saw you drink. I've never seen you drink. You went to a clinic. My mother never even admitted she had a problem, much less did anything about it."

He stopped talking and gave her time to respond. She couldn't think of anything to say. She was tired. She was hurt. It was her turn to for avoidance.

"I'm sorry," he said. "How can I make this up to you?"

"Jewelry would help." She was happy to see the sarcasm cut him.

He didn't try to stop her as she entered the apartment and closed the door.

CHAPTER 17

SHE STAYED IN BED LATE the next morning with a headache. When she came out, a flower arrangement dominated the coffee table. A black box with gold hinges sat next to it.

"Good morning," Mrs. Blackstone said. "Obviously, Saul's been here."

Jayne bent her face toward the flowers, drew in the sweet aromas.

"I'm a horrid person," she said.

"Oh nonsense. Because you gave him a hard time?"

"Because I told him jewelry would help me forgive him. I was being sarcastic."

"I'm sure he knows that. Maybe he hopes the gift will help him forgive himself."

She had to give it back. She wasn't a gold digger, and it wasn't like she came without baggage. She didn't even know what that baggage was, but it didn't require much imagination to know it was bad.

"Jayne, you can't not open it."

Mrs. Blackstone was right. And she was curious.

"Here goes." She popped the jewelry box open.

Mrs. Blackstone peered over her shoulder. "I'd say that pardons this offense and a few more to come."

Inside was a delicate gold necklace with a heart-shaped ruby dangling in the center of a larger gold heart.

It was beautiful.

She had to give it back.

She took it out and put it on.

Someone called for Mrs. Blackstone's taxi service—what she called giving rides to people who no longer drove—so Jayne was left with only her headache for company. Pressure built behind her eyes as if her head were one of Mrs. Blackstone's teapots building to a boil.

She took some ibuprofen and lay down on the sofa, wrapped her forehead in a hot, wet towel, and fell into an in-between state where dreams and consciousness weave together.

In a dream she knew wasn't really a dream, she saw herself fiddling with a napkin in a bar where they called her Anne. She sat on a high stool, elbows leaning on a brightly polished bar top, feet resting on the brass railing that lined the bottom. She saw the napkin clearly. The upper left-hand corner showed a blue spruce with "Creek City Bar" printed next to it.

A powerful, floral aroma made her jerk upright. The towel fell off her head and the headache released itself in an explosion of memory.

She was sitting on the front pew in a chapel, empty except for her, a coffin, and the mass of flowers that surrounded it. From her vantage she could only see the tip of her father's nose sticking over the paneled sides of the shiny blue and gold box. It had been closed during the service but once everyone else had gone outside, strangers in suits had reopened it, then left her to say goodbye. As soon as the lid closed she'd be alone and knew it would be forever.

She inhaled the scent from the flowers around the coffin—

No, it was the arrangement on the coffee table.

Her fingers found the ruby at her neck. She missed her father with an emptiness that would never be filled, but she'd been wrong.

She didn't have to be alone.

Saul tried to stick to duties that let him keep an eye on Mrs. Blackstone's door, but as the morning went by he had to abandon his Jayne-watch for office work. When he failed a third time to balance his bank statement, he gave up and decided to head back out to the yard. He was practically at the front door when an alarm on his master security control went off. He was relieved to discover it was for Meg's place, not Mrs. Blackstone's.

He yanked the front door open and surveyed the courtyard. No one was out. He ran back to the office, slammed open his desk drawer, grabbed the pistol—the same model Colt ACP he kept in the living room drawer—and headed out the back door. He paused on the patio, searching the open area before he moved along the wall to Meg's.

Once there, he tried the door handle. Locked, no sign of forced entry. None of the windows were open either, which meant the intrusion must have come from the front, even though he'd seen nothing when he first checked.

He looked at his watch. When he was home, the security company waited five minutes for him to investigate before calling the cops. They went off alert status if the alarm was shut off or Saul called to confirm everything was okay. He had less than four minutes.

Meg's unit was in the middle of the building, so he ran to the end and rounded the corner. A few of the tenants were standing in their doorways, looking confused. The alarm was still blaring.

He tried Meg's front door. It was locked. No windows disturbed.

What the hell?

He used the key to enter, pistol aimed, heart racing, quickly cleared her two-bedroom home, then reset the alarm. The status panel clearly stated that the front door had been opened without use of the security code.

He cleared the house again, rechecked the windows and doors.

Nothing was disturbed.

He paused as he relocked the front door. He'd been outside within seconds of the alarm's trigger, since he'd been standing at his own front door when it happened. Meg's front door was unopened.

He turned at the sound of Mrs. Blackstone's door opening behind him. Jayne ran full speed across the courtyard and into his arms. His heart flipped.

"Are you okay?" he said, pulling back to examine her face. "Did someone break in?"

She shook her head and stepped back. She was wearing the necklace.

She reached up to his face and brought his lips down to hers. He abandoned a fleeting thought of resisting and pulled her into his body with one arm. They were snapped back to earth by a low whistle.

"Whoa," Jimmy said, coming out of his place into the yard. He said nothing further as he hurried past them.

"Whoa is right." Saul took Jayne by the hand and led her to his place.

He walked toward the dinette but she pulled him back.

"Let's go upstairs," she said.

"Jesus," he muttered. He shook his head. "Something's wrong."

Jayne sighed, a low exhalation resembling a moan.

"You're such a Boy Scout. Can we at least lie down together?"

The Boy Scout in him didn't think that was a trustworthy idea.

"Well then, you need a sofa," she said. "I want be close to you while we talk."

He sat in one of the reading chairs and pulled her into his lap, her legs over the chair's arm and her head on his shoulder. They sat until her breathing slowed and some color returned to her face.

"Ready to tell me what's going on?" Saul said.

"I remembered my father's funeral and how alone I felt." She punched his arm. "You left me alone yesterday."

He absorbed her punch and tightened his hold. His nerves steadied as he realized her being upset had nothing to do with what he had to conclude was a faulty alarm.

He lifted the chain along her throat, running his fingers down it until he held the ruby heart.

"No place like home."

"What?" she said.

"Like the ruby slippers in *The Wizard of Oz*. I thought a ruby heart might bring you back home." He touched the stone. "At least I hope you think of The Courtyard as your home."

She blinked back tears.

"Come on." He pushed her out of his lap. "I'll make us some sandwiches."

She followed him into the kitchen.

"I didn't really need jewelry you know," she said

"Want to give it back?"

"Absolutely not," she said and threw her hand over it as if to protect it.

He laid out four slices of bread and turned to go to the refrigerator but felt Jayne move up behind him. He froze then turned and propped against the sink, elbows bent. She stepped close and slowly ran her fingers over the muscles of his arms. He flinched slightly and his heart raced at her touch.

He bent forward, not taking his eyes off of hers. He paused inches from her face and felt her breath before her lips. The kiss started tenderly but the gentleness quickly gave way to a hunger so fierce it left them both breathless.

She took a step back, eyes on the floor as she undid her shirt, and each button she opened stripped him of another reason not to touch her, not to discover the feel of her skin in places he'd never touched, until the last button destroyed his resistance.

As her shirt fell off her shoulders, she raised her head, gathered him into her eyes, then turned and went up the stairs.

He followed.

CHAPTER 18

THE SUN HAD SET BY THE TIME Saul got around to fixing supper: sandwiches, two bottles of water, and a bowl of grapes.

Jayne plucked a grape off its stem and rolled it between her fingers.

"Not hungry?" Saul had washed down the last of his sandwich with the water.

"I don't know," she said, popping the grape in her mouth. "I guess not."

"Or is something wrong?" He leaned his chair back, draping his arm over the edge. "Was this a mistake?"

That caught her attention.

"Oh my God, no," she said. "Not a mistake. Not even a little. I was thinking about a place I remembered right before I remembered the funeral. It's called the Creek City Bar."

"Creek City is a real place. It's in the southwest part of the state. Want to check it out?"

She stood behind him, her hand on his shoulder, while he checked with information for the bar's phone number. The person who answered the call confirmed that the logo on their napkin included a spruce tree.

"Looks like a road trip," he said.

The drive to Creek City would take eight hours, so Saul wanted to start around 5:00 a.m. He was up two hours ahead of time to assemble the gear they'd need for a trip through the mountains in October. He had everything piled in his living room when the sensor lights in the courtyard came on. He opened the door to find Jayne.

"I woke up and couldn't get back to sleep," she said. She was packed and ready.

He set Meg's alarm to silent and sent a quick email to the security company, letting them know he'd be out of town and they should respond immediately if the alarm went off again. Even though he knew how much the WPD would hate being called out for nothing, he wasn't convinced the problem was with the system.

When they were ready to head out, Saul paused next to his truck to glance up and down the street. No traffic. He made sure his jacket covered his pistol and hip holster, then got in the truck.

They journeyed south in solitude. An occasional semi rolled past, rocking the truck in its wake, interrupting the quiet with its rumble. Jayne felt the presence of the mountain ranges to the west and at about the time Pueblo materialized out of the plains, shapes began to separate from the blackness, revealing the outline of peaks against the canvas of the dwindling night sky. They stopped at Walsenburg for gas and breakfast just as the sun was rising.

Saul sat with his back against the wall, watching the front door of the restaurant. As they were finishing their meal, a pair of state troopers entered. They stared toward their table for a moment before moving on. Jayne leaned over and examined his face.

"What?" he said.

"I'm looking for an invisible badge stamped on your forehead."

"What are you talking about?"

"Those guys. The ones in uniform. I'm sure they knew you were one of them."

He laughed, showed his breathtaking smile, and motioned to the waitress for the check.

"It wasn't me they were looking at."

She waited outside in the sunlight while he paid, staring at the long, narrow road that sliced through the valley and the mountains to the west. Saul moved up behind her and she turned into his chest.

He folded her hand gently into his and pressed it to his mouth, lighting a stronger desire than any embrace could have fueled.

Back in the car, they chased never-ending lines on asphalt while she cushioned her necklace in an upraised palm, thumb-stroking the backside of her ruby heart.

They arrived at Creek City during the lunch hour. The city limits sign proclaimed the elevation to be 7,104 feet above sea level, and the sun created a golden glimmer that enfolded the town.

Two highways intersected at what seemed to be the town's only stoplight. They pulled into the gas station on the west corner of the intersection, parking to the side of the pumps.

"Recognize anything?" Saul said.

She didn't.

Saul went inside and got directions to the bar. It was at the southern edge of town, a stand-alone building with an enormous blue spruce in the front yard. The aroma of fried food and spices met them just inside the door. At the back of the room was a beautifully polished bar, exactly as she had pictured it.

The bartender gave Jayne a long look as they sat at the bar and ordered soft drinks. He flipped two glasses, filled them with ice, and sprayed soda from a hose.

"Anne. Right?" He tossed out coaster napkins with a blue spruce in the corner then served their drinks.

"You remember me?" she said.

"Knew your face right off. Took a second to remember your name. You came in all the time while you were staying out at the Sunshine Inn. That was what? About a year ago?" He moved away to help another customer then started back toward the bar.

Saul looked ready to start an interrogation, so she leaned over and whispered to him.

"Let's save the questions for someone at the inn, okay?"

He relaxed and nodded.

They ate nachos while Marty, the bartender, chatted about the town, its history, the people, old and new. He knew a lot about the area and he liked to talk.

"Say," Saul said, tossing a generous tip on the bar as they were leaving. "Anne lost her credit card when she was on her trip last year. She wouldn't have left it here, would she?"

"Nope," Marty said. "Wouldn't have been here. You always paid in cash."

The Sunshine Inn and Hostel was on the northern outskirts of town. Small, picturesque log cabins dotted the landscape around the main building, which was made from adobe. Inside was dark and cool. Framed photos and landscape paintings covered the clay walls. They could see an indoor restaurant to the right of the entrance, just over a half-wall.

In a corner booth a gaunt, middle-aged woman with a long dark ponytail scrutinized receipts and tapped on a calculator. She stopped her work as the doors clanged shut.

"Can I help you?" she said, squinting toward the dim hallway.

"We're looking for Maggie," Saul said.

The lady pushed herself up from the table.

"You've found her."

Jayne stepped into the room ahead of Saul.

"Well hello!" Maggie said as Jayne entered the light. "Nice to see you again. I'm sorry, I don't remember your name."

"Anne."

Jayne took in every detail of Maggie's appearance, but felt only frustration, not recognition.

"Yes, that's right. Anne." She led them to a four-topper by a window. "What can I get you?"

"I'd like to talk to you for a minute or two, if you have time."

"Sure," she said, joining them at the table.

"Strange as it sounds," Jayne said, "I have amnesia. We came here because I recently remembered the Creek City Bar. The bartender there told me I stayed here when I visited a year ago."

"Amnesia? Really?" She raised her brows. "Well, I'll be. I thought that only happened on TV."

"We were wondering," Saul said, "if you can tell us anything about Anne's stay?"

"Happy to share what I can."

She went to the registration desk and returned with a ledger book.

"We're old-fashioned here." She licked her finger a few times to help turn pages as she scanned. "Here it is. Anne Thompson. You checked in on July 17th and left on August 2nd, last year. Stayed by yourself in a single cabin down by the creek. You drove a 1983 Ford Taurus. I remember it was blue, and... here it is, the license plate was from New Mexico. HK-8799."

"Did she use a credit card?" Saul said.

"Both weeks in advance, with cash."

"What did I do while I was here?"

"You liked to hike. Left every morning after breakfast and returned late in the afternoon. A few times, you didn't come back until after dark."

"Do you know where I went?"

"There are trails all over the place and you never told me where you'd been. What I do know is that every time you returned, you wanted to know if anyone had been around, asking about you. I never could figure if you were waiting for someone to join you or worried someone would find you."

"You never asked?"

"You were never what I'd call open or even really friendly. So no. I didn't ask. In my business you learn who you can be nosy about and who you can't. I heard talk about you being a little friendlier with Tami Martin. She owns an art gallery downtown."

A phone started ringing from the direction of the kitchen. Maggie excused herself to answer it.

"That was Tom Hardgrove from the bank," she said when she came back. "He heard you're in town. He'd like you to drop by."

They found the bank on Main Street, between a café and a clothing store. Gilded glass windows ran the full height of the doors, surrounded by wood smoothed with age. The walls of the front office were half-glass, and they could see a heavyset, mustached man at the desk. He looked up and gestured for them to come in.

"Ms. Thompson," he said. "Good to see. You saved me some trouble by showing up when you did."

"Really? How?" Jayne said as she sat down across from him.

"The rent on your safety deposit box ran out two months ago, and the notice we sent was returned."

She decided not to tell him about her amnesia. She desperately wanted to look at the contents of that box and didn't want anything to get in her way.

"I thought I'd paid through this month. What address did I give you?"

He pulled up the information on his computer.

"10822 Claremont Street, NE, Albucuerque."

"So sorry—I'm in Denver now. I hate to say it, but I also lost my key."

"Will you be maintaining the box?" She shook her head. "Then let's just empty the contents."

He unlocked the entrance to the safety deposit box room. He used his key to open her box, slid out the oblong tray, set it on a table, and left.

Jayne opened the box. The only thing in it was a bulging manila envelope. She took it out but didn't open it until she and Saul were sitting in the shade at a small city park. Inside were two more envelopes, a big one stuffed with something, a small one with the letters NMBT and the number 853 written on the outside. Anne opened the small envelope and found a key.

"Looks like the key to another safety deposit box," Saul said. "I saw advertisements on the highway for New Mexico Bank and Trust. That could be the NMBT."

"Look. My driver's license too." She held up a plastic card for his inspection. "It says I'm from Billings, Montana."

The picture had been taken a few years ago, but Anne Thompson was definitely Jayne. Saul pulled out his cell phone and called Ben Jennings, the detective working Jayne's case. He didn't answer, so Saul left him a message with the driver's license information, along with the plate number for the car Anne had used.

Jayne opened the big envelope and tipped it upside down, dumping its contents into her lap.

"I don't believe this," she said. "It's cash. A lot of cash. Why would I leave money behind?"

"Maybe whoever you were watching for finally showed up and you ran."

"I don't think so. Maggie said I stayed the full two weeks."

"You did rent the box for a year. Maybe you meant to come back."

"Makes sense I guess." She pressed her fingertips against her closed eyelids. "So far, the only useful thing we've learned is my name."

"It's all pieces of your story," he said. "Eventually we'll get enough to figure it out."

"Maybe."

She grabbed a wad of twenties, slipped them into her pocket, and put the rest of the money back in the envelope.

"Let's put this in the truck and see what Tami knows."

The first thing Saul noticed as he walked into Tami's Gallery was the exceptional quality of the offerings. Unlike the southwestern arts and crafts on the main drag, these landscapes and portraits were from all over the world. One wall displayed a collection of African masks.

Tami was dressed in a dark blue velvet mid-calf skirt with a silk turquoise top and a silver concho belt. Even her shoulder-length black hair was reminiscent of the Spanish and Indian bloodlines common to the area, although it was thick and curly rather than straight.

"Nice shop," Saul said. "Different."

The southwest image shattered the moment Tami spoke.

"I'm Irish," she said in a thick brogue, as if it were a confession. "Black Irish," she added, flipping her thick mane with her fingers. "Most of the artwork in here comes from my friends in the UK or Europe. Truth be told, I don't sell a lot from the store. Tourists want bisons and pueblos and feathers when they stop off in this town. I make my money off Internet sales or people who drive here specifically to see my shop. It has a decent reputation."

"How did you end up here?" Saul said.

"The short version is I followed a creep who left me stranded, then fell in love with the country and the people anyway."

Jayne had moved to the back wall to study the masks. Tami raised her voice.

"But you should know that, Anne. We spent plenty of time bonding over the perils of chasing bad boys."

Jayne turned away from the masks.

"We did?"

"So the rumors are true? You have amnesia?"

"I'm sorry," Jayne said. "I only remember a little from my time here. Are you saying we bonded because I followed a bad boy here too?"

"Not you. Your sister. You're much too together for that."

"I have a sister? Is she here? In Creek City?"

"Wow. You don't even remember your sister? I'm afraid I can't help much with that. I never actually met her. I think she lives in Albuquerque now."

"Did the sister's name happen to be Cecelia?" Saul said. Maybe the alcoholic who lived homeless in Denver was this sister.

"I don't know," Tami said. "Anne just called her Sissy."

"What can you tell me about my time here?"

"You were on holiday. We met your first day in town and you joined me and my friends at the Creek City Bar every evening. You liked the music and were, let me say, a fairly wild dancer. You said you were a buyer for a small department store chain that serviced the northwest. I'd never heard of it so I don't remember the name. That's about it. You said you hoped to come back but you never did."

"Maggie at The Sunshine Inn said I was waiting on someone. Do you know anything about that?"

"As far I know you were here to unwind before heading to California for a buying trip."

They lingered long enough for Jayne to buy Mrs. Blackstone a small mask with the cash she'd pulled from the envelope.

As they walked back to the truck, Saul's phone vibrated with a text message from Ben Jennings.

The Ford Taurus with the New Mexico plates was a rental from Rent-a-Wreck in Santa Fe. Anne Thompson had secured it with her Montana driver's license and paid for two weeks with cash. It had been returned on August 1st last year.

The driver's license was a forgery. There was no Anne Thompson in Billings, Montana, or at the Albuquerque address given to the bank.

Despite all its interesting little tidbits, Creek City was a total dead end.

They watched the sunset from forest green metal lounge chairs on the porch of the cabin Saul rented at The Sunshine Inn. A light evening breeze carried the scent of pine. There was as much foliage on the ground as on the branches, but the trees were a more vivid, fiery red than any she'd seen around Denver.

As she relaxed into the cool metal, she suddenly felt the weight of exhaustion. Not surprising, when she thought about how little sleep she'd had the night before. Saul probably had even less but it didn't seem to faze him.

"What do you think?" he said.

"Nothing I heard today felt instantly wrong," she said.

"How about the sister thing?"

"I'm not sure."

The sun retreated and cold settled in around them. They moved indoors. In the fireplace, logs were stacked teepee style with kindling in the middle, practically foolproof for guests that didn't have a clue how to start a fire.

Saul had it started in seconds then joined Jayne on the sofa. She turned sideways and leaned up against him and he slipped an arm around her.

"I've been wondering something," he said, shifting to give her more room to stretch her legs. "Should I start calling you Anne? It doesn't feel right."

"I know," she said. "I may end up having to change my name. I like Jayne."

She felt a light chuckle lift her hair.

"You didn't think much of it when we first met," he said.

"That was before you added a Y and made it a gift to me."

His hold on her tightened.

She watched the crackling glow of the fire and as their breathing become syncopated, she ran through her modest catalog of memories. Her earliest memory so far was of her father's funeral. She didn't know exactly when he'd died but didn't think it was more than a few years ago.

"How old are you in your first memory?" she said.

"Around nine," he said, stifling a yawn.

"That seems old."

"I read a book on childhood memory once. It said the average first memory is between three and four. But for kids with childhood trauma, it can be as old as ten."

"What is it? The memory, I mean."

"Decorating a Christmas tree with my mother and her boyfriend-of-the-month. It was my first and only tree. Why do you ask?"

She wondered how many Christmas trees she'd decorated with her father. And with her sister. For the first time, she thought to wonder about her mother. Was she dead? Or had she left them?

"I'm tired," she said.

Saul couldn't seem to put that comment into context.

"Should we go to bed now?"

"I'm tired of not knowing," she said.

CHAPTER 19

SAUL ADMIRED MAGGIE'S ABILITY to put on a well-heeled breakfast. Many of her guests were into outdoor activities—hiking and kayaking spring through fall, snowshoeing and cross county skiing in winter. She prided herself on sending them off fueled by a substantial breakfast.

She stayed busy tending eight tables of guests, but after everyone else had left, she brought a chair over to sit with Saul and Jayne as they lingered over coffee.

"Find anything interesting?"

"Interesting but not really useful," Saul said. "What we need is some trail of Anne that leads outside Creek City."

Maggie said, "I thought of something last night. I never knew where you hiked, but one time Dick Black—he's a rancher just outside of town—said he saw you turn off the main highway toward that clinic down the road. He wondered if you were visiting a patient."

"Clinic?" Jayne said.

"For drug and alcohol rehab."

"She went to the clinic?" Saul said.

"I have no idea. She left the highway at the clinic turnoff. There's nothing else down that road. No trailheads."

"How far is it?" Saul said.

"Maybe an hour's drive south. Across the border into New Mexico."

Creek City stood at the edge of the high desert, blacktop roads set directly into a dry cracked earth, but further south a silhouette of mountains began to rise. At midmorning heat radiated over the landscape, releasing fragrant oils from wild sage.

The clinic sat next to a stream, a line of cottonwoods serving as the boundary for one side of the property. Foothills and a scrubby forest rose beyond the stream. A small woman, dark-skinned with a long raven-black braid down her back, stuck her head out of a room when they pressed the buzzer at the front desk.

"Just a minute," she said without looking at them. "I'm almost finished cleaning the coffee pot."

She came out with a smile on her face that broadened when she saw Jayne.

"Cecelia Owens! It's so good to see you back. We've been worried about you since you ran off. Especially since you left the program early. Dr. Greene's in group right now. Why don't I take you to his office to wait?"

"I'm not—"

"No excuses, we're just glad you're here." She pointed to a group of chairs then turned to Saul. "You can wait here."

When Jayne started to protest again, Saul leaned down and whispered, "Let them think you're Cecelia and tell her you want me with you."

The woman didn't argue, but from the look she gave Saul she didn't approve.

On the way to the office they passed a room with a glass wall. People sat on the floor, all eyes except the instructor's closed. The students sat cross-legged, taking in breath, holding it, and releasing it in a steady rhythm.

Saul grabbed Jayne's arm, pointing into the room with his head.

"Relaxation classes," their guide said.

She left them alone in the doctor's office.

"Cecelia must be a twin," Jayne said. "It would explain a lot."

"This doctor won't be able tell us anything about Cecelia without her approval. You need to encourage their assumption about who you are."

"I can't do that. How could I do that?"

"We tell them the truth. You have amnesia."

When the doctor entered his office and saw Jayne, he clapped his hands. He had a wiry build, fire-red hair, and moved with a bounce that reminded Saul of a male cheerleader.

"Good," he said and clapped again. "Good. I hadn't lost hope that you'd be back." He sat down and crossed a leg, his ankle resting on his knee, then straightened his pants cuff. "How are you? You look good." He turned toward Saul without waiting for her answer. "And who is this?"

"He's a friend," Jayne said. "He's helping me figure out my past." She stole a look at Saul then said, "I have amnesia."

"Amnesia?" The doctor's eyebrows jumped high.

"She's started to remember a little," Saul said. "It's what led us here."

"Where have you been all this time?"

Jayne hesitated and Saul jumped in, guessing she wasn't comfortable with her role in misleading the doctor.

"Living on the streets in Denver," Saul said.

"So you returned to the streets—that would explain why you never came back. And amnesia. Most unusual. I think we need to talk, Cecelia, and I can make the time to do it now. Your friend can wait in the family room."

"I want him with me," Jayne said. "It's okay if I say it is, right?"

"I don't recommend it."

"It's what I want."

Dr. Greene nodded. He listened to Jayne tell her story, interrupting for an occasional question, and she seemed to relax into her role as Cecelia, the former patient.

"I couldn't remember anything in the beginning," Jayne said. "Feelings sometimes. Then I remembered my father."

"Of all things, I'd have thought you'd want to forget him," Dr. Greene said. "Did he find you? That might have been the trauma that triggered your amnesia."

Jayne twisted her hair in a tight knot at the base of her neck, then let it fall back down.

"I don't know what you mean."

"Her father's dead," Saul said.

"He was alive when you were here. And you were terrified of him. In fact, you only agreed to come here if we promised to keep your stay secret."

Jayne stood up, shaking. Saul pulled her back into her chair.

"What are you talking about?" she said. "I loved him. He was murdered."

"I'm sorry, but violent men often meet violent ends."

"My father wasn't the violent one. He was the victim."

"He was released from prison, in for murder, right after you came here. I've often thought your motivation to enter treatment was as much to hide from him as it was to get well."

"What prison was he in?" Saul said.

"She never said," the doctor answered.

"What was his name?"

"Again, she never said. She talked about him only enough to let us know he was off limits for discussion. Of course, we were working toward taking off that restriction. It would have been one of her release requirements, if she'd stayed to finish the course of treatment."

"Did Cecelia have any visitors while she was here?" Saul said.

"She was close to her sister but they agreed she'd stay away to help keep Cecelia's location a secret. Too bad. Family support is so vital to success."

"The sister's name?"

"Anne."

"Anne," Jayne repeated, holding her hands to her head for a moment. She looked up at the doctor. "Does the name Sissy mean anything to you?"

"No. Should it?"

Saul began to pace. There was something nagging at him, hiding in the tangle of data.

"When was Cecelia here?" he said.

"Let me check so I can be precise," Dr. Greene said, moving to his computer. "She entered the program August 2nd of last year. She left February 26th."

August 2nd, the day Anne left Creek City.

"She was here seven months?" Saul said. "Aren't these programs usually more like two or three?"

"Most are, yes. Our minimum stay is ninety days and some stay as long as nine months. We believe time is the most important element of success, especially for people with a history of relapse, like Cecelia. Time gives the mind a chance to develop new mental habits, refine new behavioral skills."

"The lady in front said I left early."

"You planned to stay for the full nine months but you left

suddenly after seven. I felt you were borderline relapse when you disappeared. I'm not surprised you ended up on the streets."

"Did she have a car?" Saul said.

"No."

"How did she get here?"

"Our van picked her up in Santa Fe, at the plaza in front of the Palace of Governors."

"And you don't know why she left?"

"Not for certain. A private detective was here that day, asking questions about a client collecting disability. He worked for the insurance company. I know she saw him flash his ID and noticed that she went very pale. That was, in fact, the last time I saw her. She ran away between then and the evening meal."

Through the office window Saul watched a hawk circling while he worked over the information.

"What kind of documentation do you need to get in here?" he said.

"The potential client must undergo a phone interview and assessment. We prefer our relapse-prone clients to have been through a shorter program so they understand the need for the length of time we insist on here." He glanced back at the record on his screen. "Cecelia hadn't been to another clinic but her doctor had tried Antabuse treatment and her sister attested to the extent of her problem."

"Do you ask for some kind of identification?"

"We get a photo of their driver's license but that's all. It isn't like people try to sneak into this place. Would you like a copy of the license?"

He printed it from a file on his computer and handed it to Jayne, who looked and passed it over to Saul.

"We were right about a twin," she said, her voice shaky. Dr. Greene looked concerned.

Saul glanced at the license. Cecelia looked just like Jayne. There was an Albuquerque address but not the one Anne had given the bank in Creek City.

"What about payment?" Saul spoke quickly, hoping to divert the doctor's curiosity about twins. "Did she have insurance?"

"I'd like to know more about that twin sister remark, Cecelia," Dr. Greene said. "What about looking at your picture makes you think Anne is a twin?"

Saul started running through explanations like bullets out of an automatic but came up short. Fortunately, Jayne had composed herself and proved to be a better liar than he thought.

"It's hard to explain," she said. "I've been having these feelings like half of me was missing. Saul said the way I felt reminded him of something he read about twins being separated. When I looked at my picture I recognized it, like I was looking at someone I knew."

"Interesting," he said. "Anne is in fact your identical twin. I know because she stopped in here the day before you arrived to make sure everything was set and arrange for payment. She explained then why she wouldn't be visiting. Perhaps being back in this environment is beginning to jump-start your memory."

"Maybe," Jayne said.

Saul was proud of her poker face.

"What kind of arrangements did Anne make for payment?" he said.

Dr. Greene answered without looking at his computer screen.

"That's a detail I'll never forget," he said. "She left a bank check for the full nine months of treatment."

"From what bank?" Saul said. "Do you remember?"

"Not as well as I remember the shock of her handing over

that check. You need to understand, no insurance company covers a program of our length. It was a very large amount."

He glanced at the clock on his wall.

"I'm about out of time for now, Cecelia. And I'm hoping you're here to check yourself back into the program."

"Absolutely not," she said.

"We promise she'll come back if she needs to," Saul said. "In the meantime, we'd like copies of her file."

Dr. Greene tried to convince her to stay. When she refused, he tried to give her a partial refund for the time she hadn't used. She told him to apply it to the bill of someone who really needed it. That helped renew his bounce as he escorted them out.

They stopped at a roadside park a few miles from the clinic. Saul spread a map out on the hood of the truck, studying routes home, while Jayne sat on a wooden picnic table and read through her clinic file.

"We learned more about what was going on with Cecelia by talking to the doctor than we ever could have gotten from these," she said.

Saul took a quick glance when she finished, hoping to find a specific name and telephone number. When he saw it, he carried the folder back to the truck along with his map. He put both in the driver's-side door pocket.

"Santa Fe is a few hours from here," he said. "Want to stop and see if you recognize anything there?"

"We don't even know if I was in Santa Fe," Jayne said. "Only that Cecelia was."

"I don't feel like driving all the way back to Denver tonight. It's as good a place to stay as any."

***

They climbed up a two-lane road that hugged the side of a granite canyon, twisting over a path carved by water and time. The sound of the gears shifting down then back up again mixed with the rumble of water tumbling over large boulders. With her window rolled down, she could smell the decay from the forest floor.

They stopped to eat at a ski lodge close to the top of the pass. When Jayne went to the restroom, Saul ducked outside with his cell phone. First he called the number he'd found in Cecelia's folder, of the doctor who'd recommended she enter the program. Out of service. Then he called Ben Jennings with a list of new information for him to check out.

When they began their descent from the top of the pass, the eastern edge of the canyon wall still blazed with sunshine, but the winding road on which they traveled had already been claimed by cold shadows.

In Santa Fe, Saul picked a hotel across the street from the Palace of Governors. After checking in, they went immediately to the plaza park. Saul wanted to see it before night set, in case Jayne recognized something.

She didn't.

They sat on a bench beside a brick walkway that led to an obelisk at the center of the park. The sun's last touch turned the adobe walls of the surrounding buildings golden. Native craftsmen rolled up blankets filled with silver and turquoise offerings, speaking little to each other and nothing to the people strolling by.

The artists seemed pulled from centuries past yet were very much part of the present. It was as if time passed differently here, as if the distance between two time periods was traversable.

Jayne felt the ghosts of her past, but she was cut off. Like the white void of her catatonia, only this barrier didn't keep her away from the world—it kept her from herself.

The hotel they stayed in was built like an Anasazi cliff dwelling. Despite its massive, hand-carved wooden doors, sandstone walls, and sculpted staircases, it had a modern aura. Perfect in every detail, it merely imitated the age that saturated the plaza and its surroundings.

Saul got the best room available, with a sitting area and a balcony that overlooked a stand of trees. A gas kiva fireplace filled the back corner, and every piece of furniture was handmade.

"So this is how the other half lives," Jayne said, pushing down on the plush comforter and soft mattress of the four-poster, queen-size bed.

"What makes you sure this isn't the norm for you?"

"Somehow I think I'd know if I had enough money to enjoy surroundings like these on a regular basis."

"You mean it doesn't feel right?"

"That's what I mean."

She found slippers and robes in the bathroom, along with a jetted tub. She closed the door and ran hot water until steam covered the mirrors.

Jayne's long bath gave Saul a perfect opportunity to talk to Ben. He made the call from the balcony, keeping the door closed but the curtains open so he could see when Jayne came out of the bathroom.

The second driver's license number was a fake too. The doctor didn't exist. The number belonged to a prepaid cell phone.

"Any ideas on what all this means?" Ben said after giving the full report.

"Fake IDs. A made-up physician. Cash in the safety deposit box. A large amount of cash paid to the clinic in a non-traceable form. She had to have connections to make all that happen. If I didn't know her, I'd…"

"Not to burst your bubble," Ben said, "but you don't really, do you?"

Ben was right. Given the same information about anyone else, he'd assume the subject was hiding from the law. Yet he couldn't accept that his intuition about Jayne could be that wrong. And there was the Tire Man to consider. When cops found their target, they didn't stalk them, they arrested them.

"Can we keep this between the two of us?" Saul said.

"It isn't like the information really led us anywhere. By the way, I've been asked by a number of people, especially Stiles and Walters, to please by-all-the-saints-that-are-holy turn off the goddamn alarm at Meg's place. They've been there three times since you left and nothing's wrong."

When her fingers shriveled and the water cooled, Jayne forced herself to get out of the tub. Wrapped in a thick terrycloth robe, she returned to the sitting room. Flames burned in the kiva, yellow edged in blue.

"I could get used to this," she said, plopping next to Saul on the sofa.

He twirled a brandy snifter and watched the reflection of the fire in the amber.

He grunted an off-handed acknowledgment.

"Is something wrong?" she said.

"Huh? No, just hungry."

They ate room service next to the kiva, on a table covered in white linen, with a fresh flower arrangement in its center. When they were done, Saul rolled the table back to the hallway then settled in front of the kiva. He hadn't really looked her in the eye since she came out of her bath. She knelt in front of him.

"Please," she said. "I need to know what you're thinking."

"Look, Jayne. Or Anne. Or Cecelia. Whatever your name is. I don't know if you can handle what I'm thinking."

He finally looked at her, his distress evident.

"Are you angry with me?" she said.

"No." He yanked her into an embrace, holding her as if he was afraid she'd float away. "I'm afraid for you."

She pulled out of his grip and sat back on the sturdy coffee table behind her, poised on its edge.

"Why did you just call me all those names? I know why you think I'm Anne, but Cecelia?"

He ground his jaw so tightly she could hear it squeak.

"We saw those people learning the same yoga technique you use," he said.

"Maybe my sister taught me."

"It was your memory that led us to the Holy Ghost Church in Denver."

"You think I'm Cecelia and Anne is my sister? Then why do I have the memories from Creek City?"

"That's not what I'm thinking."

He was beginning to frighten her.

He kept his observer eyes on her. "I don't think you have a sister. I think you're Cecelia. As well as Anne. As well as Jayne. As well as someone else altogether different."

Of all the things she imagined he held back, that wasn't even close to one of them, and she still had no idea of what exactly he was thinking.

"What about Sissy? Am I her too?"

"Do you remember when you first met Father Ted? Before

he knew you had amnesia? He called you Ceecee. I think Tami misunderstood what Anne was saying. I think she was using a nickname for Cecelia."

"I can accept that, but I don't think that just because some of Anne's and Cecelia's memories are intertwined means they don't both exist. Sisters share things. Especially twins."

"Something kept nagging at me today in the clinic. It surfaced while you were in the tub."

He reached down to pick up the snifter of brandy he had left on the table. He knocked it off with one tilt of his head.

"The timeline is too linear," he said. "Anne shows up in Creek City and is there for two weeks. The day she leaves Creek City, she drops by the clinic to pay and say she won't be visiting, then she disappears. Enter Cecelia. Cecelia leaves the clinic and shows up on the streets of Denver. Cecelia disappears. Enter Jayne, in our tree. The pattern's been staring me right in the face. There's no overlap between Anne and Cecelia—or you for that matter.

Saul startled at a clank in front of their door and moved to look out the peephole. The wheels of their dinner table squeaked as a hotel staffer rolled it down the hall.

"So you're saying I made up Cecelia? It was really Anne in the clinic?"

"I don't even think Anne is real," he said. "Ben Jennings ran a check on her. She never lived at that address, and he found no record of her. Same story for Cecelia. Add that to both having fake driver's licenses and I think both these 'sisters' were made up by you."

"I wouldn't begin to know how to make that happen."

"Jayne doesn't. The real you does."

He returned to the sofa. They sat side by side, staring through the balcony doors into the darkness.

"Why would I do that?" she said in a small voice.

"That's the rub, isn't it?" he said. "You must be running from something serious to go to such extreme measures."

"Are you telling me we can't trust anything we've learned on this trip?"

He looked like he'd be happier if he could just beat the answers out of somebody.

"No," he said. "There's one thing we can trust because it shows up no matter whose story we're talking about. Homeless Cecelia always tried to hide her face and Dr. Greene thought she was trying to hide. Anne was always watching for someone to show up. You're afraid, even if you don't know why. I think we can trust that someone is after you."

"Someone who wants to hurt me."

"Maybe."

"What does that mean?"

"We've got someone who's watching her back, who knows how to get high-quality fake documents, someone with a stash of cash. Any cop worth his salt would have to wonder."

"You think I'm a *criminal*?"

He didn't answer right away, but when he did he sounded certain, as if closing off an argument with himself.

"Your stalker isn't from law enforcement, of that I'm sure."

CHAPTER 20

A GRAY CLOAK COVERED THE SKY as they headed up I-25. The further north they traveled, the colder it got. The clouds grew heavier and whiter. As they reached Pueblo thin white specks began to fall, melting before they reached the ground. Minutes later the specks were mixed with sleet that made a slight pinging noise as it hit the truck's hood.

They traveled over slush-covered roads with spotty traction. By Colorado Springs, Jayne's right hand clutched the door so hard her knuckles were white. Her left hand contracted into a ball and her temples throbbed with tension.

As they climbed Floyd Hill, a blasting wind angled thick snowflakes almost perpendicular to the ground and covered the passenger window so fast the wipers could barely keep up.

They descended into the Denver valley and the snow turned to heavy rain. A hint of sun spread misty light above the clouds. At The Courtyard, it wasn't even raining.

Saul had felt an inner pressure building with the cold front. The closer he got to home, the more certain he was that something ominous waited there.

He was startled when he opened his front door and found a full-sized sofa in place of his two reading chairs. He'd forgotten—it was meant to be a surprise for Jayne. Mrs. Blackstone had let the delivery team in.

The sofa was made of the same rich brown leather as his reading chairs, one of which had been moved to the corner of the room, the other he assumed to his bedroom, where he'd asked them to put it. A narrow cherry coffee table sat in front of the sofa. It wasn't large but would give them a place to set a drink and a book or two.

He continued through to the office, anxious to check his security monitor—Meg's alarm disabled. Other than its malfunction, no unusual activity had occurred while he was gone. He checked his phone and found no unexpected missed calls or hang-ups. He checked through Meg's apartment and found nothing amiss.

His prescience didn't prove accurate until he checked his mail and found a greeting card, addressed by hand and sent to his townhome address but without a recipient name. It was postmarked three days ago from Greeley, Colorado, and had no return address. The card's stock was textured, a cream-colored base with several bold strokes of red. The front was printed in a serif type: "When next I look into your eyes, I will see that I am known and understood as never before." The inside of the card simply read, "Thinking of you."

No signature.

Saul slipped the card and its envelope into a plastic bag and headed for the station.

Jayne loved the new sofa, not because it was comfortable (which it was) or because it let them sit side by side (which it did). She loved that Saul had thought to get it in the first place and she especially loved that he'd been so pleased with himself when he showed her the surprise.

That evening she curled up beside him, resting her head in his lap while he read a book on how to survive a robotic uprising. Her muscles still tense from the drive through bad weather, she couldn't concentrate enough to read. Eventually she dozed, and around midnight Saul helped her stumble upstairs to his bed.

It was warm, so warm she began to sweat under the mound of blankets. She woke long enough to push all the covers aside. As the moisture dried, her body cooled. She needed the blankets again but couldn't wake up enough to grab them. Instead, she moved into a dream.

She was in a car, gripping the steering wheel so tight her knuckles were white.

It was raining, except she was cold—so cold it had to be snow, not rain.

No, that was all wrong.

Saul drove through the storm, not her. They were in a truck, not a car. She had gripped the door handle, not the steering wheel.

But the image retained its inaccuracies and she realized the car was on the marshland road from Saul's book. Instead of the calm, still night in the picture it was raining hard and wind drove the downpour vertically. Parts of the road disappeared under water as swells rolled across the narrow pavement.

Then she was out of the car and on her knees at the edge of the road, drenched and terrified. Something bad was happening out there in the crazy, dancing water.

She woke with tears on her face, shivering.

CHAPTER 21

JAYNE'S CRYING HAD PULLED SAUL AWAKE. He covered her and held her close until her breathing calmed but never returned to sleep himself. He got up at first light.

He went into his office to check the security monitor and noticed a stack of file folders, held together with a rubber band, set out on the back corner of his desk. He grabbed the bundle. Back at his dinette he spread the pages around the table.

Jayne came downstairs, said hello, then noticed the folder.

"I moved that stack from your cabinet to make room for some current files. What is it?"

"Personal copies of a case file. This is Martha. That's her husband." Saul was pointing to the pictures laid out on the table.

"I didn't know." She pulled her eyes off Martha to look at Saul. "Did you love her?"

"Love's not something that comes naturally to me."

"Did she love you?"

He stared into space for a minute then shrugged.

"You seemed to have a hard night," he said and was glad when she accepted the change of subject.

"I had a bad dream."

She pulled a book off the shelf. Saul moved up behind her to kiss her neck. Someone knocked on the door.

"Wasn't sure you two would be up yet," Mrs. Blackstone said when he opened the door. "I thought we might go out for breakfast. I have half-price coupons for the new IHOP combo."

"Okay by me," Saul said, moving aside so she could enter, looking back for confirmation. "I'll even let Jayne pay."

She was absorbed in the book, turning pages slowly, stopping, then going back to the beginning to turn pages slowly again.

"What are you looking for?" Saul said.

"A picture of a marsh in moonlight with a road running through it. Last night I dreamed about driving down that road in a storm." She seemed almost frantic. "I was so sure it was in this Gulf Coast book…"

Saul took it out of her hands, flipped a few pages, stopped at a picture that took up both pages.

"This picture?" It was a marsh in moonlight.

"Yes but no. It had a road."

"This is the only picture of a marsh in the moonlight."

"How can you be sure? Do you know the contents of all these books?"

"Actually I do."

Jayne took the book from him and studied the picture. Her shoulders sagged and she sighed.

"I'm sorry," she said. "This looks like the right picture, except it had a single, narrow lane with no shoulder, standing slightly above the water." She ran her finger across the page, showing Saul where the road should be.

"Tell me about the dream," Saul said.

She kept her eyes on the picture.

"I was in the driver's seat of a car, on the road, but a storm kicked up and I was scared. Then I was outside in the rain, kneeling at the edge of the road. I knew there was something very bad out there and I wasn't just scared, I was terrified. I woke up cold."

"Saul?" Mrs. Blackstone was looking at the file contents laid out on the table. "Why did you have that sketch made if you had this?"

"What?" His eyes fell to the photo she was pointing at. "That's Jeff Kennedy. You recognize him?"

"That's what I'm trying to tell you," she said. "That's the man who changed my tire."

Mrs. Blackstone had barely finished her sentence before Saul had his Colt .45 ACP in his hand. He checked the office locks, then took the steps to his bedroom three at a time. When he came back he was carrying a shotgun.

"Stay there," he said, leaning the shotgun against the wall.

They both sat wide-eyed.

He walked down to his basement, pistol pointed at the bottom door. After sweeping the large unfinished room that housed his gym, he checked all the windows before returning to the main floor.

"I'll be back in through the front door," he said. "Lock the office door behind me. Reset the alarm."

In five minutes he'd covered the outside of his property. Using a key, he reentered his home and locked the door. He set the safety on the pistol, laid it on the countertop, picked up the phone, and dialed. When there was no answer, he dialed another number.

"Sarge," he said. "Saul Becker. Chuck didn't answer his direct line. Is he around? Okay. I'm coming down right now. Tell him to dig up the old Kennedy files."

He hung up and leaned on the counter.

"I've got to go talk to Chuck," he said. "You two need to stay locked in here until I get back."

"I have plans," Mrs. Blackstone said.

"Cancel them," he said.

"I don't understand," Jayne said. "The Tire Man. It's Martha's husband? Why would he be interested in me?"

"I fucked up. You don't have a stalker—I do. And he's a killer who'd love nothing more than to hurt the people close to me. So I need you both to stay safe until I get back."

Mrs. Blackstone still looked ready to argue.

"Please," he said, "this guy is crazy and *beyond* dangerous."

When she relented, he picked up the shotgun.

"Either of you know how to use this?" he said as he racked the slide, chambering a round before he set the safety.

Mrs. Blackstone did.

"Keep it close."

He handed it to her, then went to the coat closet and pulled out a hip holster. He attached it at his waist but kept his pistol out, switching it between hands as he pulled on a loose jacket.

Poised at the edge of the front window, he peeked through a crack between the fabric and the glass. He snapped around when Jayne touched his shoulder.

"Don't do that." Sheer willpower had kept the pistol down at his side.

She stepped away.

Chuck waited for Saul at the front desk, his jovial attitude nowhere in evidence. He led the way, looking for an empty room. When they found one, he closed the door behind them.

"You were right," Saul said. "The shit going on is from my past, not Jayne's. My Tire Man is Jeff Kennedy."

"You sure?"

"I had an old file out this morning. Mrs. Blackstone saw his picture. She's certain."

"Shit. Damn. Fuck." Chuck opened the door and yelled out, "Danny. Get in here. Bring those files."

Ben Jennings burst into the room right behind Danny.

"You'll never believe this," he said. "That card you got? It had a partial print. Guess who it belongs to? No less than Jeff Kennedy."

"What card?" Chuck said.

"What card?" Ben said. "That's all you have to say? I just told you Kennedy resurfaced."

"Saul's already figured that out," Chuck said. "It's why he's here. Have a seat, you two."

Saul quickly summarized the events since Mrs. Blackstone's flat tire. It was news to Ben and Danny, a refresher for himself and Chuck.

"So that was the sketch you showed me," Danny said.

"Showing it didn't get us anywhere because Mrs. Blackstone was right. It didn't really look like him."

"We'll get a real picture down to The Corner Store along with an official uniform. See what kind of response it gets," Chuck said.

"Hey, does the date October 20th mean something special?" Danny asked.

He was looking at the front page in the file.

"It's the Kennedy's wedding anniversary."

"The kidnapping and murder were both on that date?"

"Yeah," Saul said. "Sentimental son of a bitch."

"So," Danny said, "that date is next week."

"Great catch," Chuck said. "Saul, I hate to run but we've got a commander to brief and a manhunt to start."

"Keep in touch," Saul said.

"Like you were my one true love."

CHAPTER 22

JAYNE AND MRS. BLACKSTONE STAYED at Saul's until he returned, then spent the rest of the day locked in their own home. They put more time than necessary into deciding where to hang the mask Jayne had bought in Creek City, after which they had nothing to do but read books from Saul's shelves and build up resentment at his acting like a prison guard.

When evening arrived, so did Saul. He'd told all of the tenants to keep their alarms on and circulated Kennedy's picture. Everyone at The Courtyard was on alert.

He insisted on staying the night. When Mrs. Blackstone got up the next morning, Saul was gone and the sheet and blankets she set on the sofa hadn't been touched.

"What did he do? Stand by the window all night?" She gave the pillow a particularly strong fluffing. "You'd think we were the criminals the way he's acting." Mrs. Blackstone returned the bedding to a hall closet. "At least he's left us alone for now."

Through the window, she could see Saul sitting on his porch step, see his holster and pistol. He wasn't drinking coffee. He wasn't reading. Just sitting, watching over them.

Some part of her wanted to defend him, knew he was crazy with worry and had fallen back on well-worn habits. The louder part of her inner dialogue was less charitable. His protective measures chafed like scratchy wool on a hot, humid day.

Mrs. Blackstone rattled around the kitchen while Jayne tried to watch daytime television. Saul said there was nothing to watch at two in the morning, but it wasn't any better eight hours later. Mrs. Blackstone joined her and lasted about three minutes.

"I have to get out of here," she said. "Here's my plan. You have to stay. Then he'll be split between going with me or staying with you and I know he'll pick staying with you."

Mrs. Blackstone got no further than the edge of the lawn before their personal gargoyle intercepted. Jayne watched from the window.

At first she couldn't hear the words, but the tone was angry and Mrs. Blackstone's gestures large. Soon she was loud enough to hear clearly.

"I *will not* put up with this. I lived through the Great Depression and the Second World War—I know how to take care of myself. Now move out of my way!"

Saul said something in return that caused Mrs. Blackstone to stamp her foot and cross her arms, her purse dangling at the crook of her elbow. But she came back in.

She tossed her keys into a bowl on her buffet. They landed with a loud plunk. She went to the kitchen, pulled out one of her tea steeping balls, and began loading it while she muttered.

"Passionflower calms irritation. I need lots of passion-flower."

***

When the sunlight reached the porch, Jayne took a book and a dinette chair outside. Saul was standing in the middle of the courtyard, able to see both the bridge to the parking lot and the trail coming up from the lake. His face was implacable, his eyes methodically searching the area, never staying on her longer than a second. He registered her presence with a frown but didn't order her back inside.

When a half-hour passed and he hadn't so much as said hello, she stood up and took a few steps toward the bridge. Saul's shoulders tensed and his eyes narrowed but he stayed in place. She took a few steps the other direction, toward the trail. Saul shook his head and walked over to her.

"What are you doing?" he said.

She smiled and shrugged.

"Getting some sunshine?" she said.

"You know what I mean."

"Oh really?" she said. "All I know is that one day there's this great man in my life, then bang! He's replaced with a maniac that insists on imprisoning the two people who care most for him in their own home."

"Would you rather be dead?"

Exasperated, Jayne gestured at one of the benches.

"Can we at least sit down and talk about this?"

"I'm hearing you just fine."

"No, I don't think you are. What would you do if I decided to take a walk around the lake?" She took a few more steps toward the trail. "Throw me over your shoulder? Shoot me?"

"Don't do this."

"Why not?"

She turned her back and started walking. He grabbed her arm, twisting her around. His face was crimson, his pupils so wide they covered his irises. This was the black-eyed Saul.

"You think I'm making this up just to mess with you?" he shouted.

He let go of her arm, held up his hands, and took a step back.

"The risk is real," he said. "*Don't you get that*?"

Her eyes filled with tears and she turned her anger on herself, furious at being so vulnerable. Almost immediately, she was mad at him again for being unmoved by her vulnerability.

They stood at an impasse until he said, "What do you want from me?"

She realized, with a grab at her heart, what she yearned for most was the thing that had been ripped from her without warning.

"I want you back," she answered, then took off at a run.

He didn't stop her because she was running to Mrs. Blackstone's.

Saul relented, without explanation or apology, and took them to the grocery store. He'd barely spoken other than to lay out the rules of their outing. No running around the corner of the aisle. No splitting up. If he were to yell out a command, they were to execute it immediately, without argument. They were happy to agree if it meant they could get out.

They made it to the store and back without incident. Jayne had been waiting for him to yell out something like "Drop to the floor!" just to see if they would. He didn't. After their return he cleared the house, reset the alarm, and left. She didn't open the curtains to see if he was out there, watching. She didn't need to.

They were still putting up groceries when they heard laughter and a knock. Mrs. Blackstone opened the door.

"Hi there, Mrs. B," Chuck said. "Thought I should introduce myself to Jayne."

"You must be Chuck," Jayne said. "I'm…"

"Jayne with a Y. Yeah, I know. I saw you at the station the day you were found. Don't guess we've met though."

"Please come in," Mrs. Blackstone said. "Would you like some tea?"

"Sure," he said, stepping over the threshold and shutting the door. "I've heard a lot about your teas."

Delighted with the notoriety, Mrs. Blackstone excused herself and went into the kitchen.

"Thought I'd let you two know the department's approved extra security around here for the next few weeks," Chuck said. "My partner Danny and I will be staying in the empty townhome. How are you holding up?"

"I feel like I went to sleep and woke up in another life." She paused, recognizing the irony in her statement. "Again."

"Kennedy is ruthless, Jayne. You're lucky to have Saul watching out for you."

"Was he like this when he worked with you?"

"Like what?"

"Cold? Detached?"

"I'd say focused and watchful."

"You know what I mean. Wasn't it hard to work with someone so, I don't know, single-minded?"

"This Saul is closer to who he used to be than how he's been since meeting you. As his friend, I sometimes saw the part of him he shows you, but I don't think anyone else did."

"He didn't act this way just at work?"

"Saul's life was his work."

She looked at the closed window.

"I miss the other Saul."

"I assure you the degree of his single-mindedness is in direct relation to the amount he cares for you."

"You think so?"

"Lady, if you don't know how much you mean to him by now then you're missing a few cards in your deck."

Jayne plucked at the fuzz on her sweater. "Still, this seems… excessive."

"Excessive is appropriate."

Mrs. Blackstone entered the room carrying a tray of mugs and cookies.

"I heard what you said and I understand Saul is trying to take care of us, but I can't live like this. I just can't."

"Let's take it a day at a time, Mrs. B," Chuck said, taking a deep whiff of tea before his first sip. "I'd ordinarily say leave town for a while, but that might cause an entirely different concern."

"What?"

"With no one to watch over, Saul might go hunting without a license."

Someone rapped against the door then unlocked it from the outside.

"Danny's here, Chuck," Saul said. "He's asking for you."

Saul turned to leave but Jayne intercepted, forcing him to meet her eyes. When he did, she smiled, stood on her tiptoes, and kissed him. His eyes softened briefly.

Then he was gone.

CHAPTER 23

KNOWING HIS PRESENCE AGITATED Mrs. Blackstone more than it comforted, Saul left her and Jayne alone for the night after he double-checked all the window locks and the alarm system.

He spent the night on his sofa, pistol at his side, curtain open, watching the front entrance to their place. When he heard movement outside, he picked up his weapon and pushed the safety off.

"Don't tell me, you weren't asleep." Chuck said when Saul opened the door. "Does that mean you have coffee on?"

"Not yet," Saul said, moving back to let him by.

Chuck went into the kitchen and started rinsing out the coffeepot.

"Several clerks at The Corner Store identified Kennedy. He always walked to the pay phone, so he had to be staying around here some place close. We haven't found where yet. And get this—he checked into a motel in Lincoln, Nebraska, early this morning. Used a credit card with his real name but gave a phony plate number for his car. Surveillance cameras caught him in transit so we know he's driving a Dodge Stratus. It had a fleet license; Danny's tracking that down. Kennedy was already gone by the time the locals got there."

"He must have wanted us to know he was there."

Having set up the coffee, Chuck opened the cabinet. Found cups, not mugs, and turned around to open the dishwasher.

"He uses his real name, gives fake plates but lets the car get caught on video." He pulled a travel mug out of the dishwasher. "What's he up to?"

"He'd never want to make it too easy." Saul rolled the data around his head. "Maybe he wants us to think he's running east."

Chuck poured coffee into the mug and took a sip like it was his life's blood.

"And then he'll head back here." He nodded. "Sounds like something he'd do. By the way, what should we do with your prisoners?"

"No one's a prisoner."

"Don't think they see it that way. And Julie, who's quite the cook by the way, and very kind to people staked out next door to her, is chomping at the bit about the party."

"I've got my hands full of angry women."

"Interested in a suggestion for at least one of them?"

"Do I have a choice?"

"Have the party in the place we're staying. It's empty, there's quite a kitchen to cook in, even room for dancing."

"You planning on dancing, are you?"

"I might." He grinned. "Julie said she likes to dance."

"Ah."

"Look, Saul. Your tenants will revolt if you try to turn this place into Fort Knox. There are only two doors in that town-home and we can easily keep a close watch on both."

"It's still a distraction."

Chuck slapped Saul on the back.

"The party's in three days. The anniversary is another four days after that. I don't think we'll see Kennedy before then."

"You won't have enough men to watch everything," Saul said.

"You're right on that point," Chuck said, "which brings me to the real thing I came here to talk about."

Saul sat on the bench in the courtyard. Chuck and Danny were down at the station. An unmarked car was parked at the lake, next to the trail. A patrol car periodically checked the parking lot.

Jayne came out of her apartment and crossed the courtyard toward his bench.

Some days her beauty was simply what he expected, but this morning he felt like he was seeing her for the first time. If she hadn't worn the ruby heart around her neck, he'd wonder if their time together had been a dream.

She approached him with a smile but the brightness faded when he didn't respond in kind. He wished she understood. He was either in the zone or out of the zone. Jumping between the two the way she wanted him to had never been one of his talents.

It seemed as good a time as any to share Chuck's purpose for the early morning visit.

"I'm hiring some twenty-four-hour security for the complex."

"More security?"

He could hear the wail in her voice.

"The results might surprise you." Saul said, "in a good way. If I know someone capable is watching in my place, maybe I'll be able to let my guard down. A little. I'm not promising anything big here."

Jayne looked skeptical and he didn't blame her. He wasn't sure of the effect himself, but for her sake he was prepared to make the effort.

"If I get these people hired by tonight," he said, "would you like to go out to dinner?"

The brightness returning to her eyes was all the answer he needed.

Saul insisted that Mrs. Blackstone join them for dinner, an apology for her confinement. She tried to weasel out, saying he and Jayne should be alone, but for once Saul got his way with his elderly neighbor.

As they left the complex he stopped to talk to Bob Ellington, the owner of Ellington Security, who'd been in the courtyard for a couple of hours. Another man was around somewhere, a shadow moving from one darkened corner to the next.

Bob was the first person Saul had ever met who seemed more observant than him—the first thing you noticed about Bob was that his eyes continually swept over his environment in a left-to-right pattern. He was average height, lightly muscled, with gray in his hair (what was left of it). Saul got the impression he might not be the strongest guy on the block, but that reflex and technique made him deadly. Bob always worked the first night of surveillance to ensure the plan they'd come up with was what his client needed. His personnel included both former military and former law enforcement.

They took Mrs. Blackstone's car but Saul drove. After securing both women in their seats, he surveyed the parking lot. He was leaving the place in good hands. He could relax.

The gun at his waist and his own constantly searching eyes proved the concept more theoretical than real.

***

They went to a restaurant not too far from home, with superb food and service. When he'd made the reservation Saul had requested a corner table. It had a clear view of most of the room and the front door. Other than the waiter ogling Jayne, which annoyed the hell out of Saul, it was a nice enough evening. He was happy to see Jayne and Mrs. Blackstone laughing, though he didn't join them.

After dinner Jayne returned with him to his place. When he came out of his office after checking for messages, Jayne was leaning against a bookshelf in the dining area, the Time-Life book opened to the picture from her dream.

His property, his tenants, and his friends were as safe as they could be. For just one night, Saul wanted to let go. He didn't want to think about his past or Jayne's.

He moved behind her, looking over her shoulder.

"Anything we need to talk about?"

She closed the book, set it on the dinette, and turned so she could wrap her arms around him. He felt the rhythm of her heart against his chest and his own heart began to race.

They moved at the same time, her reaching up and him leaning down.

Their kiss fueled his already racing pulse. Desire turned to hunger, and he lost connection to everything but her.

When the hunger was satiated, they made love again, slowly this time. He drank in their closeness and let the boundaries between them fall away until only two parts of one whole remained.

With the heat from Jayne's body seeping into his own, Saul slept soundly the rest of the night.

CHAPTER 24

SUN STREAMED THROUGH THE BEDROOM skylight, bathing Jayne in muted radiance. Saul sat at the edge of the bed and studied her face, then touched her arm. It was cold so he pulled the covers up and watched her sleep for a while longer, happy to steal an early morning respite from the day ahead.

Once downstairs, he was back to business. He went outside to introduce himself to the new team of guards that had replaced the night shift. He was talking to John, a Latino man with sharp dark eyes and a thin, licorice-black mustache, when a car door slammed in the parking lot. A woman stormed over the bridge, picking up speed when she noticed them.

John stepped in front of her.

"Can I help you, ma'am?"

She tried to push past him, but he held his ground.

"I need to know who you're visiting, ma'am."

As much as Saul would have enjoyed watching Lorel fume, he told John to let her through.

"Would you please ask Detective Leonard to come over to my place?" Saul said.

"He's already left for the day. The younger one too. I'm not sure why, but he was surprised that your lights weren't on when he came by this way."

"Go figure," Lorel said, jerking the strap of her purse back onto her shoulder.

She followed Saul into his place but erupted before he could offer coffee.

"We had a deal," she said. "You said you'd give me an exclusive if a story developed."

"So?"

"So you don't call Jeff Kennedy being back in town a story?"

"It isn't a story about Jayne. I said we'd give you an exclusive when something developed about Jayne."

Lorel clenched her fists then unclenched them. "I'm working on a story about the incompetence of you, your old partner, and the whole frigging department." She pulled out a recorder the size of a cigarette lighter and held it up. "Any comments?"

"It's Chuck's case. Talk to him."

"I already have," she said, smirking as she pressed the play button.

"Good morning, lazy ass," Chuck's recorded voice said. "You awake now?"

Lorel captured his stunned expression with her cell phone camera.

"For Detective Leonard," Lorel said. "The price of a good quote. He said to tell you he'll call when something comes up. I'll let myself out."

She put her hand on the front door knob, but turned to speak as she held it.

"And be glad I don't work for a tabloid. Otherwise, you hooking up with Jayne would be newsworthy."

"How in the hell—?"

"Don't worry," she said. "I'll keep that one safe in my back pocket."

Julie decided to change the menu because the party would be inside. They were having beef tenderloin with caramelized onions and mushrooms, corn-on-the-cob, green beans with a mustard dressing, and a kitchen-sink salad. For dessert, she was baking peach pies with fresh peaches from the Western Slope.

The day before the party, Jayne, Julie, Mrs. Blackstone, and Leslie sat in the gazebo shucking corn. George, a barrel of a man with eyebrows thick enough to braid, stood just outside the entrance, legs spread slightly apart, hands clasped behind his back. His head and eyes were in constant motion and he rotated his body regularly to keep the entire layout under observation. When they returned to the party townhome to put up decorations, George stood in the living room, where he had a view of both the front and back doors.

Saul joined them for dinner and they all worked on pies late into the evening. Chuck and Danny still hadn't returned by the time the group dispersed that night, which troubled both Julie and Saul.

Around midnight Jayne was half asleep, curled on Saul's sofa, her knees pressed to his thigh. He had a book but spent more time looking out the window than at the pages, so he was up and opening the door as soon as the motion sensor lights at the edge of the courtyard turned on.

Jayne pushed herself upright in time to see the door open. Chuck came into the living room, looked at Jayne, then back up to Saul.

She knew they wanted to talk alone. She started putting on her shoes.

"We found the rental car," Chuck said. "Abandoned just outside of Lincoln."

Evidently that was as much as he was willing to share in her presence.

"It's bedtime for me," she said. "I'll see you guys tomorrow."

She went to Mrs. Blackstone's and left them alone.

"I'm really sorry."

Saul wished he'd stop saying it.

"Obviously, I have to tell Jayne," Chuck said. "But I wanted you to know first. I mean, well, you can tell her if you want." When Saul didn't reply, he added, "Or I can. Jesus. Whatever you want."

The muscles in Saul's jaw clenched so tight his cheek began to twitch.

They sat at his table as Saul read two newspaper articles, faxed copies of those found in Kennedy's car. One was from *The Denver Post*, the article Laurel had written about Saul and the woman in the park, Jayne. The original, Chuck said, was worn soft and thin, like it had been read a million times. The other article was printed off the web site for the *Houston Chronicle*, from July of last year.

It covered the story of a missing woman: Jane Calender, wife of Dean Calender, partner in a prestigious law firm in Houston and a member of the James Michael Calender family. Old oil money. She'd disappeared, presumably from an upscale shopping mall. Her car was found in the parking lot. Surveillance cameras didn't show her entering or leaving the mall, and she hadn't been seen or heard from since. Nobody matching her description had been found.

It didn't take long to match the photo of Jayne Doe in Denver with Jane Calender in Houston, even though they didn't look exactly alike. The hair was different, the face from Denver more gaunt, the eyes unfocused. Of course, she'd been catatonic when the Denver picture was taken.

"When did you say Calender will get here?" Saul said.

"Late tomorrow."

"If she were my wife?" Christ, it was hard to say that word. "I'd be here on the first flight out."

"Airline scheduling isn't his problem. He's flying into Jeffco on his private jet, but he needed time to rearrange some things in his schedule. To be honest, after he heard about Jayne's amnesia I think he wanted to give her a little time to adjust."

"Are you sure he's…?"

"Positive."

Saul studied the photo in the Houston article. He had no doubt about the identification. He did have doubts about her husband.

Dean.

The name of the man who killed her father.

"And Ben asked about her dad?"

"Died almost two years ago," Chuck said. "From lung cancer."

"There's something off about Calender," Saul said.

"I understand you want that to be true," Chuck said. "I checked the obituary myself. He's telling the truth."

"Her deceptions were elaborate," Saul said. "Fake IDs, hiding in rehab clinics. She's running from something bad. What if it's him?"

"I don't know what to tell you."

"How the hell did Kennedy get this? How did he know?"

"I don't have an answer yet."

Saul's index finger caressed the picture of the beautiful Houston socialite.

"Her name really is Jane," he said. "What are the odds?"

Chapter 25

It was almost noon the next day before Chuck went to see Jayne. She knew at a glance that whatever he'd shared with Saul would devastate her.

Mrs. Blackstone sat on the couch and pulled Jayne's hand into hers. She didn't even offer tea.

"We know who you are," Chuck said.

She waited.

"You're…" He shifted in his chair. "Well, believe it or not, your real name is Jane. Jane Calender. You're from Houston."

The information fell flat, like a bad joke.

He handed Jayne a copy of a newspaper article.

"This was in Kennedy's car."

Mrs. Blackstone held it out so they could both read.

Jane Calender, missing. Jane Calender's husband Dean Calender offering a substantial reward. Dean Calender a rich, important man.

Jayne looked at the dates and calculated. Jane Calender went missing about the same time Anne Thompson had shown up in Creek City.

"Your fingerprints match. There's no doubt it's you."

"Dean. That's the name I remembered."

"I know," Chuck said. "Your father wasn't murdered. He died two years ago of cancer."

"Cancer," she said.

She looked again at the article.

"Why would Kennedy have this?"

"He wanted us to know who you are. I don't know how he knew it."

The woman in the picture—Jane Calender—was beautiful. Perfect hair, perfect makeup. She wore a glittering evening gown and dangling emerald earrings. There was a small, gracious smile on her lips, but Jayne sensed a numbness behind the façade.

"You've talked with… him? Dean Calender?" She couldn't bring herself to call the man her husband.

"Ben has."

"What did he say?"

"Considering the circumstances of your amnesia, he was willing to wait until we had a chance to talk before speaking with you. He's flying into town this evening."

Jayne looked out the window. Chuck followed her gaze.

"I left him around two this morning," he said. "When I went back at seven, he wasn't there. He must be out running." Chuck took a breath and let it out slowly. "I think Calender might want to take you home right away. He's coming out in a private jet."

Laughter filtered in from the courtyard. She moved to the window and pulled back the curtain to watch the activity outside.

"I don't want to see him."

Chuck came up and stood beside her, waiting until he had her attention.

"I can't keep him from coming to Westglenn. I'm sorry."

She turned back to the window, rubbing the ruby at her neck.

"What if it's him?" she said. "What if he's the one I'm hiding from?"

Chuck put a hand on her shoulder. "We can't keep him from coming here, but there'll be plenty of people around to support you if you decide not to go back. He can't make you do that."

Jimmy and another neighbor carried speakers and other sound equipment over to the empty townhome. The party was that night.

"Don't tell anyone," she said. "We've worked so hard on the party—I don't want to ruin it." She looked from Chuck to Mrs. Blackstone, silently begging them to agree.

"I can't do this!" Mrs. Blackstone stifled a sob, ran to her room, and closed the door behind her.

After Chuck left, Jayne headed to Saul's office. An internet search for Dean Calender produced hits in the tens of thousands. He'd pitched for the University of Texas baseball team in his undergraduate years. They won the national championship his senior year. He was top in his class at the UT law school, joined the most prestigious law firm in Houston, and was the youngest person to ever make partner there. During her absence, he'd won an election to the state legislature.

She thought he looked older than her by at least a decade. His face was lean, his jaw square, his eyes green and piercing. Handsome with a heavy touch of arrogance. His brown hair showed no gray and was perfectly styled. Even his posture shouted privilege, which made her wonder what she was doing with him. She was a mechanic's daughter, of that she was certain. Their engagement and wedding announcements didn't mention her family, only his.

Jane Calender often made the society column. Her Thanksgiving party was a highlight event of the holiday season.

In every picture she was smiling.

In not one of them did she look happy.

Once she learned her maiden name, she was able to find her father's obituary. It included a small photo of him, upper body only, with his hands posed across each other, resting on the top of a table. It pained her that she didn't recognize his face, but her heart twisted at the sight of his hands.

She didn't look like him. James Pousson was dark skinned with black, curly hair. His smile showed in his coffee-colored eyes, not on his lips.

He was seventy-two at the time of his death. She had learned that she was thirty-six, so he'd been older when she came along. He was born in Happy Jack, Louisiana, but had lived in Houston for thirty years. He and Tomas Mendez owned The Bay Street Auto Shop together. She was his only survivor. Her mother, Mary Ellen Pousson, was only mentioned as having "preceded him in death." She couldn't find any further information on her.

She looked up The Bay Street Auto Shop and stared at the listing, biting her bottom lip. There, right there, was a number she could call and talk to someone who knew her father, someone who must know her too.

She dialed but her courage failed before the first ring finished. She still had no idea who she could trust.

She needed fresh air. She needed comfort.

She knew where to go.

***

She sat with her back to the dry, rough surface, the smell of charcoal stronger than on her last visit to the tree. George's shadow fell across the opening.

She needed this dark, small space to think.

A stranger was coming to take her away, to a place she'd been desperate to leave, a place she remembered nothing about but the need to escape it.

One moment she was certain she'd refuse to even see Dean, then she thought she'd see him only long enough to tell him to get lost. Then she was curious about whether seeing him would produce any memories, because there was one thing of which she was certain: she would never be free to pursue the future until she faced her past.

Her memories—good, bad, or deadly—were the key. She stretched her legs, arched her back to stretch those muscles too. Then she closed up into a tight ball.

"Jayne?"

Someone was calling out to her.

Saul squatted at the entrance to the tree. Jayne huddled against the bark inside.

Exactly how they started.

He crawled in and sat beside her, legs bent, pressed against her side.

"Where have you been?" she said.

She lifted her head but he couldn't pick out the details of her face.

"I drove to Eldorado Springs for a run," he said. "Then I went by Ellington Security and talked with Bob."

"I want you, not him."

He took her hand in his, felt the physical conduit that had bridged the gap between them even while she was catatonic.

"I can't be there when you meet tonight," he said. "I'd never be able to hide how I feel about you."

"He's going to know about us soon enough."

"You need to greet him alone. You might remember him."

"And that I love him?"

"Or why you ran away."

An eerie quiet seemed amplified inside the tree. No birds were singing in its limbs, no leaves rustled.

"I used your computer to find the number for my father's business partner. I even dialed it but I hung up before anyone answered. The truth is I won't trust anyone until I remember who I ran from and why."

"That's a healthy attitude."

She took her hand back.

"I'm thinking about going with him tonight," she said.

He jerked upright, head slamming against the bark.

"You're what?"

She crawled past him and out of the tree. He followed her to the lake's edge.

"You're afraid of someone finding you," he said, "and you don't even know if you can trust your father's business partner. You think someone with the same name as your husband killed your father, but you want to go back?"

"Not want to, need to. Don't you get it? If I don't find my memories, I'll never be free. Since my memories are there, that's where I have to go."

"Understood." He spoke his next words slowly. "But you aren't safe on your own. Wait for this Kennedy fiasco to play out—then we'll go together."

She just stood next to him, shaking her head, until she saw how low the sun was hanging.

"What time is it anyway?" she said.

Saul checked his watch. "Almost five."

"I need to go," she said. "I'm helping Julie get things ready." She gave him a shaky smile. "I'll talk with you again before I make up my mind."

Then she moved up the trail, with George close behind.

A loud blast of music rattled the windows of the party house, followed by a shout of "sorry" as the volume was lowered. Mrs. Blackstone asked when she could listen to Frank Sinatra.

Saul caught a glimpse of Jayne as she moved behind the thin drapes. It hit him hard. She'd soon be face-to-face with Dean Calender, probably within the hour. She might remember a life with him, one she preferred over the life she had here. He had a little money but nothing compared to the Calender fortune. She wouldn't be the first woman in history to be lured into marriage by wealth. Hell, she might even love the man.

He turned at the sound of someone crossing the bridge. It was Chuck. He nodded toward Saul's townhome and together they went inside to the kitchen.

"Learned some things," Chuck said. "Finally got a hit on someone seeing Kennedy around here. Two hits, in fact. First, we know he was staying at a motel about five miles from here. Clerk says he checked in back in July and stayed over a month."

"He's been here since July?"

"Yeah. Can't say that's comforting."

"What else?"

"We traced the rental car. Paid with a stolen credit card. Guess the return date."

Saul grimaced.

"His anniversary?"

Chuck nodded as he answered his buzzing phone. He listened then snapped it shut. He hesitated but eventually let it out.

"Calender's plane just landed," he said.

CHAPTER 26

JAYNE SAT IN A CORNER, watching Chuck flirt with Julie and tensing every time the door opened. When Julie left to refill the buffet trays, Chuck came to sit next to her.

"You doing okay?" he said.

A woman Jayne had never seen before entered the party. Julie called out from the other side of the room.

"Meg! You're finally back. I expected you last week."

"I took some vacation before I came home," Meg said. "Needed some down time after New Orleans. Is Detective Leonard here?"

Julie pointed him out and Meg moved through the crowd, responding to the greetings of her neighbors with nods or a distracted hello. She stopped in front of Chuck and Jayne.

"You're Chuck Leonard?"

"I am. You the infamous Meg?"

"We've talked on the phone."

"Of course," Chuck said. "Something wrong?"

"I just got home… just now." She pointed at the wall, toward her place. "This was sitting on the top of my kitchen counter."

She handed him an envelope. Chuck examined the contents.

"An unsigned thank you note," he said. "For the use of your home."

"I don't know who put it there."

"I do," Chuck said. "Shit. That was Jeff Kennedy squatting in your house."

"You mean the murderer on the front page news today?"

"Listen, I know you just got back, but do you have a friend you can stay with for a few days? I don't want you in your place until we figure out how he got in—or, better yet, we catch him."

With Jayne's attention on Meg and Chuck, she didn't notice the stranger until she heard his voice.

"Excuse me," he said. "I'm looking for my wife."

Jayne recognized her husband from the pictures online and shrank into the shadows. Chuck walked over and shook his hand.

"I'm Detective Leonard. You must be Dean Calender."

"Are you the detective I spoke with?"

"No, that was Ben Jennings. He's been working on Jayne's case. I'm working the other side, the one with the murderer who led us to you."

"I still don't understand how that happened," Calender said, glancing around the room. He moved through the crowd, searching.

"Jane?" He stopped in front of her. "It's me. Dean."

He pulled her from her seat and hugged her. She stiffened. His arms didn't fit. Saul's arms fit.

Most of the partiers watched them, from the corners of their eyes if not outright. Whispers spread like germs on a playground.

Mrs. Blackstone introduced herself to Dean as the friend

who'd invited Jayne to share her home. He thanked her, then offered to reimburse her for his wife's keep—as if he wanted to pay for boarding a dog.

"She's my friend," Jayne said, fighting off a surge of bitterness. Dean gave a short, uncomfortable laugh.

"My apologies," he said, with a slight bow to Mrs. Blackstone. "I hope I didn't offend you."

Jayne bit her tongue.

"Perhaps you two need to talk alone," Mrs. Blackstone said, handing Jayne the key.

Jayne waved a hand toward the buffet table.

"Are you hungry?" she said.

"I'm not here for food," he said. "I'm here for you."

Jayne's fingers trembled as she fumbled with Mrs. Blackstone's key. It took several attempts, and when the door was finally open, the arm she unfurled toward the living room, inviting her husband to enter first, felt stiff.

"After you." He smiled and nodded toward the interior.

It was an innocuous gesture; gentlemanly, in fact. Yet it galled her. Being near Dean Calender affected her like fingernails scraping across a chalkboard.

She watched him look around the room and tried to see it through his eyes. It was filled with comfortable furniture and mementos, testimony to a life well-lived. What was he thinking? That the contents were old-fashioned and shabby?

He didn't have an expressive face. She had no clue what was going on in his head. Saul wasn't expressive either, but from the first day she saw him, she saw him all the way through.

He lowered himself to the sofa and patted the empty space at his side. She sat in the recliner.

"It's hard for me to picture you here."

She bristled. "You can stop with the attitude."

His shoulders dropped.

"It isn't attitude," he said. "It's just that your closet is likely as big as this whole apartment."

Several responses, none polite, ran through her head.

"I want to know what happened to you," he said. "Why you left me."

"I have amnesia," she said. "Why don't you tell me?"

"We had problems but it wasn't all bad. You never really adjusted to my social status and I guess I worked too many long hours, left you alone too much. But I never thought you were so unhappy you'd leave."

None of his words connected. They didn't feel real.

"You don't know how hard it's been, not even knowing if you were alive. Not knowing if you were in danger and needed me to find you or if you were fine and just didn't want me to know where you were."

He seemed desperate for something. Maybe he really cared about her. Maybe her reaction was unreasonable. Of course he'd want to know what happened to her over the last year. He was her husband. He'd even been honest about their marriage: it hadn't been perfect.

"I'm not pretending to have amnesia, Dean. I don't remember you. And I don't remember anything about a life with you. The only thing I remember is my father."

"Your father." His tone hardened. "Why did the detective think he'd been murdered?"

"Because that's what I remembered. That someone…"

She barely caught herself before saying someone named Dean had killed him.

"He died from lung cancer," Dean said. "Completely natural, considering he smoked all his life."

That truth had been eating at her since she first heard it. How could her father's death be so far removed from what she remembered with such certainty? And if she was wrong about that, what else was she wrong about? Her instinctual negative reaction to Dean? Did he deserve it? Was there even anything from her past to fear? Maybe she'd just run away from what Dean described as a troubled marriage.

"Tell me about us," she said.

"What would you like to know?"

"Anything. How did we meet?"

"I took my car to your father's shop. He was well known for his work on sportsters, old and new. You were there, digging around inside an engine compartment. Your hair was in one long braid down your back and your hands were covered in grease. I was accustomed to well-groomed women, but you struck me as the most beautiful thing I'd ever seen in your coveralls and T-shirt."

"And I liked you?"

"I don't know how to take that."

"You're older than me; you come from a different world. It seems a strange match."

"No one approved except us. My family didn't. Your father certainly didn't."

The bond with her father was strong, she was sure of that. At least, she *had* been sure of it.

"I married you against my father's wishes?"

"He was a tough old Cajun but you had him wrapped around your little finger. You convinced him you loved me, so he walked you down the aisle. Does any of this help?"

His eyes were bright orbs, boring into hers. The attention was uncomfortable and frightening, but his words belied any sinister interpretation.

"Under the circumstances," he said, "I'm not sure where to go from here. I have a room for us at the Peak View Hotel for the night. I want to take you home tomorrow..."

She twisted her hair in a knot off her neck, then let it fall down her back.

"I see you haven't forgotten your nervous habit of twisting your hair," he said.

"I don't want to leave."

His only reaction was a small tick at the corner of his mouth. He rubbed his jaw with his hand, as if to massage that tell from his face.

"I'm afraid to ask, but I feel like I have to," he said. "Is there someone else? Someone here? Is that what this is all about?"

His directness flustered her. She wanted to tell him about Saul on her own terms, but here it was, the elephant in the room.

"Yes. No. I mean, I've met someone but he's not why I ran away."

"If you have amnesia, how can you be sure?"

"Because I just met him. He had nothing to do with the rest of it."

"Who is it? Wait, it's the detective, isn't it? The one sitting next to you when I came into the room?"

"No. Detective Leonard is a friend. It's someone else."

"Are you in love with him?"

Was she? They'd never named their feelings and she had never expected Saul to make a commitment without knowing who she was. She assumed all of that could wait until she got her memory back.

"The situation hasn't… we've not…"

He stood and turned away, taking two or three steps to nowhere in particular, his back straight, his shoulders rigid. When he turned around, his face was neutral, his composure regained.

"It's not really fair," he said. "After everything you've put me through in the last year. I want you to come home with me.

We'll hire the best doctors to help with your memory. We can go to counseling." He looked painfully earnest. "If you don't want to stay once your illness is cured, I'll let you go. I'll give you a divorce."

It was a reasonable offer. Since she couldn't trust a thing from her memory, there probably wasn't any reason to be afraid of him. Dr. Frank had told her the usual treatment for amnesia was working with people who knew the patient. She couldn't get that here.

She felt a searing pain from no physical cause.

Dean came back across the room and knelt at her side. He hung his head and didn't look at or touch her.

"Please," he said. "Don't you owe me that much? I'll do whatever it takes to make sure you're comfortable. I'll stay at a hotel until you tell me to come home."

"No," she whispered, "I can stay at the hotel."

"That won't do. You need to be in the house. It might help you remember. Say you'll come?"

It made sense to go back to Houston, at least for a while. She still hesitated.

"He lives here, doesn't he?" Dean said. "At this place?"

He meant Saul.

"I want you to come with me tonight, to the hotel. I'll get a separate room. Just come and think about these things in a neutral setting. Away from him. Make your final decision in the morning. Can you give me that much?"

Everything he asked seemed understanding and respectful. He was so damned nice about it. And earnest.

But if he was so wonderful, why had she run away?

Saul stashed himself at a small corner table in a coffee shop several miles from home. Conversations filled the place, forcing people to raise their voices, increasing the noise level until Saul wondered how any of them could hear anything.

Not that it mattered. He wasn't listening.

He worked to keep his thoughts off the reunion happening back at The Courtyard, but every train of thought he followed wound back to Jayne and Calender, leaving together, forever.

If thinking wouldn't keep his fears at bay, maybe not thinking would. He stared out the window, watching two squirrels chase each other through the trees, emptying his mind.

Until something clicked.

"Oh, fuck."

Mutilated squirrels at the lake, found only hours after Jayne was rescued. As a teenager, Kennedy had been arrested several times on charges of animal mutilation.

He'd been in town for months. He must have been nearby when Jayne was found, must have seen the potential, then watched from the sidelines, patiently waiting to see what grew between them.

Saul knocked into a woman as he sprang from his seat. With a murmured apology, he ran to the door, barely avoiding another collision.

He'd been protective of Jayne ever since he found out Kennedy was in the area, not wanting her hurt as collateral damage. He couldn't have been more wrong.

Jayne wasn't a bystander.

She was Kennedy's next target.

Jayne put her single bag on the ground, next to Mrs. Blackstone, who sat on a bench in the courtyard. She glanced up just long enough for Jayne to see her eyes were red.

She sat down and put an arm around the older woman's shoulders.

Chuck came out of Meg's, headed back to the townhome until he saw them. He walked over.

"Did you remember him?" he said.

"No, but he's given me information, things I need to think about. I'm going with him to the hotel. I'm staying in a separate room and I'll decide in the morning what to do."

"Where is he now?"

"Waiting in the car."

Danny leaned out the front door of the party and yelled, "Chuck, need you in here."

Chuck raised a hand in acknowledgement. "I thought you and Saul agreed to talk tonight."

"I need time to think," she said. "Tell him... tell him I promise I'll call in the morning."

"Are you taking George with you?"

She hadn't thought about it. The threat from Kennedy was still real. It didn't come from her faulty memory. Still, she was going to the hotel to get away, from this place, these people, these tensions. Taking George felt wrong.

"I'll be fine. We'll go straight there. I'll lock myself in the room and not go out or open the door." She glanced down at her bag. "And I have my taser."

"I'd try talking you out of this if I thought I could." He shook his head. "Just be smart, all right?"

He turned on his heel. Jayne heard a low "fuck me" as he walked away. She looked back at her friend on the bench, who hadn't said a word.

"Mrs. Blackstone?"

Jayne reached over and held onto those soft but strong hands that had seen her through the roughest traumas. Mrs. Blackstone looked up, her eyes sunken, her cheeks puffy.

"Don't be sad," Jayne said. "Even if I decide to go, I'll be back. I promise."

Mrs. Blackstone tried to smile.

"Should I save your room for you?" she said.

"Absolutely." Jayne squeezed her hands. They felt like thin velvet in her palm.

"Are you sure you'll be okay, dear?" Mrs. Blackstone said. "I don't like him."

"I don't either. But he's nice—just different from us."

"I already miss you," Mrs. Blackstone said.

Saul pulled into the parking lot as a black Lincoln with tinted windows pulled out. A shadow moved at the edge of the lot. Saul eased his pistol out of its holster then relaxed when he saw it was George, headed to one of the Ellington vehicles parked in the lot. George changed his trajectory as soon as he recognized Saul.

George had been assigned as Jayne's personal bodyguard for the day. Saul fought a surge of fear, could feel the muscles harden under his skin. He crossed the lot to meet George halfway.

"Where's Jayne?" he said.

"She left with her husband," he said, "and told me not to come. I know they're staying at the Peak View Hotel so I gave them a minute to get ahead of me. I'm on my way there now."

"What happened?" He stared after the black Lincoln. "She said she'd talk to me first."

"You'll have to ask Detective Leonard."

Saul expelled an audible breath. Nodding, he said, "Okay. I assume there's been no sign of Kennedy?"

"No immediate sign. The detective has a status update for you."

"I'm on my way. Make sure Jayne's okay but stay out of sight. I'm not sure where her mind is right now."

***

Saul was headed for the party when he spotted Mrs. Blackstone in the gazebo.

"It's a little dark to be in here alone," he said, sitting beside her.

"There's a guy right over there." She waved at the shadows.

"I saw the car leave," Saul said.

"She hasn't decided to go back," Mrs. Blackstone said. "Just wanted to be alone, think. She said something about needing to be in a neutral environment."

That didn't reassure him.

"I need to talk with Chuck. Would you come back with me, please? I don't like you being out here, even with a man in the shadows."

"Can I just go home? I don't feel like a party."

Saul checked out the apartment before watching her lock herself in for the night. She turned on one dim light and sat next to a box of tissues.

Saul stopped inside the door, searching the crowd for Chuck.

"I'm pretty sure Jayne is Kennedy's next target," he said when they connected.

Chuck looked confused, but before Saul could explain, Jimmy walked up.

"Mr. Becker?"

"What is it?"

"I just heard, about Jayne leaving and all. I didn't think about it before. Now it seems a little weird."

"What are you talking about?" Saul said.

"This." Jimmy showed him the music sign-up sheet for the party.

About halfway through the handwritten titles was a song with a note asking that it be dedicated to Saul. "Last Day" by Delta Deon Slade.

"I don't know who requested it," Jimmy said, "but it was written in weeks ago. I mean, the timing's just... weird. How did they know Jayne was leaving tonight?"

"What's it about?"

"A guy whose girl leaves him and he's afraid she'll never come back."

Saul's mouth went dry and he had to lick his lips to get his words out.

"Let's hear it," he said.

Jimmy led them back to his media station and put on the song. An outright mournful blues number, it was a perfect match to how Saul felt.

He had no doubt Kennedy had left the request, but how had he known all those weeks ago what would be happening tonight? Could he really have manipulated all of them that precisely? To get that answer, he only needed to look at the night Kennedy murdered Martha. His manipulation was precise enough to keep her alive until Saul got home.

It took all of Saul's self-control to keep an icy terror from taking over as the song concluded.

"There's too much badness out there, it'll keep you far away,

And I just can't shake the feeling that we've shared our last day."

CHAPTER 27

THE PEAK VIEW HOTEL WAS AN in-town resort with golf course, spa, and a five-star restaurant. Brass gleamed throughout the lobby, bellmen hovered over designer suitcases, and the atrium was filled with flowering trees that reached up six stories. Dean had booked a penthouse suite for himself and a single room for Jayne several floors down. They rode the elevator up together. Dean pressed the hold button when they got to her floor.

"You know how to reach me if you need anything, right?" She nodded. "Let's have breakfast together in the morning. Around eight? I'll meet you at the restaurant."

The doors closed on his "Sleep well."

As soon as she entered the room, she threw the bolt and privacy chain, then jammed the wooden chair from the desk under the doorknob.

For the last six days she'd been watched constantly, a shadow always tailing what little movement she was allowed. She expected to feel light and free with her sudden privacy. No such luck. Her heart didn't stop racing until she reached in her bag and pulled out her taser.

She opened a split of champagne from the minibar and went out on the balcony. She clutched the glass in one hand and her taser in the other, waiting for the chilled alcohol to calm her nerves.

She was here to think, but her mind wandered, refusing to concentrate. Mostly it kept drifting back to Saul, imagining his face when he found out she'd left.

Bob Ellington came to get an in-person update on the situation.

"Has anyone other than Meg been out of town lately?" he asked.

"No. Why?"

"Kennedy couldn't have broken into your place and messed with the master control without your knowing, but he could have compromised other tenants from their individual controls, if he had access to them."

"I never even knew he was at Meg's, so I can't guarantee he didn't access other places. What are you thinking?"

"Kennedy's supposed to be a smart guy, right? He probably has a backup plan, ways to hurt you if he can't get Jayne. If it were me, I'd be targeting other tenants for that backup."

"You think we need more men?"

"No, I'd like to bring in an expert and have him audit your security system, see if he can figure out how Kennedy got through. He can also tweak the code, eliminate any backdoor Kennedy might have planted. We'll need him to reset all the security codes too. I can have him here in fifteen minutes."

"Do it," Saul said. "I'll stick around until your guy gets here. Then I'm going to the hotel to see if I can talk some sense into Jayne."

A blast of music from the party felt intrusive, irreverent even. Julie was going to hate him when he interrupted the fun to tell everyone their security codes would be changing that night.

Maybe Chuck should handle that.

Jayne was sitting on the side of the bed when a soft knock on the door startled her.

She crept toward the middle of the room and aimed her taser at the door. The knock repeated, slightly louder.

"Jayne, it's Saul. Open up."

She moved the chair and looked through the peep hole, then leaned against the door. She didn't think she could be in the same room as Saul and not fall apart. She opened the door a few inches, the chain still on.

"Call me."

She closed the door.

The phone next to her bed rang.

"Please let me in."

"I can't," she said. "I need a clear head."

"I have something important to tell you. Let me in."

"Just say it."

"Fine. Kennedy knew about you from the start. And about us. He's been squatting in Meg's place. There *is* no better way to get at me than hurting you. You're his next target—I'm certain of it. I'm not talking about being in the line of fire or about danger from your husband. I'm saying Kennedy's coming after you."

She crumpled to the floor beside the bed, phone still to her ear. A thin band of pain wrapped around her skull. She should ask how he knew. What she should do.

She just wanted everyone to go away.

"I'm locked in here till morning," she said. "I'll be okay."

"Jayne, you can't go to Houston. Not alone."

"I need to think. I'm sorry. I'll talk to you later."

She hung up.

He didn't call back.

She fell asleep on the floor, her back to the bed, her throbbing head on her knees. When she woke several hours later, her muscles were stiff. She ran a hot bath and soaked in the steam.

The only thing she was certain of? She needed her memories. Going to Houston was the best way to get them back. People there knew her. Dean would pay for doctors.

She didn't even need to resolve her conflict over whether she should fear someone from her past. Saul had convinced her to be afraid of his.

Fortunately, she'd seen firsthand what kind of protection money could buy.

Her hands were prunes and the water lukewarm by the time she got out of the tub, but she knew what to do.

The security system expert, Mark Long, had found a wireless trigger device on Meg's security box, which explained why it kept going off when no one was there. The technology was similar to the rig used on the ATM machine. Fortunately, no other homes had been tagged.

Mark was still hard at work when 4:00 a.m. rolled around. He'd suggested Saul get some sleep earlier.

"I understand insomnia," he said when Saul declined. "Most veterans do. Still, I'd rather you not stand over my shoulder while I work."

That left Saul to pace his living room. When the phone rang, he and Mark both jumped.

"Hi," Jayne said. "I know it's late, or maybe early. But you were awake, weren't you?"

"You okay?"

"I'm fine. Can we talk?"

He waved at Mark to signal nothing was wrong. At least, nothing Mark would need to be concerned about.

"Go ahead."

He sat on the bottom step of the stairs to his bedroom.

"I've decided."

There was a long silence.

"I'm going," she said. "I've got to. You can't even imagine. I'm exhausted and I'll stay that way until I remember. But I heard you earlier. My goal is to come back and be with you, which won't happen if I get myself killed. So I'm wondering— do you think Ellington security would send a man with me? I'll have Dean pay."

Her plan knocked his arguments right out from under him.

"What if he won't agree?"

"Then I won't go. Would you arrange that? If possible I'd like for it to be George. I'm comfortable with him. Can you have him meet me at the airport in the morning?"

He was left with only one argument, and it was one he couldn't use. How could he say he loved her over the phone when he'd never said it to her face?

CHAPTER 28

JAYNE WOKE THE NEXT MORNING to a call from Dean—she was late for breakfast. He sounded upset until she told him her decision. She'd go back, as long as he hired someone from Ellington to protect her. He agreed immediately.

She met him in the lobby, her bag strap over her shoulder and her taser on her belt. He was dressed in a suit and adjusted his tie as he glanced at her waist. He took her bag without comment and set it down next to his luggage and briefcase.

After settling into the car, Jayne glanced sideways at Dean. It wasn't hard to see what she must have seen in him. He was handsome; he exuded confidence and authority.

"Ready?" he asked.

"As ready as I'll ever be," she said.

He started the engine and pulled out through the parking lot. At the end of the row, he swung in next to a large SUV and rummaged through his jacket pockets.

"I need to let the pilot know we're on the way." He leaned over to pop the trunk lid open with a button. "Would you mind getting it for me? From my briefcase, in the trunk."

The briefcase had slid out of reach. She placed one hand on the carpeted floor and leaned in.

She heard footsteps behind her.

George went home to pack for a lengthy stay in Houston and Saul took over his watch at the hotel. He spent the remainder of the night on the end of a sofa, next to the fireplace in the lobby. He was exhausted.

Dean came down to breakfast alone. Saul struggled to keep hope at bay. Just because she didn't join her husband for food didn't mean she'd changed her mind. Still, when she met her husband at the lobby desk, Saul felt a gigantic letdown. The valet brought their car around, the luggage was packed in the trunk, and they pulled away.

His plan was to tail them to the airport, to make sure Kennedy didn't make a move before Jayne could fly out of reach. Saul hung out near the door until Dean started the car. Then he moved outside, keys in hand, ready to follow. He was surprised to see the Lincoln stop at the edge of the lot.

What was that about?

A large SUV with tinted windows obstructed his view. He walked quickly to his truck and by the time he reached it, the Lincoln had started up again and moved toward the exit.

Saul's internal alarm started screaming. His tires squealed as he threw the truck into gear and stomped on the gas. When he came within sight of the large truck, his vision spun, then his training took over.

He laid on the horn then jumped out, leaving his door open. He waved at a couple that turned toward the noise.

"Get medical help. Now!"

He ran to Dean, who lay on the ground twitching, and yanked the taser wires off his shirt.

Saul took one quick look around the area, confirmed that Jayne wasn't there, and jumped back into his truck. He dialed 911 as he drove.

She felt vibration. Her eyelids were too heavy to open, but she could wiggle her fingers. They brushed across a rough carpet. Her lips tasted sweet. Convinced it was a dream, she let herself drift away.

She was thrown against something sharp and it sliced her shoulder. An arc of fire seared her skin.

A sudden lurch pulled her away from the pain, then something heavy slammed her back again. Instinct caused her to twist, but that just dug her shoulder deeper into the sharp edge.

Movement stopped. She struggled to wake as cool air brushed her skin. She jerked when something stung her arm.

CHAPTER 29

SHE COUGHED AS SHE INHALED FUMES and her head ached. She remembered being grabbed from behind, a cloth being pressed against her face.

So not a dream.

She shifted her position and jerked at the pain in her back. Her palm burned and when she brought it close to her face, she smelled blood.

She coughed again and recognized the fumes as exhaust. She was in the trunk of a moving car.

Panic coursed through her.

She wasn't restrained and so explored the space around her, expecting to find Dean's suitcase. There was nothing. She felt along her belt for the taser. It was gone.

Her panic increased.

She tensed as she heard a vehicle close in behind them, coming fast. It might be someone chasing them, coming to rescue her, and she braced for the kidnapper to speed up.

The approaching vehicle passed with a swoosh. Another one passed, then another. Every car she heard passed by without even knowing she was there.

She screamed and pounded the lid of the trunk until her throat was raw and her arms ached. She screeched until it dawned on her: her kidnapper knew she was awake.

If she'd stayed silent, he might have opened the trunk less prepared. Or stopped for gas, thinking she was still unconscious.

Making noise had given her away.

Eventually, the sound of the road went from a smooth roar to a long, continuous crunch. She smelled dust and pictured it gathering in a cloud around the car.

After maybe a half-hour, they crossed over something bumpy, like a cattle guard or railroad track. A short distance further they came to a halt.

She braced her hands to push outward and hopefully surprise whoever opened the trunk.

It was a lame plan, but it was all she had.

Someone got out of the car. Footsteps moved away. Then she heard what sounded like a screen door squeak open and bang shut.

Without movement to create circulation, the air became dense, suffocating. Heat built in the trunk like an oven and still no hint of activity outside.

She scooted to the back of the trunk and felt along the wall, looking for a panel that opened into the backseat. There was nothing. Returning to the outer edge, she probed with her fingers until she found the lock mechanism. She pried until her fingertips were bloody but it never budged.

The heat continued to build until a sense of lethargy overcame her. She reached a nadir of hope and energy. That's when she heard the squeaking sound again, followed by the bang of a door as it slammed shut. Fear jolted her awake.

"I assume you can hear me. Knock on the lid, so I know you're listening."

If she was quiet, he might think she slept or was passed out. She pressed against the floor, ready to spring.

"I only have one rule," the voice said. "You always do exactly what I tell you. No more, no less. You didn't know, so I'll give you a do-over. But if I open the lid before you knock, I'll shoot you—not to kill, but it'll hurt. That might not seem fair if you're passed out, but that's how it's going to be. You have five seconds to knock."

She heard a pistol hammer being cocked. He meant what he said. Escape would be impossible if she was shot. Heart beating so hard it hurt her chest, she rapped on the lid.

"Much better," he said. "I'm about to open the trunk. When I do, you stay perfectly still until I tell you otherwise. If you move at all, I shoot. Now close your eyes. Knock if you understand."

She knocked then locked her muscles, listening as he slid the key into the lock and opened the trunk lid.

"Good girl," he said. "Open your eyes, get out, and stand still."

She stumbled out of the trunk and lost her balance when she put her full weight onto trembling legs. She grabbed at the car and braced herself against it to stay upright.

Rapid blinking helped moisturize her dry eyes. The car she leaned against was a faded white, with rust spots along the back fender. Not the Lincoln.

She was inside a barn, empty except for a pile of boxes and two suitcases stashed near the entrance. The roof had missing shingles and the holes let in a harsh light. There was a mild stench of ammonia. When she regained her ability to focus, she turned.

Her abductor pulled off a wig of shoulder-length stringy hair, tossed it onto one of the suitcases, and ran his hand over his natural hair to straighten it. Then he pulled off an oversized fake nose and stuffed it into in his pocket.

His real nose was long and thin to match a long thin face with prominent cheekbones. His hair was brown, medium length. His eyes were piercing. As they connected to hers, she felt as if he could read her mind. He wore tan slacks and a well-pressed linen shirt, light yellow with tan stripes.

He gave her a rather boyish laugh and a shy smile. If he hadn't been pointing a large revolver at her, she might have thought him both friendly and nice looking.

"You know who I am, right?" he said.

She knew. It was Martha's husband.

When she didn't answer, his sweet demeanor slipped and he tightened his finger on the trigger. She knew, without doubt, this was a maniac who would carry out any threat he made.

She nodded and the motion made her head spin, prompting a wave of nausea.

"Not feeling well?" He looked and sounded concerned. "Understandable, given the circumstances. I'll do my best to keep you comfortable but you have to do your part. Do exactly as I say or I'll be forced to hurt you." He shrugged. "Now step out into the open and look around."

She followed his instructions, stopping at the edge of the barn door. Everywhere she looked the land was flat and empty, save for a small copse of trees in the distance. No other houses were in sight. The short driveway connected to a one-lane dirt road that carved a thin, pale vein through an ocean of brown grass as far as the eye could see.

"There's nothing out here," he said. "You could scream at the top of your lungs and no one would hear. Go ahead. Give it a try."

She hesitated.

Sparks exploded in her vision from a full-force, backhanded slap to the side of her head. He watched as she fell to her knees, arms flying out to her sides. Her stomach, already unsteady, relieved itself of all its contents. She rolled over on her side, heaving.

She stayed as she was until the spasms passed, then pushed her hands off the ground and sat back on her heels. The shine in Kennedy's eyes woke a primordial terror beyond anything she'd ever felt.

Another spasm produced nothing but a string of yellow bile. When she stopped gagging, he helped her to her feet. She hugged her arms around her torso to steady herself.

"We'll pass on the scream," he said. "The point is, the closest town is forty miles away and has a population of eighteen. It's so small you can't buy food or gas there. There isn't anything of substance between us and that town but the wide open plains. The name of the town is Last Chance. I know—don't you just love it?"

He reared his hand back.

"Yes," she said, hating herself for giving him what he wanted, but not wanting to pay the price if she didn't.

"What I want you to understand, without any doubt, is that you are far, far removed from help of any kind. Your situation is hopeless and completely under my control. Smile if you get this."

She got the feeling he'd be happier if she disobeyed so she gritted her teeth and gave him the very best smile she had.

Which wasn't much, but it satisfied him.

CHAPTER 30

THIRTY MINUTES LATER, SAUL RETURNED to a parking lot filled with a fleet of blinking lights and the crowd to go with them. Dean Calender sat on the back of an ambulance, a blanket wrapped around his shoulders. No one was administering to him. The aftershock of a taser would leave the victim sore but that was usually it.

Chuck spied Saul getting out of his truck, left the civilian he was questioning, and jogged over.

"No sign of them anywhere," Saul said. "What have you got?"

"Dean Calender stopped so Jayne could get his phone out of the trunk. When she took too long, he opened the door to go check on her. That's when he got zapped."

"Did he see his attacker?"

"He was taken out too fast to see anything."

Danny came over to join them.

"I can't find anyone who saw a thing before Saul blared his horn," he said.

"Whose SUV is that?" Saul said, pointing to the vehicle Calender had stopped beside. "Kennedy had to be inside. He couldn't have come from anywhere else."

Chuck looked around the parking lot. "It makes no sense that someone would hide there to kidnap Jayne. It was pure happenstance that Calender stopped next to it."

"Some kind of coincidence that he stopped next to a vehicle so big it blocked my view."

Danny had ventured over to a patrol car during the conversation. He came back.

"Saul may be on to something. I ran the truck's plates—came from a dealer lot a few miles from here. Reported stolen this morning."

Chuck waved over a crime scene tech and asked him to process the truck, then turned back to Saul.

"Still, no way for someone hiding inside to know Calender would stop here to get his phone."

"There's one way," Saul said. "Calender was working with Kennedy."

"Far-fetched, at best," Chuck said. "How would they even know each other?"

"Someone could have been hiding in the back seat of the Lincoln," Danny said. "That makes more sense than Calender working with someone to kidnap a wife who was already going back to Houston with him."

Chuck released a long breath. "That taser was Jayne's. Any chance she ran away on her own?"

Saul's eyes narrowed.

Stiles, who was on his car radio, called out to Chuck and waved him over.

"Look," Chuck said, "You used to do this job. I need to stay open to any possibility. You get that, right?"

Saul gave him a grudging nod before Chuck took off to see what Stiles wanted.

***

Saul approached the ambulance. When his shadow fell across the ground, Calender looked up. Saul held out his hand.

"Hello, Mr. Calender," he said. "I'm Saul Becker. I own the place where your wife was staying."

"I recognize you." He didn't take Saul's hand. "I saw your picture in the articles those Westglenn guys showed me about my wife."

"I was there when she was found."

"You were a cop," Calender said.

"A detective."

"They seem to think Jayne left on purpose," Calender said. "Why would she say she was going with me, then run?"

"I don't think she ran away either," Saul said.

"She was afraid of some guy named Kennedy. I hired a bodyguard for her even though I thought it was ridiculous. I guess he's waiting for us at the airport. Too little, too late. What she needed was someone to guard her here."

A flush climbed from Saul's neck to his scalp.

"Why did you pick that spot to stop?" he asked.

"It's out of the flow of traffic."

"And you didn't see anyone? Didn't see a door from the SUV open?"

"No."

"Is it possible someone was hiding in the back seat?"

"What did you say you were doing here?"

Saul ran his tongue over his teeth, taking time to get himself under control.

"He's a consultant with our department, Mr. Calender," Chuck said, placing a hand on Saul's shoulder. Under his breath Chuck said, "Need to talk." To Calender he said, "I understand the medical team has released you. What are your plans?"

"I'm getting back my room here for the night," he said. "My family is working to get the FBI involved, but they need this case to be declared a kidnapping. What can I do to convince you of that?"

"I'm working on it." Chuck handed Calender a business card. "I'll get in touch this afternoon with an update. Meanwhile, if you hear from anyone with demands, call me right away."

Calender flipped the card between his fingers.

"Are you even looking for her?"

"Of course. You'll hear from me in a few hours. Go back to your room and get some rest. You've had a difficult morning."

Chuck took Saul's arm and moved him away from the ambulance.

"Found the Lincoln," he said when he was out of Calender's earshot. "It's in the parking lot of an empty building in the Interlocken Business Park."

"Do you really think she ran away?"

Saul sat up front with Chuck as they drove to the park. It was only a few minutes from the hotel.

"With Calender's influence, all I have to do is say the word 'kidnapped' and the Feds are all over this," Chuck said. "I'd like to have proof before that happens. That might buy us some good will, encourage them to keep us in the loop."

The empty building was a four-story square of red brick, abandoned due to finances before the interior had been completed. They drove through the front parking lot, empty of cars, and around back. There they found the Lincoln, parked next to a wall where it couldn't be seen from any of the neighboring buildings.

Saul scanned the ceiling and ledges.

"No cameras?"

"Didn't get that far in the setup."

The patrol team had already opened the trunk. There was

a small pool of blood on the carpet, and some blood and skin on an exposed screw in the side wall.

"Someone was in there, probably not of their own free will," Danny said.

Chuck moved up to the front of the car to look inside and talk with the guys who'd found it. Saul stayed at the trunk, his vision tunneling until all he could see was blood.

"It isn't a lot," Danny said.

"No," he said, turning away. "It's meant to worry me. She's still alive."

"You sound sure of that."

"I'm sure Kennedy wants me to suffer."

As soon as they returned to the car, Chuck said, "I'm briefing Commander Morris as soon as I get to the station. He'll make the call to the FBI, and that's not a bad thing. They have a lot more resources than we do. And we still have jurisdiction over Martha's murder. They can't keep us from working the case if we find a Kennedy connection." He caught Saul's eye. "*When* we find one."

Saul's first stop back at The Courtyard was to check the missed call log in his office. Nothing. He then went to Mrs. Blackstone's, braced for a scolding for not calling to let her know what had happened. She surprised him with a look of pity, a hug, and sobs.

He'd have preferred a lecture.

"All this time," she said, dabbing at her eyes with a tissue, "I didn't really believe he'd try to harm us." She braved a look at Saul. "Even when we knew who he was, he seemed so..." She glanced around the room, as if looking for an explanation somewhere on the walls. "Do you know where she is?"

"Not yet."

"Do you think she's still… I can't bear to say it. Saul?"

"I think so."

"But you can't be sure."

A fissure cracked the foundation of Saul's composure.

He patched it with a healthy dose of denial. And for them both a dollop of hope. Or bullshit.

"I'm sure," he said. "If she weren't, I think I'd know."

CHAPTER 31

KENNEDY LED HER TO A WOOD-FRAME HOUSE, weathered gray except for a few specks of dirty-yellow paint around the windows and door. A decrepit cottonwood slouched in a front yard covered with dead leaves.

A wave of heat rolled over her as she entered the front door, Kennedy following right behind. Dust covered the floors, rising in puffs as they walked across the creaking wood. Mixed in was the same ammonia smell she'd noticed in the barn.

A dining table and chairs sat at the back of the room beneath a bare bulb that hung from the ceiling. A vase with a filthy plastic flower bouquet sat on the table. Spider webs trailed from flower head to flower head.

The only other furniture was an ancient armchair covered with faded blue corduroy and a battered buffet piled high with broken plates, glasses, and knickknacks. The walls were bare.

"Sit there." He gestured toward the armchair with his pistol.

She sank deep into the chair, the cushion long ago molded to a much larger bottom than hers. Dust collected in her nostrils and she sneezed. Then she froze, afraid her unauthorized movement would be punished. Kennedy's grin was so big his right cheek dimpled.

"I only have the one rule, but let me clarify it for you. If I ask you a question, I want an answer. If I haven't told you to do something, I want you to do absolutely nothing. Is that clear?"

She nodded. When he frowned, she quickly added a verbal answer.

"Yes."

"Your responsibility in this relationship is to follow the rule. My responsibility is to enforce it. Is that clear?"

"Yes."

"Don't worry," he said. "When I say relationship, I'm not talking about love."

He folded his arms, studied her.

"Not that I'd object. What do you think—could you fall in love with me as fast as you did with Saul Becker?"

The question was dangerous. She stammered, unsure how to answer.

He laughed. "Ah, I'm just messing with you."

He paced the room, tapping the pistol against his shoulder, occasionally glancing at her. He noticed her looking at the slice on her hand.

"I cut that so you'd bleed in the trunk of your husband's car," he said. "Becker will worry more if he knows I've hurt you, especially if he can't guess how badly. The scrape on your back came from an exposed screw in the trunk so you can't blame me—but hey, the more blood the better. Now, would you like to use the bathroom? This may be your only chance for a while."

She didn't have to go but she grasped at the idea of going into a room and closing the door. Even if the windows were barred and there was no way out, she could still get away from his mocking eyes.

"Yes."

He led her down the short hall.

"In there," he said, leaning against the door jamb, barely leaving her room to get through.

He waited until she'd almost squeezed by, then pinned her against the door frame. He leaned his forehead into hers until their eyes were less than an inch apart and stayed like that until she nearly collapsed from fear. Then he shoved her sideways into the bathroom. She staggered a few feet before recovering her balance.

"Have at it," he said.

He moved into the hall. She looked at the door but knew better than to close it. He turned his head up and whistled at the ceiling.

She steadied herself with a hand on the yellowed sink and moved to the toilet. When her jeans and panties were hanging below her knees, she stole a glance in his direction. He was looking right at her.

Her muscles ached with tension.

There was no toilet paper so she simply pulled her clothes back up. Her necklace, resting under her shirt, slapped against her skin when she stood.

It made her think of Saul. That only increased her humiliation.

"You might want to rinse your mouth out after all that upchucking by the car." He pointed at a sink so filthy just the thought of touching it repulsed her.

She turned the grimy faucet with the tips of her thumb and forefinger, cupped her hands, held them under running water. She took a small sip, let it swish around her mouth, then spat it out. It was frigid.

"Cold, huh?" he said. "Comes directly from a well. The

pump runs on a small gas-powered generator I brought out when I prepped this place. It's all the power we have here."

The tiny dose of water she got from rinsing out her mouth was a tease to her dehydrated body. She turned the water off to reduce the temptation of drinking more.

He opened all the windows as she returned to her spot in the armchair. The outside light was fading and a cross-breeze cooled the house.

"I have a problem," he said, standing behind her and placing his hands on her shoulders. "My original plan was to keep you in the attic. But now I think I want you close."

She shuddered at the thought of what might inhabit the attic. And shuddered again at what Kennedy meant by keeping her close.

"So as long as you behave, I've decided to let you stay down here."

He retrieved a backpack from the floor by the dining table and rummaged through it.

"Stand up and turn around," he said.

He pulled a smaller bag from the pack, bent her over the arm of the chair, and pushed her shirt up. It stuck where the blood had dried, and he ripped it off the wound. She could feel the bleeding start up again.

"This might sting," he said, then poured something over her injury.

The liquid streamed down her sides in tiny, cold rivulets. The chair's fabric absorbed the runoff and her nostrils flared at the odor. Rubbing alcohol? He applied an ointment, then put a large square of gauze over the injured area. He dried her skin and gently pulled her shirt down.

"Okay, you can sit now." He zipped his bag up and put it back in the pack.

He pulled out a plastic restraint and set it on the floor by her feet. Kneeling, he took off her left shoe and sock then ran a fingernail across the sole. She flinched.

"Ticklish, huh?" he said and repeated the routine on her right foot.

She eyed the pistol on the floor by his knees. She wasn't restrained yet. If she jerked up with her knee she might connect with his jaw. Would that give her time to grab the pistol? And if so, did she know how to shoot it? She knew guns had safeties but couldn't tell by looking if it was on or off.

While she struggled with indecision, he snapped the plastic tie around her ankles. He caressed the gun as it lay on the floor, then picked it up and stood.

"You were thinking about taking my gun. That seriously pisses me off. And after I was good enough to treat your wound."

He yanked her up and threw a punch that landed on her left eye. She fell back into the chair.

"Your job is to follow the rule. Not to get creative. My job is to enforce the rule."

He pulled her up by one arm, over-rotating until the pain made her scream. His hand slid up the back of her shirt and he yanked the gauze off, pulling skin and hair with it. He scraped his fingernails across the wound until it started bleeding again, then cuffed her arms behind her and shoved her back in the chair.

"Are you starting to understand?" he said. "You follow the rule or you pay a price."

He dragged a dining room chair across the floor and set it in front of her. He sat straight-backed, the pistol resting on his lap. A vein in his neck began to pulse.

"You only stay out of the attic if I think you'll behave," he said.

He rolled his head to the side. The vein looked like a worm squirming along his neck.

The cut on her palm rubbed the back of the chair when she shifted her weight. The bindings at her ankles bit into her flesh and her bare toes turned cold, as an evening breeze snaked across the floor. Blood from her back soaked through her shirt and into the fabric covering the chair.

"I don't understand what's so hard about a little discipline," he said. "Are you so weak-bellied and self-centered you can't even control your impulses? You worthless piece of shit."

He jerked his arms and rubbed them.

"Holy shit, I sounded just like my dad."

He stood up, set the pistol on his chair, and shook his arms again.

"It's getting a little chilly in here, isn't it?" he said.

He went into the front bedroom and came back out with a sweater. After he put it on, he picked up the pistol.

"I'm sure you're full of questions," he said. "Just to pass the time, go ahead and ask me one."

She wasn't prepared to hear the answer to "Do you plan to kill me?" Asking after Saul would be insane. Kennedy sighed at her hesitation, and before he could call her on not obeying an order, she blurted out, "Why?"

"Okay," he said, laughing. "Why. Good choice. It's such a big question, you'll get plenty of information. And I get to choose the topic, since a simple 'why' isn't specific. Keeps you from accidentally bringing up a subject that's... sensitive to me."

He began to pace and his eyes took on an insane sheen.

"I choose to address the question of 'why am I doing this?' I'm doing this because I need to make Becker suffer in a big way. He ruined my life. I lost my wife to him and when my business partners believed the things Martha said about me, they kicked me out of my own company. I meant to kill him two years ago, but then Martha showed up while I was casing his place. It seemed so much better to kill her and let Becker live. But then I had to go underground and start over again. That's on him too. Granted, I've landed on my feet, but hate's been eating at me and I needed to do something about it."

He stopped and faced her, crossing his arms, tapping the pistol against his side.

"I have my own 'whys.' Why did Martha fall for that fake white knight and leave me? We had a good life together. Why were my business partners so self-righteous? It wasn't like the board was filled with saints. Why did the papers make Becker out to be such a smart guy when he never even caught me?"

He stared out into space for a moment, lost in thought. She took a deep breath, grateful at the reprieve from his attention. It didn't last long.

"Everyone thought he was such a great detective," he said. "Fucking Sherlock Holmes reincarnated, a master of intuitive leaps of logic. Yeah, right. I had to practically hit him over the head before he figured out I was in town. Mysterious calls, smiley faces in the dirt. How much more in-his-face could I have been? Pushed plants, bogus police reports—too subtle for his legendary instincts. Bet he was totally clueless until I sent a card with my DNA. You were there, you tell me. It took forever for him to figure it out, right?"

"He knew there was someone. He didn't know it was you."

"See what I mean? I put my John Hancock on the deal the first day of contact. You know, the mutilated squirrels? How many people from his past would show up around this time of year that have a record of animal cruelty?"

She felt the blood drain from her face.

"The state made me go to a dime store psychologist as a kid. His brilliant analysis was that I had no interest in conforming to social norms. Duh."

Her stomach rumbled. She hadn't eaten since the party.

"You know," Kennedy said. "I'm getting hungry too. What would you like for dinner?"

Before she had time to come up with an appropriate answer, he waved his hand.

"Just kidding. You don't get food tonight."

He stood up and tilted his head, assessing her like a piece of prized livestock. His gaze settled around her neck before he looked back at her face. He leaned forward and stroked the hollow of her neck, then undid the top button on her blouse.

She let her focus shift, trying desperately to disconnect. Her attention wasn't gone for more than a few seconds when Kennedy slapped her across the face. Her nose began to bleed, the blood running across the curve of her chin and down her neck.

"No disengaging," he said. "It isn't polite."

He pulled her shirt open. Several buttons popped off and clattered to the floor.

He ran his finger across the chain on her necklace and held the gold heart in the palm of his hand.

"Is this supposed to be a sign of Becker's everlasting love?"

She said, "It's just a gift."

He ripped it off her neck.

"No tokens of hope allowed."

After that he left her alone.

The blood from her nose caked and began to itch. With her hands behind her back, she couldn't scratch.

Night crawled by and the house turned cold.

CHAPTER 32

COMMANDER MORRIS THOUGHT SAUL acting as a consultant while they worked on catching Kennedy was a good idea. After getting two hours of sleep, Saul headed down to the station.

Chuck met him at the front desk.

"How you holding up?" he said, as they walked back to his desk.

"What do you think?"

"She's going to be okay. You know that, right?"

"Give me something to do, Chuck. I… need it."

"Kennedy's prints are on the taser and in the Lincoln. That means we're still very much in the game, ostensibly looking for Martha's killer. And the Feds are here with the commander right now, setting up a task force. I'll be the WFD rep."

Saul avoided eye contact with everyone as they walked. He couldn't handle the looks of pity.

"The kid had an idea."

Chuck dragged a spare chair next to his desk. Danny stared at his screen but looked up as Saul took the seat.

"I went over the area crime reports," he said, "and found four other skimmers at work in the Metro. All but the one at our Corner Store were in high-income neighborhoods. I'm downloading pictures of the hardware now."

Saul leaned across the desk so he could see. Chuck was standing behind him.

"Looks like the same setup," Chuck said.

"If these are all Kennedy's work," Danny said, "he's managed to clean out some hefty accounts."

"Then we have to assume there's no limit to his resources," Chuck said. "What do you think he's up to?"

"He's setting up a cat-and-mouse game," Saul said. "The starting point should show up any time now—we need to keep our eyes open."

Commander Morris stuck his head out his office door and waved Saul over.

"Special Agent Prescott heard you were here, Becker," he said. "He wants you in interrogation room two."

There was an upside to Jayne's being a member of the Calender family: the Bureau had every available resource working on finding her. They were canvassing the neighborhood where the Lincoln was stashed, trying to figure out what car Kennedy had switched to and which way he went. They circulated photos of Kennedy and Jayne in public transportation areas and towns along the major highways. They were checking traffic cam video for facial recognition. And they'd set up a tip line and given out the number to TV stations and newspapers.

Calender offered a hefty reward for information leading to her rescue.

How many men had to do that twice in the span of a year?

***

Saul eventually forced himself to go home. When he opened his front door, the emptiness hit him like a wall. He couldn't help thinking he stood at a crossroad—if he took the wrong turn, he could never come home again.

Right there, she'd unbuttoned her shirt before they made love the first time. Over there, she teased him about his disorganized office. She leaned against the wall there when she asked if he'd loved Martha. He told her he wasn't sure what love was. Why hadn't he just said no? That the only time he'd ever been in love was with her?

His vision blurred. Bracing himself against the wall, he stumbled into the bathroom and splashed cold water on his face.

As he stared in the mirror, he saw Martha. Her bloodied and beaten face became Jayne's. Way too little sleep and way too much pressure for way too long. He wasn't at a crossroad—he was at the edge of a cliff.

His eyes burned and his hands trembled. His legs started to give way. He caught himself on the edge of the sink and hung there, undone by doubt.

When he checked on the security monitor, he remembered Jayne saying she'd tried to call her father's partner from his office phone. He scrolled through the outgoing call log until he found a Houston area code. He got an answer after several rings.

"Bay Street Auto Shop, Tomas Mendez here."

The voice was brisk, with a slight Spanish-influenced accent.

"Mr. Mendez," Saul said. "I'm calling from Colorado. Saul Becker. I'm a friend of Jane Calender's."

A long pause.

"A friend of Jane's, you say?"

"She's been staying with my neighbor these last few months."

"What the… she knows better. Don't call me…" His voice faded, like he was about to hang up, then strengthened. "Wait, is she okay? Put her on the phone."

Tomas Mendez didn't seem surprised Jayne was still alive after being missing for over a year. He sounded more like a father about to scold a child than someone who meant to hurt her. Saul took the plunge and gave him the truth.

"I can't," he said. "She's been kidnapped."

"Goddamn son-of-a-bitch. How'd he find her?"

"You mean her husband?"

"Of course her husband. Who else does she have to be afraid of?"

"Ever heard of Jeff Kennedy?"

It would have been surprising if he had. Saul gave him the short version.

"Kennedy took her while she was with her husband. I think he might be involved. Unfortunately, I haven't convinced the FBI of that. Do you have any clue as to how those two might have met?"

"None. Are you telling me Jane went with Calender of her own free will? Why would she do that?"

Jayne's amnesia was such an integral part of the woman he knew, he hadn't thought to mention it. Saul filled Mendez in.

"She worked so hard to get away," he said. "It breaks my heart he found her."

"You helped her escape?"

"She came to me for help in getting fake papers. Other than that, she kept the details to herself."

"Why was she so scared of him?"

"Do you have any idea the power that man and his family wield? She asked for a divorce and he told her he'd have her committed before he'd let her go. She believed him. She's not much of a fighter, you know?"

"Would you be willing to talk to the FBI? Tell them what you know?"

A long silence.

"There a problem?" Saul said.

"Yeah," Mendez said. "He's a Calender and I'm the ex-con that got her fake papers."

"Let's not tell them that part," Saul said. "Just convince them she was afraid of him. I'll take care of the rest."

CHAPTER 33

THE SOUND OF A BIRD CHIRPING woke her up. She kept her eyes shut, fearing Kennedy watched her and that to open them would be the same as waving a red flag at a bull.

She didn't remember curling up, but she was sideways in the chair. She straightened her legs and pushed upright, eyes still closed. Her nose and eye felt swollen but the night was over and she was still alive. That simple thought helped her open her eyes.

Kennedy sat in front of her, legs crossed, pistol gripped with both hands and steadied against the platform of his knees. He raised his hands a little and she swallowed as the muzzle pointed to the middle of her forehead.

"Bang," he mouthed, and seemed pleased as her face paled.

Kennedy went outside for a while, then she heard him stirring in the kitchen. When he returned to the living room, he deposited a canteen and small pack on the ancient buffet. He was no longer dressed in business clothes—he was dressed up to play army. He wore a tight green T-shirt and camouflage pants, along with a heavy leather utility belt with a hip holster. He pulled out a multi-tool knife, opened one of its many blades, and cut the tie off her ankles.

He led her to the dining table, went to the kitchen, and returned with a sandwich. He hand-fed her bite-sized chunks that dropped like thick, dry balls into a turbulent stomach.

"Come on, now—you need to keep your strength up," he said.

He tipped a glass into her mouth and she savored the feel of water sliding across the desert of her tongue. Some dribbled down her chin. He wiped it dry with an intimate touch that almost made her throw up.

"We're going out." He took the cuffs off her hands. "Take off your shirt."

She hesitated only in her mind. Her arm was black and purple where he'd grabbed her the night before. She pulled gently to separate the material from her back wound. It didn't start bleeding again.

"Here's one without the buttons yanked off." He held the new shirt for her like a gentleman holding a lady's coat. "Put it on."

She had to turn her back to slide her arms in. He ran his hands down her arms as if to smooth the fabric, but he put extra force on her bruises.

"I like the open shirt look," he said. "What do you think?"

"Whatever you want."

He wrapped his arms around her from behind and kissed the top of her head.

"Button it, if you want."

She wanted nothing more than to button the shirt and he knew it.

"That's my girl," he said when she left it unbuttoned.

He brought her shoes and while she put them on he went

to the buffet, picked up the canteen, and slipped the strap over his head. He also grabbed the small pack. Once outside, he marched her to the barn and then to the car, where the trunk was already open.

"Get in," he said.

She scanned the horizon. There was nowhere to go, nothing to hide behind. Every direction was flat, vacant, exposed, except for the small copse of trees too far away to reach and much too small to hide in.

Somehow she managed to crawl into the trunk. She tried to hold back hysteria when he closed the lid.

She didn't succeed.

They drove for a long time. When they stopped, Kennedy immediately opened the trunk and helped her step out. The landscape was still mostly flat, but there were intermittent swells as if waves of soil had frozen in time as they rolled across the plains. It was every bit as isolated as at the farmhouse.

They took a short walk, stopping at a shallow gulch that cut through the dry ground. It was only about a foot wide but twice as deep.

"There's a present for you in the gulch," Kennedy said, motioning with his pistol.

She moved closer and looked down. It was a shovel.

"That sandwich should give you some fuel to work with," he said. "I want you to dig. Expand the hole about two feet on each side, from here to here." He marked a section about six feet in length. "You don't need to make it any deeper."

Her lacerated palm hurt when she grabbed the shovel, and the wounds on her back pulsed with pain. She labored slowly, chipping away. Her tongue grew thick. She almost gagged on the taste of old blood as it mixed with her sweat and dripped into her mouth.

Her unbuttoned shirt kept falling off her shoulders as she worked. When it got to her elbows, she'd shrug it back up again. Her tormentor seemed to find this little ritual amusing.

The sky was clear and she felt the sun's heat burning her skin. Kennedy rummaged through his pack, brought out a baseball cap, and secured it on his head. He held up a bottle of sunscreen.

"You're looking a little pink there," he said. "Want me to put some of this on you?"

She suppressed a shiver at the thought.

"Thank you, no."

She was relieved when that answer didn't make him mad.

By the time she finished expanding the first side of the gulch, she was exhausted and sunburned from digging what she felt would become her grave. She straightened and wiped the perspiration off her nose with the back of her hand. She ran her swollen tongue over cracked lips, jerking at the sting from the salty sweat.

Kennedy made a production of studying the sun as he opened his canteen, drank from it, and closed it back up again. Then he walked over to the edge of the hole, looked in, then back at her.

"Good enough." He reached out his hand for the shovel.

She couldn't force herself to let go. Kennedy had to peel her fingers off. Then he motioned to the hole.

"Lie down, face up," he said.

She hesitated, head down, tears muddying the dust on her face. She wanted to lash out at him, tear out his eyes. Overcoming him was hopeless but that didn't mean she had to let him have it all his way. She could choose the moment of her death.

She turned and ran.

CHAPTER 34

SAUL FELL ASLEEP ON THE SOFA after his talk with Mendez—not for long, but long enough to get through the day.

He was getting ready to head to the station when he heard shouting at the parking lot bridge. He pushed the safety off his Colt .45 and went to investigate.

A large, heavily muscled black man with tattoos up and down both arms was arguing with the guard. They both turned around when Saul's door opened.

The newcomer was Tee Mack, the gang banger from The Corner Store.

"Yo, Becker," Tee said. "Get this asshole off me. Got something for you."

"He won't tell me who he is or show ID," the guard said.

"It's okay," Saul said. "I've got this."

Tee sauntered over to Saul, flipping the guard a finger.

"It's a little early for you to be out, isn't it?" Saul said.

"Don't want nobody seeing me." Tee glanced around the darkened courtyard. "Ask me in."

"Just talk."

"Okay, be that way," he said. "Here's the thing. I've got me a few boys who think it's okay to take freelance jobs. That makes me look bad and they need to be taught a lesson. A few of them go down, the rest will get back in line."

"I'm short on time, Tee."

"I'm getting there. Jesus. So some of these pikers hooked up with that guy whose picture's been in the paper."

"Kennedy? Some of your boys did a job for Jeff Kennedy?"

"Stole a car. Left it parked at that fancy hotel with this Kennedy dude hiding inside it." He reached into his pants pocket and pulled out a sheet of paper. "Here's their names and where you can find them."

When Saul reached for it, he snatched it back to his chest.

"Your source is anonymous, got that?"

"No problem."

"And just these guys. You don't use this to disrupt the rest of my business."

"Any part of your business associated with helping Kennedy is in my sights. Other than that, I don't give a fuck what you do."

"Fair enough."

Tee handed over the paper.

"Of course, I can't speak for the WPD."

Tee laughed, which made his hardened face look ten years younger.

"Ain't them I'm worried about."

Saul and Danny took over a small conference room and set up a war room. The first thing Saul did was tape an oversized, detailed Colorado map from his personal collection on the wall. He called Chuck to tell him about his late night chat with Tomas Mendez and the early morning talk with Tee Mack. Chuck was on his way to the first task force meeting.

"This should convince them to look at Calender," Chuck said. "Who went to round up the car thieves?"

"Mathews and Roan."

"If I'm not back when they get there, go ahead and start without me."

Saul was waiting for the car thieves to work their way through processing when Chuck showed up. He popped the tab on a soda, threw himself into a chair, and downed half the can in three gulps.

"Thank God I work in a small department." He rolled his eyes. "It'd drive me nuts to coordinate with so many people on a regular basis. They have a task list so long it would take a year to actually look at everything."

Danny arrived, balancing three cups of coffee. Chuck pointed to his soda and launched into an update.

"I think we might have actually impressed the Feds with our work—Saul's work, I should say. Unfortunately, by the time we did, Calender's plane had already taken off for Houston. They'll pick him up for questioning when he gets home."

"But they're convinced he's working with Kennedy?"

"Maybe not convinced, but based on your conversation with Mendez, they're certainly suspicious."

"Any sign of Kennedy on the traffic videos?"

"Nada."

Saul's cell phone rang. He answered it while Chuck crushed his can against the tabletop, aimed it toward the trash, then flipped his wrist. The can disappeared in the makeshift hoop.

"Calender's plane just landed in Houston," Saul said. "Guess what? He's not on it."

"The Feds are sure he left this morning," Chuck said. "They're waiting for him in front of his house."

"I had an Ellington guy follow him to the airport, so I know he got on the plane, but he wasn't on it when it landed. I know, because I had a guy waiting to follow him there. Ellington checked with a contact at the FAA and learned the plane filed a new flight plan ten minutes after take off. They stopped in Colorado Springs. On the ground for fifteen minutes, then on to Houston—without Calender."

Saul's phone rang again. He listened then said, "Hold on. I'm putting this on speaker." He laid the phone on the table. "Go ahead," he said. "Repeat what you just told me."

The voice was tinny but still identifiable as Bob Ellington.

"Someone met Calender when he got off at Colorado Springs. We showed the staff a picture of Kennedy but it wasn't him. The person delivered a car and a large manila envelope."

Saul's antenna went up.

"And not just any car. A red Lamborghini Murcielago. Our source thinks it had a fleet license. Turns out there's only one place in Colorado that rents Lamborghinis and it's in Denver—Prestige Auto Rentals."

"A red Lamborghini?" Chuck said. "That's like driving around with neon lights."

For the first time since Jayne disappeared, Saul felt he'd found his footing.

"That's the point," he said. "Kennedy wants us to follow Calender."

"Why would Calender agree to that?" Danny said.

"I imagine Kennedy's manipulating him too," Ellington said. "Want me to check out Prestige Auto?"

"Chuck, do you think Ben can handle the auto theft interviews?"

"Sure. Morris said use whatever resources we needed."

"We'll take Prestige Auto." Saul got up and stuck a red push-pin into the map at Colorado Springs. "You start searching for signs of that Lamborghini."

CHAPTER 35

SHE WAS ON HER BACK, shoulders and hips lodged against a hard surface on both sides. With time, she remembered.

Running. Dread. Waiting for the pain of a gunshot.

Instead, an arm had hooked her from behind and slammed her into the ground, knocking the breath out of her. A cloth clamped over her nose and mouth, and she'd slipped into darkness.

But here she was waking up, still alive.

She opened her eyes to a clear blue sky.

Turning her head, she saw the upper edge of the gulch. She tried to raise her hands but her arms were pinned against her stomach. As she struggled, she realized her torso was covered in dirt.

Panic gave her strength to push through the soil. Dirt scattered and she gasped for air even though her face wasn't covered.

"You're such fun to play with," Kennedy said from behind her. "You never disappoint."

Twisting around, she saw him perched on the edge of the gulch. He had a small camera in his hands and was flipping through displays on the digital screen.

She brushed off her skin and clothing, trying to rid herself of a sense of decay. Dirt mixed with sweat covered all her open wounds. If she lived long enough, infection would fester.

Kennedy stood up. "We're done here."

He dragged her to the car by her arm and threw her into the trunk.

Back in the farmhouse, he had her button her shirt and then he cuffed her wrists in front. He shoved her into the armchair and spun the cylinder on his revolver. He clicked it open, peered inside, then snapped it shut and half-cocked the hammer to spin the cylinder again.

"You know what I don't understand?" he said. "How that sap Becker managed to charm you and Martha."

He opened the cylinder again, placing a finger over one hole as he dumped bullets out of the other five.

"Did he ever say he loved you? No? He never said it to Martha either. I know because I asked her. The guy has commitment issues. But enough of that—we have our own issues to address, don't we? Look." He held out his hand to show her the bullets. "Just one left."

He snapped open the front pocket on his utility belt and dropped the bullets in. Then he tapped the pistol against his cheek.

"You tried to run away," he said. "You know I can't just let that slide."

He spun the cylinder and brought the barrel to her forehead. The hammer fell with a click as he pulled the trigger.

A shriek caught in her throat and her ears roared. He spun the cylinder and pulled the trigger again.

Click.

The roar ratcheted up to a high-pitched whine. She was

paralyzed, her concentration fixed on the pistol barrel, a long dark tunnel holding death.

"I calculated the odds for Russian Roulette once, just for fun. The simple version is this. If you spin the cylinder, the odds of being shot stay consistent at one in six, about seventeen percent. If you don't spin the cylinder, the odds of being shot go up each time you fire. I'll show you."

He pointed the pistol and held it in front of her eyes.

"I've fired once already and I'm not spinning again, so your odds are one in five—that's twenty percent." He pulled the trigger.

Click.

"One in four, or twenty-five percent."

Click.

"Thirty-three percent."

Click. Click.

She pressed into her seat. There was one more shot. Pressure pushed against her eyes so hard it felt like her eyeballs might explode from their sockets.

Click.

The sixth shot but no bullet.

"Damn," he said. "How did that happen?"

He looked puzzled for a second, then pulled a bullet out of his shirt pocket.

"Oh, I remember now. I took a bullet out while you were in the trunk."

She slumped forward, covering her face with her hands, knowing how much he enjoyed her fear, knowing that had been the only point since the weapon was empty, angry with herself for being duped again, even angrier when she thought about what he'd have done if she *had* caught on.

"No more trying to fuck me over." He reloaded the pistol. "I mean it. Think you can handle that from now on?"

"Yes," she said, wondering how long "from now on" was.

"Here's your final exam," he said. "Stay."

He didn't put any bindings on her feet before he left. She heard the car pull out of the barn and drive off.

She stayed.

When he returned, he walked over to the junk-ladened buffet and uncovered the camera she'd seen at the gulch.

"It's a video cam too," he said.

He watched the playback, sitting on the arm of her chair.

"Good girl," he said.

He moved through a number of pictures on the camera's display.

"You're very photogenic but I knew that already. I make my living off the Internet. Identity theft mostly. It's part of my work to pore over online subscriptions to major newspapers, to find potential targets, keep up with things. You were all over the *Houston Chronicle*, front page, for weeks. That's why I recognized your picture when it showed up in *The Denver Post*."

He stopped scrolling and held the camera out to show her a picture.

"This one's my favorite," he said. "Like it?"

It was a still shot of her in the dug-out gulch while she was unconscious. She was on her back, covered in dirt, her pale face visible. She looked dead.

"No."

"Too bad. It's the last picture Becker will have of you. He gets to live knowing another lover died at my hands. That way, he and I can play another round someday. Think he'll have the guts to ever get involved again?"

The sound of a car approaching interrupted his gloating. He jumped off the chair and slid his pistol out of the holster. She heard gravel spray in the driveway.

Kennedy saw who it was, lowered his weapon, and flung the door open.

"Welcome to our humble abode."

Dean Calender swaggered into the room.

CHAPTER 36

PRESTIGE AUTO RENTALS' WINDOWS were smoked glass, the chairs deep leather, the receptionist tastefully dressed. Through the glass wall of a waiting room, they saw a man about Saul's age with a well-trimmed beard. He drank from a bottle of Perrier while he read the *Wall Street Journal*.

Chuck showed his badge. "I need to talk to the manager."

The receptionist jumped out of her chair and pushed the badge down as her eyes cut toward a waiting customer. She pressed a button on the intercom and whispered.

It didn't take long for a rotund man to come hustling down the hallway. His bald head shone. Most of his extra weight was packed around his belly.

"*Right* this way, gentlemen," he said, smiling as though they were his favorite customers, herding them down a long hall. "I'm George Levy. The manager."

Chuck pulled out his ID again and Levy reacted the same as the receptionist, quickly pushing it back toward Chuck's chest.

"No need for that," Levy said. He took a few steps up the hallway, motioning for them to follow. He stopped as soon as they were out of view.

"We need to know about the Lamborghini delivered to the Colorado Springs airport this morning," Chuck said.

Mr. Levy kept his face polite and open.

"I'm *truly* sorry," he said. "Our contracts don't *allow* us to give out information without a warrant."

"Not even if your car's involved in a kidnapping?"

"What? Oh my. Really? My Lamborghini?"

"It's highly possible."

Levy mopped his head with his sleeve as he led them into his office and motioned them toward a conversation pit by one of the windows.

"If that's true, then all privacy concerns are void, naturally. I'll do whatever I can to help, but tell me why you think my asset is involved."

"The man driving it is likely on his way to meet a known kidnapper and murderer. Now, what can you tell me about the rental? And the guy who rented it?"

Levy looked back and forth between Saul and Chuck.

"I need to be certain it's involved before I give you information. Or see a warrant, of course."

"Let's start with something easy," Saul said. "I know you don't just let people drive off in these things. What does it take to rent one?"

"We confirm identity, run a credit check, and get a large security deposit, usually on a credit card. Occasionally, some of our more eccentric customers pay in cash. If so we get payment in advance too."

"Has anyone ever tried to run off with one?"

"They can't really. We monitor them closely via GPS and can disable the car remotely, should we feel we're at risk."

Saul sat up straight.

"You mean you can tell us exactly where the car is and make it stop running?"

"From the control room, yes."

Chuck reached into his jacket pocket, pulled out two photos.

"Do you recognize this man?"

The picture was of Dean Calender.

"No. Should I?"

"He's driving your Lamborghini."

Levy looked distressed. "The man who rented it doesn't look anything like that."

"Is the driver who dropped it off still around?"

"Yes, of course. Excellent idea. I'll have him sent in."

The driver was a clean-cut young man who looked nervous when Chuck showed him Calender's picture.

"He's the one," he said. "Did I do something wrong, Mr. Levy? He had the paperwork."

Chuck jumped in over Levy's answer.

"How about this guy?" He showed a picture of Kennedy. "Either of you seen him?"

The driver shook his head, but Levy blanched.

"That's the man who handled the rental. He said his name was Mike Laughing."

"Let me guess," Saul said. "One of those eccentrics who paid in cash?"

Levy nodded mutely.

"Hate to break it to you," Chuck said, "but he's the kidnapper we're looking for. A known killer."

Levy's breath turned shallow. His pallid face went even whiter.

"Would you excuse me for a moment?" he said. "I'll get the current location for you right now."

Levy returned less than five minutes later, his dome glistening with sweat. He sat down with a thud.

"Both the tracking and remote control systems on the

Lamborghini appear to have been disabled," he said. "This has never happened before."

"Is that a hard thing to do?"

"Unfortunately no. All it takes is a jamming device that plugs into your power outlet. Anybody can buy one on the Internet."

"I'm surprised it doesn't happen more often then," Chuck said.

"Well, it also disables a phone or any other such device. Most of our clients are absolutely wedded to their gadgets. And really, it's quite an expensive way to steal a car."

"So you have no idea where the car went?"

"I don't know where it is now, but he didn't install the device until he'd been on the road for an hour. Thanks to that, we know he headed south on I-25 and turned east at Pueblo onto state highway 50."

CHAPTER 37

"WHAT THE HELL WERE YOU THINKING?" Dean yelled. She heard an *umph* from Kennedy—Dean must have shoved him.

She held her breath.

"If you're going to whine, at least tell me what you're whining about," Kennedy said in an even tone.

"You fucking tasered me. That was *not* part of the plan."

"Not part of *your* plan," Kennedy said.

"You were supposed to put a rag over my face and drug me."

"That someone my size could overtake you long enough to drug you wasn't believable."

"And you didn't feel the need to mention that before you left me twitching on the ground?"

"I left you angry and surprised. That helped convince the cops you were a victim, didn't it?"

They were co-conspirators. She searched for an element of surprise in that revelation, but failed.

"Did you follow my instructions?" Kennedy asked. "Exactly?"

"Yes, I followed your ridiculous instructions."

"I'm just making it easier for you to prove I was messing with you," Kennedy said. "Speaking of the ransom…"

Kennedy held out his hand. Dean passed him a briefcase. After inspecting the contents, Kennedy snapped it shut and set it down by his pack. He gestured toward Jayne.

"Well, there she is. As promised."

Dean looked at her for the first time. He seemed so cold she thought the temperature would drop as he approached her. He cupped her chin and titled her head up, frowning at the dried blood still on her face. He wiped his hand across his pants leg when he released her.

"You said you'd keep her healthy until I got here."

"I said I'd keep her alive and motivated to talk," he said. "Trust me, she's motivated."

Dean shrugged then leaned in toward her. She resisted an urge to spit in his face but not because she cared what Dean thought. Kennedy was watching like a praying mantis poised to spring.

"I thought it would be harder to get you away from your bodyguard boyfriend," Dean said. "It was a breeze. As easy as it was to get you to lean into the trunk. My idea worked quite well, don't you think?"

"My idea actually," Kennedy said.

Dean frowned. "We're done for now." He waved him away without looking back.

Kennedy blinked, then winked at Jayne from behind Dean's back. He went outside.

"What are you doing here?" she said.

"I've brought your ransom."

"No really. What are you doing here?"

"You have information," Dean said. "I want it."

"How did you find me?"

"You will tell me what I want to know."

The fool. He thought he was in control.

"You first," she said.

He shrugged. "Kennedy recognized your picture and contacted me. He kept asking me over and over again what I really wanted. He knew things about me I'd prefer he didn't, so I told him, and that's when he came up with this plan. He'll tie me up when we're through and the world will think I came here to save my wife." He leaned in and whispered in her ear. "Unfortunately, I was too late." He stepped back. "How's your memory now?"

She hadn't thought about her memory for days. Amnesia was irrelevant. The past didn't matter, only the fight for survival.

Dean sat in Kennedy's favorite spot, the dining room chair in front of her.

"Well," he said. "Don't you have anything to say?"

"You're a good actor. You must be a great politician."

"I am. I guess I should thank you, Plain Jane. The grieving husband played well with the voters. Becoming a widower might be enough for a senate seat."

He put his hands on her knees, leaned in toward her face.

"I need to know how you stole my money."

"I didn't." Then she thought of the cash and safety deposit box key in Creek City. "Why do you think I did?"

His grip on her knees tightened. Beads of sweat ran down his face.

"Because, my darling Plain Jane, you took $650,000."

Something about the amount resonated. It meant something, something she could almost grasp.

"You took it from a numbered offshore account." Each word was crisp, condescending, impatient. "My problem, Plain Jane, is that I need to know how you got to it. There are millions more where that came from and if you were smart enough to figure it out, then anybody could."

The veil over her past began to weaken.

He leaned back and started up a new tack.

"You surprised me," he said. "I married you for your looks, but it turns out you have a bit of a brain too. Isn't that why you did this? To prove how wrong I was about you? So tell me about it. Impress me with you smarts."

She shrugged. "I can't tell you what I don't know. And even if I could, I wouldn't."

"That's quite blunt to have come from you, my little Plain Jane," he said. "You seem to have reinvented yourself since I saw you last, so let me refresh your self-image. I wiped the grease off your face, literally and figuratively. I did it because you were the most beautiful woman I'd ever seen, probably ever will see."

"Then why do you call me Plain Jane?"

"I'm describing your personality, obviously, not your looks. I never cared that you weren't overly bright. As long as you were on my arm, every man I met envied me."

He ran a hand lightly up her arm. "I think I could learn to like the new you. I might even forgive what you did, if you tell me how you did it."

He leaned in and kissed her. It felt like a hard-boiled egg rubbing against her lips. She shoved him away.

"Come on," he said. "You know the significance of $650,000."

He cupped her chin in his hand and squeezed.

The gesture was familiar. He'd used it on her frequently, but only in private. He increased pressure on her jaw, and—

What felt like an electric probe sizzled through the middle of her brain.

She remembered.

How much she hated him, how much she feared him—him and the wealthy elite he belonged to. Their money, their influence, their power over everyone, including her: an emotionally battered wife who just wanted to go home.

She remembered the murderous rage she'd felt at her father's funeral—no, it was more than remembering. She felt it, every bit of it.

$650,000 was the amount she'd asked for to take her father to Germany for six months. It would cover a new treatment protocol, experimental but proving to be surprisingly successful with his type of cancer. Dean refused to pay.

Fury turned her vision into a tunnel with only Dean at its end. She raised out of the chair, intent on finding a way to hurt him.

"You killed my father." Her voice cracked.

"He died of cancer, you idiot," Dean said, shoving her back. Her hands were still bound in front, and she stumbled into the armchair. "Just because I have a lot of money doesn't mean I'd throw it away on your whim."

"My father's life was not a whim, you bastard!"

A sour acid coated her throat, a byproduct of having too many memories.

Fifteen years of private humiliation. Fifteen years pretending she was lucky. She smiled for the world and acted her part, then cried herself to sleep with Dean in bed beside her. He knew she cried because of him and he liked it.

"I paid for his funeral," he said. "And now that you've stopped pretending, answer my question."

Her anger was replaced by terror when she heard the boards of the porch moan. Lost in her emotional vortex, she had forgotten about the only man who mattered in this house.

Dean slapped her, opened-palmed and hard. The blow reverberated in her skull.

"TELL ME!" He put his hands around her neck and started squeezing.

She heard the screen door squeak. And then all she thought about was air, wanting, needing air. She flailed her legs, thrashing the only part of her body that could move. Her vision grayed, black at the edges with silver sparks…

Suddenly she was back in the chair, her famished lungs full of beautiful oxygen. When her vision returned, she saw Dean on the floor, a crimson spot blooming on his thigh as blood pooled and spread beneath his leg.

"You know," Kennedy said, "I can appreciate your feeling insulted by all that talk about how stupid you are, but I've got to ask. How smart was it to admit to getting your memories back, when amnesia is the only thing that's kept you alive?"

CHAPTER 38

KENNEDY DISAPPEARED INTO THE BEDROOM and returned with a wadded up piece of bedding he pressed to Dean's wound. Pale with shock, Dean threw it aside and spoke through clenched teeth.

"What the fuck do you think you're doing?"

Kennedy righted the chair Dean had knocked over, sat down, placed his right ankle over his left knee, and folded his arms.

"Jayne, your husband doesn't seem to understand the situation here," he said. "Why don't you enlighten him?"

"There's only one rule," she said, bending over the chair's arm so she could see her husband. "Do exactly what he tells you. No more, no less."

Disbelief and anger brought a tinge of color back to his face. "And if I don't?"

Kennedy took aim and shot him in the other thigh.

Dean struggled to access his Blackberry, face bathed in sweat, lines of pain etched deep along his face. The effort sapped the last of his strength and he let the hand holding the phone fall across his chest.

"You won't have service," Kennedy said. "You're in range of the signal jammer I gave you for the GPS. It kills cell phones too. Now lie still."

Dean raised the phone again, his breathing harsh, as he checked the reception. Kennedy stood and pressed his foot into the most recent gunshot wound. Dean screamed.

She searched for pity on his behalf and found none. Twice he had separated her from the man she loved. First her father. Then Saul. Dean deserved Jeff Kennedy.

"What do you want from me?" Dean said.

"Money of course," Kennedy said, "but I want to earn it. That should make you happy so stop being such a surly bastard."

Dean flinched but held his tongue.

"What I want," Kennedy said, "is two million of that off-shore money. Since you said there were millions more there, I'll assume I'm not asking for much. In return, I'll get Jayne to answer every question you have." He cocked his head. "You seem to have lost your grip on her but I assure you, I have not. So what'll it be? I suggest you not think about it too long."

Dean clenched his hand in a fist, pounded it on the floor. He spoke through ashen lips.

"How?"

"Easy. I've already set up my own unnumbered account for you to make the final payment—by the way, that's all set to happen at midnight tonight, right?"

Dean moaned as he nodded.

"Good. Then all you need to do is give me the account number, access information, and password. I'll drive far enough away that the signal jammer won't influence my Wi-Fi. If the information's accurate and the money's really there, I'll come back and we'll finish up."

"How do I know..." He paused for a shuddering breath. "How do I know you won't just take it all?"

Kennedy squatted next to Dean and patted his cheek.

"We're just going to have to trust each other."

He was gone about thirty minutes and when he returned, he gave Dean a bottle of water.

"The shock has worn off by now," Kennedy said. "It'll hurt more and more until I give you some medicine. I'll do that when we're through with the questioning. Don't want you to miss anything and think I cheated you."

He sat across from Jayne.

"All right, let's get started. How did you get his money? Don't leave out any details."

Jayne kept her eyes on him while she answered.

"Dean liked to brag about the money he hides in offshore accounts for his dummy corporations. He dared me to tell anyone, since I was listed as the majority stockholder and primary officer on most of them. He said I'd spend more time in prison for tax evasion than he ever would if we were caught."

"Sounds like I should have asked for a lot more than two mil," Kennedy said.

Dean started to protest, then shut up.

"Keep going."

"I knew where he kept the keys to his home office, so I started searching it when he was gone. I found a list of passwords and combinations taped to the bottom of a drawer, so when I found a hidden floor safe, I kept trying the numbers until it opened. Inside was information on every one of those dummy corporations and their offshore accounts. When I was ready, I did what you just did, created my own account and transferred the money."

"I saw the balance of that account. Why did you only take $650,000?"

"I meant for it to be symbolic." She shrugged. "Plus, I thought it was little enough that he'd eventually give up looking for me. I didn't realize he'd fixate on how I got to it."

"There you go, Calender, problem solved. Stop trying to hide behind your wife. Put your name for hers on the paperwork, change your passwords and combinations, and be a little more devious in how you hide the information. Are you satisfied?"

Dean mumbled something that might have been "Yeah."

"Tell me about your escape," Kennedy said. "How did you plan it? Where did you disappear to?"

"I put in a lot of time at the library, researching how to disappear. I learned if you want to stay hidden, you can never go back to the places or people you love. To leave Dean, I'd have to leave my father. That's why planning my escape was just a hobby until my dad died. I also learned how to create misinformation, like telling people my father was a murderer and I was deathly afraid of him. Things like that."

"Where did you hide?"

"In a rehab clinic."

"Really? Why?"

"More misdirection. No one would look for me there because I'm not an alcoholic. I was admitted under a false name. It gave me room and board for nine months."

Kennedy seemed impressed. She stole a glance at Dean. Despite the pain, he looked astonished.

"My plan," she said, "was to come out after nine months. Jane Calender would be forgotten. I have identity papers stashed in a safety deposit box in Albuquerque. I meant to use them and the money I had left to start a new life."

"My, my, my. What a crafty girl. What went wrong?"

"A private detective showed up at the clinic. I saw his ID. I thought Dean had found me, so I ran. When I got to Denver,

I decided living on the streets would be as good a hiding place as the clinic. I still meant to go back to Creek City for the key to the box in Albuquerque."

"How did you end up in Becker's tree?"

"I heard someone sneaking up on me while I was going to sleep and they yelled 'I've found you' or something like that. I thought it must be the private detective so I tried to get away. A guy grabbed my arm but I twisted out of his grip and ran as far and hard as I could. I left everything behind, even my shoes. I wandered around until I found the tree to hide in."

"The P.I. wasn't from me." Dean had to pause for breath halfway through the sentence.

"I get that now. I was so frightened I stayed hidden in the tree and then kept on running all the way into catatonia."

"That amnesia thing. It was real?"

"Yes."

"Where's my money?" Dean rasped from the floor.

She answered to Kennedy.

"I spent a lot of it on my escape. The clinic was $20,000 a month. I paid for nine months in advance. I had two minor fake identities made, ones that would stand up to a traffic ticket, $20,000 each. Then there's the identity I meant to use to start my new life. It could stand up to a full background and credit check, and it cost $60,000. I paid for forged medical records, a used car, and kept out some traveling money. I put $25,000 in cash in the safety deposit box in Albuquerque. The rest is sitting in the Caymans account."

"What's the account number?" Kennedy said.

"I didn't memorize it. It's with everything else in Albuquerque. The key to that box is with Saul."

"You've got two extra million," Dean got out between ragged breaths. "You owe me. Get that key."

"You're a fucking idiot." Kennedy bent over Dean and took

his phone. He scrolled through the menus. "Bingo. I thought you might be dumb enough to keep your passwords on here. Named the file *numsandpass*—very sneaky. At least it's protected. Want to give me the password?"

Dean shook his head.

"No worries," Kennedy said. "I can hack it."

Dean's hand stretched out in supplication as Kennedy cocked his pistol, the cold intent obvious on his face, a decision made that Dean's money and power and influence couldn't touch or undo. His arms flew out wide and he jerked like he had been shocked by a defibrillator when Kennedy shot him in the gut.

Kennedy straightened Dean's legs and folded his hands across his bloody midsection, making him look like he was already laid out in a coffin.

"I'd love to stay and watch," Kennedy said, looking up at Jayne, "but I've got things to take care of. You get comfortable and rest, if you want."

He left her alone with a dying husband.

CHAPTER 39

BACK IN THE CONFERENCE ROOM, Saul added a pushpin at Pueblo, and one along highway 50, heading east from Pueblo.

Ben Jennings came by.

"Didn't learn anything from those interviews," he said. "At least nothing that's going to help us find Jayne. One of the guys met Kennedy down at The Corner Store. When Kennedy offered money to steal a car, he and a few of his buddies jumped at the chance."

"Did he say anything to them that could be meant as a message for me?"

"If he did, they're too stupid to know it."

As Ben was leaving, Saul got a phone call. When he hung up, he took a highlighter and drew a yellow line along state highway 50, heading east until it intersected with state highway 287. He continued the line north, stopping at Kit Carson, where he placed a pin.

"What's with the yellow?" Danny asked as he and Chuck came in.

"It's the trail, so far. Ellington called. The Kit Carson town sheriff noticed a red Lamborghini at a tourist trap. No video surveillance, but it's got to be Calender."

"What was he doing there?"

"Not buying cheap souvenirs. I think Kennedy must have told him specific places to stop. I don't know what excuse he gave Calender, but he's leaving us a trail of breadcrumbs."

Danny moved up to the map.

"He can go straight north on county highway 59 or head east or west on state highway 40," he said. "Are you thinking east? Otherwise, he's practically heading back to Denver."

"Look," Saul said, tracing a semicircular line on the map. "The east and west ends of highway 40 both curve north and intersect I-70. So does the county highway north from Kit Carson. I think he meant to define our search zone. I'll have the Ellington guys focus on the place between the points where 40 intersects I-70."

"Do you really think Calender will lead us to Kennedy?"

"I think Calender will lead us wherever Kennedy wants him to. I hope to hell it's to him."

Within an hour, there was another pin on the map. An Ellington agent confirmed a sighting of the Lamborghini in Limon. Calender was caught on a convenience store's video surveillance paying for gas, and the attendant was certain he headed north from there.

When he didn't show up in Houston, FBI agents there executed a full court press on Calender's staff and attorneys, trying to figure out where he was and what he was up to. They discovered he'd withdrawn $25,000 in cash from a bank in Westglenn just before the plane took off that morning, suggesting possible contact from Kennedy and a ransom demand. Saul believed the money was more likely a payment for services rendered than a ransom, but he didn't care. Finding Calender meant finding Kennedy, which meant finding Jayne.

The bad news was, by the time the information got sorted out, it was too late for the FBI to start a full on search. Jayne would have to endure another night under Kennedy's control.

CHAPTER 40

THE LONG, DARK ROAD IN THE BAYOU she'd dreamed about all her life was a road where people died. In the dream, she didn't know why; she just knew it was true. She developed a fascination with dying, often trying to envision the moment of her death. Would dying hurt? Would she be afraid? Would she rather see it coming or be surprised?

She knew the answer. Surprise was best. Knowing gave you time for regret.

She heard a whisper from the floor.

"Jane."

Dean's shirt and hands were covered in blood so dark it looked black. A thin line of brighter red dribbled from the corner of his mouth and down his cheek.

His eyes fluttered open.

"It hurts."

He sounded vulnerable, like a little boy calling out in the dark for his mother.

She had no feeling left, no anger or pity for Dean, no terror over what Kennedy might do, no love for Saul. All she had was waiting.

"It'll be over soon," she said, sympathy no more accessible to her than a hanging piece of fruit in a tall tree.

She laid her head back down until her stupor was disturbed by a scraping sound. Looking over at Dean, she saw one leg in spasm. When it stopped, his eyelids opened.

"Thirsty," he whispered.

The bottle of water Kennedy left lay sideways on the floor, cap on. It was still half full.

She should give him the water. She'd do as much for an injured animal.

She knelt next to Dean, braced the bottle between her thighs, and twisted the cap with her cuffed hand. It took several rotations to get it off. She tipped the bottle at his mouth but pulled it back after a short splash across his lips. His eyes begged for more.

"I'm thirsty too," she said. "And I might live more than an hour."

She drank until there was only an inch left. She looked at the bottle, at Dean, then the bottle. He opened his eyes and his lips began to move, but no sound got out. Then he paused for so long she thought he might be dead until he gasped out his words.

"Didn't know... forgive?"

Anger shook her hands so hard the water sloshed in the bottle.

"Forgive you for what? Not loving me? Abusing me? Or hiring someone to kill me?" She tossed the remaining water into his face.

She watched as the color drained from it, listened as his breathing became irregular.

She remembered the way her heart had jumped when he first brought his car to their shop. She thought him a bright light in her dull and boring life and she'd loved him fiercely.

What a long way they were from that unhappy fairly tale.

His body jerked. He sighed but didn't take a new breath, his eyes open but no longer seeing, no longer pleading.

She clutched the empty water bottle to her chest, staring back at the dead eyes, and felt an eruption building. She struggled to stop it, damp it down, knowing if she gave in she would lose all control and not be able to stop. Struggled so hard that she barely noticed when the door creaked.

Kennedy reached down to raise her from the floor.

Was it her turn?

He wrapped his arms around her, stroked her hair, and murmured, "Shhhh, it's okay. Let it all out."

The dam burst. She would have fallen to the floor but Kennedy's arms held her up as she released giant, gasping sobs.

He picked her up, carried her to a mattress in the front bedroom, and gently laid her on it.

She held her breath so she wouldn't cry. At some point, she fell into an uneasy sleep.

She woke when the walls began to rattle and she heard the same squeaks and clicks as the day before. She opened her eyes to find Kennedy lying beside her, listening.

"Bats," he said. "In the attic and the walls. They're going out for the night."

He touched her hair. She flinched.

"You know, we aren't that different, you and I. We've both plotted to get free of the person we hate. I'm curious—how did it feel?" he said. "To watch him die?"

To hell with the rule. She refused to give him the satisfaction of an answer to that question.

He swung his legs over the edge of the mattress, stood, and pulled her up by her hands.

"You didn't answer me but I don't have time to deal with you right now. Tomorrow's a big day," he said. "I need a good night's sleep."

They stopped in the hallway in front of the bathroom. He took her cuffs off, stashing them at the back of his belt, and let her pee. He wouldn't let her near the faucet to wash her hands. She stood in the bathroom doorway as he pulled a collapsible ladder down from the hallway ceiling, exposing a hatch to the attic.

Three stout boards, about three feet long, leaned against the wall, and a flashlight sat on the floor next to them. She noticed heavy-duty brackets mounted on the ceiling alongside the opening. He must have rigged the boards and brackets as a lock.

He motioned her up, then reached down to pick up the flashlight.

She thought of wild, winged creatures, red-eyed with sharp teeth, hanging in hordes above her. She froze.

"Up," he said. "Now."

She needed no further encouragement.

"Lie down on your stomach when you get in," he said as she climbed.

She dragged herself over the edge and into the shadows. The scent of ammonia was worse up here, strong enough to gag her. She glanced at the rafters but it was too dark to see anything.

Kennedy climbed until he was halfway through the hatch and panned his light around the room. From what she could see, it looked like the attic had a solid floor all the way across. The middle of the room was clean.

"No bats now," he said. "You should meet them around

sunrise. They like the walls, but I've seen them flying around in here too."

He wrinkled his nose.

"That ammonia smell is bat shit," he said. "Glad I don't have to stay here and smell it all night. You have my permission to move around however you want up here, since there's no way out. Now, goodnight and sweet dreams."

He disappeared but briefly poked his head back up.

"Look on the bright side," he said. "My original plan was to take the old biddy, but then you came along and Becker fell in love. I'm sure you're glad I took you instead of her, right?"

Even though night had already begun when Kennedy locked her in, the day's heat was still trapped in the close attic space. Within minutes her clothing was soaked with sweat. Her thirst was maddening.

Her back and her palm burned. Her tongue felt thick. It was hard to concentrate—she felt lethargic, dizzy from dehydration and hunger. And Kennedy was right about bat shit. The smell was beginning to make her nauseous. She curled around her stomach, hoping the queasiness would subside.

All too soon the heat began to leach away, letting in the cool October night air.

Her sweat dried and she curled up even tighter, trying to stay warm.

Chapter 41

The manhunt cranked up in earnest at first light. Based on Saul's work with Ellington, the FBI defined the search grid as a rectangle with Colorado Springs and Pueblo as the western anchors. They started at the northwest corner and worked their way south and east, looking for abandoned houses in remote locations, as well as the Lamborghini.

They'd already put together a list of likely properties in the grid from tax rolls and utility records.

Representatives from the Westglenn Police Department were not invited to participate.

All those times Saul had worked on missing person cases, he had thought he understood what the family went through. He realized there was no way, without experience, to comprehend how long a minute could drag on, while every second of that minute you waited for news. And there was no way, without experiencing it, to realize how every phone call, knock on the door, or call of your name could flood you with dread that news had finally arrived and it might not be good.

Since there was nothing to be gained by hanging out at the station while the FBI executed their search, he went home.

Hoping to keep his mind off of worst-case scenarios, he started in on the punching bag in his basement. He struck at it until sweat dripped. He worked until his hands were sore and he was exhausted. Then he rehydrated and started up again.

He didn't stop until his phone buzzed. He took it off his belt, surprised to discover a text message. He seldom texted anyone.

The number was blocked. When the message opened, everything blurred but the picture on the phone.

It was a photo of Jayne, partially covered in a shallow grave. The necklace he'd given her lay on top of the dirt piled over her torso.

Her eyes were closed, her face pale.

The phone buzzed again. This time it was a voice call, from Chuck.

He answered with, "What?"

"Just letting you know we got a status call from the FBI," Chuck said. "They're halfway through the grid, still coming up empty. What's with you? You sound strange."

He closed his eyes, but still saw every detail of the photo.

"Get over here," he said.

Saul answered the door, red-faced, jaws clenched.

"What the hell?" Chuck said. "What's happened?"

Saul's hands were still taped from his work at the punching bag. He unwound the tape, bloody in places, yanked it off his palms. He nodded at his phone, on the table.

"Take a look." He crumpled the tape in a ball and threw it across the room as hard as he could. It hit the wall and slid to the floor.

Danny picked the phone up first.

"Fuck." He turned his head away to hide how upset he was.

Chuck took the phone, looked at the photo closely, and frowned.

"It isn't real."

"I agree," Saul said, clenching and opening his hands. "Goddamned son of a bitch."

Danny grabbed the phone and looked again.

"It isn't Jayne?"

"It's Jayne," Chuck said. "But she isn't dead."

"It's too early in the game," Saul said. "He's taunting me."

"And if she *were* dead," Chuck said, "he'd have left her eyes open. So we'd know it was a..."

He stopped.

"Call the Feds," Saul said, jumping into the uncomfortable lapse out of a superstitious need to keep them from picturing Jayne as a corpse. "This has to be traceable."

The text came from a mobile phone and it didn't take the FBI long to trace the cell tower that broadcast it, or to identify the originating number. Using reverse 911, they located an address outside Lamar. The house, at the furthest point of their search grid, was already on their site list. Positive they had Kennedy's and both the Calenders' current location, the Feds started loading their Hostage Rescue Team on helicopters. ETA to the house in Lamar was ninety minutes.

Representatives of the Westglenn Police Department were told to stay away from the hot zone. This was strictly an HRT operation. Saul, Chuck, and Danny had no recourse but to settle in at Saul's and wait for updates.

Less than an hour into the excruciating monotony, Saul got a call from George Levy at Prestige Auto Rental. The GPS for the Lamborghini had come back online. It was stationary, north of Jackson Lake State Park. The park was in north-central Colorado, in the opposite direction the HRT was traveling.

Chuck was immediately on the phone to the FBI task force coordinator.

Saul had taken his largest Colorado map down to the station but he still had one close to its size. He pulled it out of his closet and spread it out on the dining table. He grabbed two large red tacks from the office, stuck one on Lamar and the other on Jackson Lake State Park, some 250 miles to the north.

The FBI remained committed to its course of action. The Hostage Rescue Team was only forty minutes from its destination, convinced the car was an attempt at diversion by a suspect unaware the Feds were closing in. They requested that the State Patrol check out the Lamborghini, something they expected to result in minor evidence at best.

Kennedy had the full force of the FBI bearing down on Lamar and the State Patrol tied up in the north. Saul suspected both were merely diversions to keep everyone busy while Kennedy carried out his final manipulation. Saul was certain about only one thing—whatever Kennedy planned, he'd want Saul there to see it.

Saul moved his eyes across the map, back and forth between the marked sites. North to Jackson Lake, south to Lamar. Back and forth. He leaned forward, stared intently at the midpoint.

And found a speck of a town by the name of Last Chance.

A name dripping with irony.

He could already imagine Kennedy's call: "Meet me at Jayne's last chance."

He grabbed a Colorado road atlas from a bookshelf and yelled over his shoulder as he ran for the door.

"Let's go. I'll explain on the way."

CHAPTER 42

THE ROOF SHOOK, AND JAYNE HEARD a hundred tiny flutters. The bats were coming home. She tensed, put her arms around her head, and peeked out.

She knew she should be terrified but she wasn't. Perhaps she had run out of terror.

They slipped through holes in the ceiling with soprano squeaks, creating a rustling movement of the air she could feel. Very subtle, like a faint breeze. Most of them disappeared into a half-finished wall, but others dipped and flapped around her, a choreography that struck her as graceful, even beautiful.

The rumbling stopped. A half-dozen or so remained hanging from rafters. They were furry, not something she expected. Tucked up in the shadowy corners, wrapped in their wings, they seemed as vulnerable as she was.

Discomfort forced her to uncurl. The skin around the cut in her palm was inflamed and leaked a sticky yellow fluid. From the feel of it, her back was doing even worse. She was so thirsty she could barely swallow, and when she did, it hurt.

As if the bats' return had been an alarm clock, she heard movement downstairs. Water ran. The toilet flushed. The screen door banged. Something was dragged across the floor. Soon, an engine turned over and gravel grated as the car drove off.

She was drifting in and out of consciousness when a cramp in her calf contracted until her toes stiffened to a point. The wooden floor groaned as she rolled, moaning, and grasped her lower leg. She massaged the muscle and the knot slowly relaxed, but the cramp still hid there. Any sudden movement of her foot or leg and it would start all over again.

She was hot from the inside out but she'd long ago stopped sweating. Her eyes burned when she thought of Saul. And Mrs. Blackstone. Everything she'd worked so hard to find.

Her eyes burned but no tears fell.

Her body no longer had the moisture to spare.

CHAPTER 43

CHUCK DROVE WHILE SAUL CONSULTED the atlas for directions to Last Chance from Westglenn. Thirty minutes in, Saul's phone rang.

"It must be hard," Kennedy said, "being kept at home like a child while the big boys go rescue your lover. At least I hope they left you behind. Otherwise, you won't make it in time."

"What do you want?" Saul said, careful to keep a growing excitement out of his voice. Kennedy thought they were still in Westglenn. If Saul's guess was right, they were a half-hour ahead of schedule.

"If you leave now, and hurry, you find can Jayne's last chance before she dies—you'll understand the humor soon enough. My watch says 12:30. I'm sending directions to your phone. She dies at 3:35. Don't be late."

Kennedy disconnected.

Saul punched the dashboard hard enough to hurt his hand.

"We've got you, you bastard!"

"It's a straight shot until we get off US 36 at County Road LL," Saul said once he'd scrolled through the directions. "It's all county roads from there."

A few minutes later, Commander Morris called to inform them that what looked like a grave, dug into a gulch, had been found beside the Lamborghini. The state guys secured the scene for the FBI, who dispatched a forensic team from Denver. They'd be there within an hour. The HRT was only minutes away from their target location.

"It's a diversion," Saul said. "The grave is probably empty, but it's definitely not Jayne."

They rode in tense silence. The landscape looked the same in every direction: flat and empty, a string of utility lines running parallel to the highway, an occasional fence. Saul had never seen so many variations on the color brown.

As they passed through Last Chance, a hole-in-the-road with a faded old Dairy King, but no gas station, Commander Morris called again.

"Feds came up empty," he said. "There's nothing at their target location. They didn't share what they plan to do next or when. I don't think they even know."

"How much time's left?" Danny said.

"Two hours by Kennedy's reckoning, but our head start should get us there in ninety minutes." Saul studied a road sign as they passed it. "Keep watch for the next intersection. That should be our turn."

They navigated the directions easily. Time passed and apprehension mounted as they drove on gravel roads through miles of nothing. So far they'd seen only two farmhouses along the way.

He looked at his watch. "We should be there by now."

Over the last ten miles, their speed had slowed as the road they bounced along deteriorated.

"Here's CR JJ," Chuck said. "That's the last turn, right?"

"Yeah. It should be three miles from here, on the left."

The road became little more than two ruts in the unrelenting dirt.

"Twenty minutes left," Saul said about the same time Danny yelled, "There!"

The road came to a dead end at a house, not much more than a rambling single-floor shack. A small copse of trees sat some distance to the south. There were no vehicles in sight and no outbuildings.

The car crunched to a stop and they all got out, pistols drawn. Saul and Danny went for the front door while Chuck circled to the back. They entered within seconds of each other, finding nothing but two empty rooms with rotted floors. Jayne's necklace hung on a two-way radio with a note.

Call me when you find this.

CHAPTER 44

THIS WASN'T HER WHITE WORLD of catatonia, but it felt similar. It was inside her head more than outside, the body a disposable vessel for her thoughts. She sensed her mental connection grow thin, like a single strand of a spider's web strung across space in a last-ditch effort to hold onto life. Any disturbance and that tentative connection would break.

The siding rattled as a wind kicked up, battering the house in its path. Air slipped through cracks, brushing against her skin like feathers. Occasionally, a blast would form a high-pitched whistle. Was someone calling for a dog?

She felt it was time to leave.

The dog must have found its way home because she heard it knocking about below. It climbed the stairs, opened the a hole in the floor, and said something about needing to wake up. She wanted to explain she wasn't asleep, just leaving, but that was too much effort.

Water splashed across her face and she sputtered. She was shoved back into a body that ached and burned.

She opened her eyes, just a slit. Colors swirled around her.

"Here. Sit up some." A hand cradled her neck. "Take a drink. Slowly. Not too fast."

The colors began to take on focus.

Kennedy. He laid her head back down on the floor.

"Better. You rest a minute, then we'll talk."

He gave her more water. Her lips and tongue soaked it up. She took only tiny sips until he pulled the bottle away. He moved slowly, keeping an eye on the bats hanging above them, and retrieved a mug sitting on the floor next to the pull-down stairs. He fed her its contents—beef broth, cold and mostly flavorless. Her mind cleared a little.

"That should hold you," he said and settled crossed-legged beside her. "Becker will try to comfort himself with the idea that you were unconscious at the end, that you didn't suffer. I can't have that so I need you to stay awake enough to know what's happening."

She wondered why he didn't just leave her alone.

"It's not just about tormenting Becker. I could have played out the end game without involving you at all, but *I* would have known the difference. I need to know you suffered. It's important to my well-being."

He glanced at his watch.

"We're out of time, you and me. I know I've made you think that before, but it's for real now. Like I said, it's very important to me that you know when you die. Tell me you understand this? Promise me you'll stay awake."

He was making no sense—she was alert enough to know that. How could he kill her and not know if she was awake?

His shadow fell across her as he stood. She felt a vicious kick to her ribs, heard a popping sound inside her chest. Her scream was weak, pathetic. He reared his foot back for another blow and stopped himself, shaking his head.

"I don't have time for this," he said. "Here's what's going to happen. There's a bomb downstairs. It doesn't pack a big boom but I'll douse the place in gasoline before I leave. Between that and how dried-out this house is, the fire will be spectacular. The bomb is rigged to set off an alarm two minutes before it blows. Got that? A two-minute warning. You'll have that long to anticipate your death. Now tell me you understand."

She turned her face away from him.

"Answer me!"

He kicked her again, and she felt a rib give way with a tearing pain that caused a loud scream as another gust of wind rocked the house. He kept kicking until he'd forced her nearly to the wall. Then he squatted next to her, grabbed her head and made her look him in the eye.

"I want you to know that Becker will be close enough to watch the fireworks. He'll have to live with the knowledge that if he'd only known where you were minutes earlier, he could have saved you. And there's this."

He pulled a bottle off his utility belt and dumped the contents over her. The fumes made her eyes water.

"I was torn about whether to do this part or not," he said, "because I happen to like you. So you just remember as you're turning into a human bonfire, I would have left you to die from the smoke if you'd just answered my fucking question."

CHAPTER 45

"HE WANTS YOU TO CALL?" Danny held the note. "What the hell is that about?"

Saul slipped the necklace into his pocket and picked up the radio.

"This is a Midland camo GRMS radio. If he can communicate on this, he's within a thirty-mile radius right now."

"Do you think we're that far from Jayne?" Chuck glanced at his watch. "We've got less than fifteen minutes. In fact, if we hadn't left early, we'd be past the deadline already."

"Maybe he wants to give you the next set of instructions," Danny said. "We should get on with it. Call him."

A gust of wind came screeching out of nowhere. Saul barely noticed as he moved from the house to the yard.

"Let me think a minute," he said.

If they had not left early, the deadline would be already be past. Had Kennedy meant for them to get there too late? Was the radio a way to gloat?

No. If Jayne were dead, Kennedy would already be out of range and on the run.

"Ten minutes left," Chuck said. "Call the bastard."

Saul began squeezing his fingers to engage the radio.

The effects of the water and broth were wearing off, but adrenaline kept her conscious. All part of the plan, she was sure.

The thought made her so angry she kicked the wall. Excruciating pain raced through her body. The wall shuddered and she heard a chorus of high-pitched squeaks.

She reached for her necklace, a sign that she had really been loved once in her life. It wasn't there of course. It was no more accessible than the man who gave it to her.

Wait a minute. What had Kennedy said?

Saul was close enough to see her die.

If only he'd known where she was a few minutes earlier.

Maybe he could know.

With the last of her strength, she pushed herself up the wall and smashed her fists against it, screaming through her pain. She kept at it until her fists were bloody and her parched throat emitted nothing but a strained rasp. Then she slunk to the floor, back to the wall, and curled into a tight ball.

Kennedy wanted him to call, which was exactly why Saul wouldn't do it, not without knowing why. What advantage would his call give Kennedy?

"I get it." Saul dropped the radio into his shirt pocket. "Contingency plan."

"What?"

"The deadline was to get us out here as quickly as possible, but anything could have gone wrong. An accident, getting lost on back roads. He couldn't be sure I'd be in the right place at the right time. Calling on this radio tells him I'm in position."

"Okay, but where's Jayne?" Chuck said.

"Close."

Beyond the copse of trees, thunder started rumbling.

Saul braced himself for another gust of wind and glanced at the sky. There was a thin white haze but no storm clouds. All three turned toward the trees.

"What the...?"

An undulating stream of black began to swirl through the sky, folding into itself then spreading out again, always moving forward. Finally, as it swarmed above their heads, it could be distinguished as a mass of fluttering, squeaking bats.

"In daylight?" Chuck said.

Saul and Chuck sprinted for the car at the same time. Saul slid behind the wheel and Danny barely had time to get in the back seat before Saul floored the gas, spraying gravel as he drove like a maniac toward whatever had disturbed the bats.

CHAPTER 46

ONCE THEY REACHED THE TREES, Saul could see they had hidden the view of another, larger house. It looked to be in better condition than the shack they'd just left.

A barn sat behind the house, door wide open, but it was hard to tell if a vehicle was inside.

"Time?" Saul said as he slammed the brakes and ground the transmission into park.

"Five minutes after the deadline," Danny said, "but I thought it was bogus."

"Not totally," Saul said. "Whatever he's going to do, he'll do any time now."

They scanned the area around the house but saw no sign of Kennedy.

"I'll take the barn." Chuck took off in that direction, pistol aimed toward the open barn door.

Saul and Danny moved to opposite sides of the front door. There was smeared blood across the porch and down the steps. On a nod from Danny, Saul jerked the rusty screen door open. It squeaked as it banged against the siding. Pistol level and extended, he moved into the house, eyes searching the room. Danny positioned himself to Saul's right.

The living room was clear but the smears of blood stopped at a brownish-red pool on the floor. Saul frowned. It was a lot of blood, not fresh, but not that old.

They split up, Saul heading to the hallway and Danny taking the front bedroom.

After a quick look in the bathroom, Saul moved to the back bedroom. From there he entered the kitchen. It had a door to the yard and a view of the barn from the window. There was no sign of Chuck. Saul circled through the living room and back into the hallway, where he met up with Danny.

"Jayne's shirt is in the bedroom," Danny said, "It's got blood on it but not enough for that spot on the floor to be hers."

Unless she wasn't wearing it when the blood was spilled.

"What's that smell?" Danny said.

The house was filled with the odor of rot and dust and decay, but since Danny mentioned it, Saul identified another one. It seemed strongest in the hallway.

"Gasoline," Saul said.

Kennedy must have wanted him to see the place go up in flames from the shack.

"Jayne's in this house." He reviewed the layout.

No basement. No root cellar.

And no idea how long before Kennedy tired of waiting. He was bound to be getting impatient.

Where was she?

Saul thought he heard a sound, riding on the wind as another heavy gust kicked up. Then he heard it clearly: a low moan.

He looked up.

Three boards fitted into L-shaped brackets latched across an access door in the ceiling. He stretched his arms, found he could reach them without assistance, and knocked the boards free. They clattered to the floor. In four quick steps he was up the collapsible ladder, through the opening, and into the attic, his pistol moving with his eyes.

Jayne was on the floor in a corner. He holstered his weapon and sprinted to her side, alarmed at the blood seeping from her mouth and nose, more alarmed at the smell of gasoline her pale skin exuded. He felt the carotid pulse in her neck. Weak but still beating.

Jayne grabbed his arm. She didn't open her eyes but said his name and seemed to relax when he answered with hers. A loud alarm went off downstairs. Her eyes popped open, wide in panic.

Danny was waiting below the opening, looking around wildly, searching for the source of the alarm. Saul called his name as he slid Jayne down.

"We have to get out of here. Now."

They bolted for the door, Danny carrying Jayne, Saul right behind him, and they didn't stop until the car was between them and the house. Saul put his hands on his knees, bent over while he gasped for air. Danny laid Jayne on the ground and joined Saul in taking deep breaths.

Saul looked up at the barn while his breathing returned to normal.

Still no sign of Chuck.

He straightened and drew his pistol again, taking a step toward the barn just as Chuck walked out, one arm around the waist of a stranger whose arm was draped over his neck. They stumbled into the open air.

Saul pointed at the house and yelled, "It's about to blow."

Danny touched Saul's arm and moved past him.

"I'll help," Danny said. "Stay with Jayne."

Danny reached Chuck and slipped the man's other arm across his shoulders. The group limped along for another four steps before a deafening boom erupted and the concussion wave knocked them to the ground. The air blazed briefly, then the flames collapsed back into the house.

Black smoke from the huge bonfire formed a giant cloud that stretched for the sky.

Saul had flung himself on the ground, over Jayne, at the sound of the explosion. He performed a mental check of his limbs and took a quick look at Jayne. She seemed undisturbed. He touched her cheek, then pushed off the ground and ran.

"Chuck!"

"I'm good," he said and slowly pushed off the ground. "Danny?"

An answering groan. He was crumpled in a heap on his side. Wood fragments from the house dotted his back like shrapnel, ranging in width from toothpick-sized to one almost as thick as a knife. The entry wound was bleeding heavily. Saul squatted next to him, put a hand on his shoulder.

"I'm still here," Danny whispered.

The stranger stood. He seemed unscathed.

"Who are you?" Saul said.

The guy looked bewildered.

"He's what took me so long in the barn," Chuck said as he folded his jacket and placed it under Danny's head. "Best I could get out of him was that he was knocked out while unloading his car this morning at Jackson Lake. I heard him calling for help when he came to just a few minutes ago in the trunk of his car."

"That's how Kennedy got back after staging the Lamborghini," Saul said.

Chuck's gaze moved to the still body on the ground by their car.

"Jayne? Is she…?"

"Alive," Saul said, a catch in his voice.

"I'll keep watch on these two." Chuck pulled out his cell phone. "Go."

Saul returned to kneel beside Jayne and his breath stopped briefly when he saw the full extent of her blood-caked body and beat-up face. He could hear Chuck shouting over the wind and the roar of the flames.

"We're south and east of Last Chance. You can't miss us—look for the huge pillar of smoke."

Saul heard the distinctive whump-whump-whump of helicopter blades only minutes after Chuck's call, so it couldn't possibly be the medical evacuation team from Denver. When the craft got close enough, he identified it as a UH-60 Blackhawk with FBI painted on the side. The Hostage Rescue Team must have been heading north to Jackson Lake after coming up empty in Lamar.

The chopper neared the ground, but wind forced it to circle back up. It came in on the next attempt and landed by the barn just as two fire trucks pulled into the dirt and gravel driveway. They were followed by a county sheriff's vehicle.

There was no house left to save. The best the local fire crew could do was protect the barn and keep the wind from spreading the flames across the dry prairie.

As the roar from the chopper died down, Saul felt a buzz from the phone in his pocket. He read the text message, grunted, and closed the phone.

Chapter 47

"We've got injured!" Saul yelled when the first man got off the chopper.

He recognized Special Agent Prescott, who turned and said something. Two men carrying large black trauma bags jumped from the bird and ran up. Medics, thank God.

"One here," Saul said when they reached him. "And over there."

He pointed to Chuck and Danny.

"What happened?" the medic asked as he unzipped his trauma bag. Then he frowned and leaned in to sniff Jayne's arm. "That gasoline?"

Saul ground out a "yes" from a rigid jaw.

The medic whistled under his breath as he glanced at the blazing house, then turned to the business at hand. He did a quick assessment, opening Jayne's shirt, exposing bruises over her rib cage. He put a blood pressure cuff around her arm and tossed Saul a bottle of water from his bag.

"Give her a few small sips of water and wipe down her face."

Saul tilted the water bottle against Jayne's mouth and it dripped from her closed lips down her chin. He took the edge of his shirt and dried the moisture.

Her eyes blinked open, searching until they settled on him.
He held up the bottle and tried unsuccessfully to smile.
"Looks like I'm in charge of your water again."
She shuddered and touched his face.

The medic ran a rapid check of Jayne's vitals, then yelled at the
chopper pilot.

"I want us airborne and inbound to Denver Health and
Hospital's Knife and Gun Club in five minutes." He used a
nasal cannula to set up a small oxygen bottle, then moved on
to an IV setup. "Go tell them I need a gurney. Check with the
other medic first. He may need one too."

It took all of Saul's self-control to let go of Jayne's hand.

Danny was on his stomach, barely conscious. The HRT medic
worked to secure four gauze sponges around the largest of the
wood fragments in his back.

"Yeah, I need a gurney and some extra hands to get him on
it," he said in answer to Saul's first question. Saul then asked
him about the man Kennedy had kidnapped at Jackson Lake.

"He's in shock, but he can walk."

As soon as Saul relayed the medics' instructions, the pilot
stuck his head out the door and yelled, "Ready to lift in four
minutes."

Saul waited at the chopper for Jayne and Danny. Chuck
came to wait with him.

"Special Agent Prescott is staying here and driving my car
back," Chuck said. "I'm coming with you guys."

Prescott came up from behind them.

"You know, the whole Lamar thing was a ruse," he said.
"Kennedy used a remote server to spoof the caller ID on that
text message, deliberately pointing to the Lamar address as the

originating point. We'll eventually find the server, but at this point we're assuming he used a non-traceable, disposable cell. I doubt we'll ever know where he was when he sent that picture."

Saul watched the HRT team and the medic put Jayne on the gurney.

"I want your opinion, Becker," Prescott said. "What's Kennedy doing right now? Close by and watching? Waiting at your place? How do we get him?"

"He's on the run," Saul said, keeping his eyes on Jayne as he pulled out his phone and opened the latest text message. "This came in as you guys were landing."

The message read, "Sorry for your loss. I've got to run, but we'll dance again some day."

"She didn't die," Prescott said.

Saul stepped back as the team members lifted their patients into the cabin and began to secure them.

"He obviously thinks she did. If you get word out that Jayne's alive, I think his pride will bring him racing back to finish the job."

Prescott started nodding. "Our media experts can get the story of her survival circulating within the hour. How do we find him?"

"Make sure you say what hospital she's been taken to. He'll find us."

"You're willing to use her as bait?"

"He'll know I'm with her. You keep her safe and I'll be your bait."

"It's a deal." Prescott laid his hand on Saul's shoulder. "I'll have guards waiting for you at the hospital."

As the turbines began to whine, Prescott stepped back. Saul and Chuck jumped into the chopper and buckled up for the ride.

***

When they reached the ER, Mrs. Blackstone was already there, pacing between the reception desk and the ER entrance, purse swinging on her elbow. She cried out when she saw them and ran to Saul's side. He put an arm around her shoulders as Jayne disappeared behind the automatic doors.

"Is she okay?" Mrs. Blackstone asked.

"She survived," Saul said. "We'll see about the rest."

"Has she said anything?"

"She's been conscious, Mrs. B," Chuck said, "but she couldn't really talk. I can tell you nothing good happened."

"Oh my..."

Mrs. Blackstone looked ten years older. Saul pulled her into his chest. She sniffed against his shirt, then moved back and tried to look stoic.

A few minutes later, a nurse came and told them Danny was going upstairs for surgery. Saul walked Chuck to the elevator.

While they waited for it, Chuck said, "Oh hey. Forgot to tell you what was in that grave up at Jackson Lake."

"It wasn't empty?"

"Dean Calender. Shot multiple times with a .357 magnum."

"Kennedy killed Calender? I didn't expect that."

The elevator bell dinged as the doors opened.

Chuck got in but held his hand against the door to keep it from closing. "She's going to be okay. You know that, right?"

Saul pushed Chuck's hand off the door but as it closed, he nodded. And unlike earlier when Chuck had said pretty much the same words, this time Saul almost believed it.

"How're things in here?" Chuck said, sticking his head into Jayne's room in the ICU.

She was asleep. Saul stood beside her, holding her hand. Mrs. Blackstone sat straight-backed in a corner chair, trying to maintain composure at the sight of Jayne covered with bruises and bandages.

"Two broken ribs—one almost collapsed her lung—severe dehydration, some infection, but she'll pull through." Saul glanced up at the clock. "Danny still in surgery?"

"Yeah," Chuck said. "Shouldn't be much longer. I'm just here to check in. I better get back. Since Danny's got no family that gives a shit, I'm it for him." He motioned his head toward the hallway. "You take care of yourself, Mrs. B." He moved out of the room with Saul close behind. "Any news on Kennedy?"

"Not yet," Saul said.

"I don't like leaving you alone as bait."

Saul glanced at the guard posted by Jayne's door. "I'm hardly alone."

"You call me the minute you know something, right?"

"Get back to Danny," Saul said. "And when he wakes up, tell him I said he can partner with me any day."

"Hell no," Chuck said. "I finally got me a good one. I'm not letting him get away."

CHAPTER 48

SAUL HAD GIVEN HIS BEDSIDE SEAT to Mrs. Blackstone, who looked as though she was hovering even though she sat perfectly still.

"You look exhausted," Saul said.

"I am." Mrs. Blackstone sighed. "It's been a long few days, hasn't it?"

"Go home and get some sleep. She won't wake up anytime tonight. How did you get here?"

"I drove."

"By yourself?"

"George followed me. He said he'd wait and escort me home."

"Come on," Saul said. "I'll walk you out."

"No need," she said, rising and moving to the window. "See? My car's right up front and there's George parked at the exit."

He let her go but watched from the window. She turned as she put her key in the lock and waved. He waved back.

A bus let out a crowd of riders at the stop and most of them moved in groups toward the hospital. One passenger moved in the other direction. He stopped on the corner, staring down the street Mrs. Blackstone had just entered. Then he walked back to the parking lot, got in a silver Honda, and drove off.

About an hour later, a nurse walked in and spoke quietly to Saul.

"I have your brother on the line at the nurses' station. He says he needs to talk to you right away."

Saul started to refuse, then nodded. Kennedy knew he was an only child. This was just a way to get Saul's attention. He followed the nurse out and took the call.

"You're a crafty bastard, aren't you Becker?" Kennedy said.

"And you're predictable," Saul said.

"I'm not stupid enough to think I can get to Jayne again. At least not any time soon. But how about you and me take care of our business right now?"

"Sure. Tell me where you are and I'll send the Feds over to say hello."

"You could do that, but then your old lady friend would die."

Saul hesitated and Kennedy laughed.

"Go ahead. Try to call," Kennedy said. "She can't answer because she's in a car trunk with a bomb strapped to her chest."

All of Saul's emotions went into shut-down mode.

"What do you want?" he said.

"Simple. You for her."

"I don't trust you for shit."

"Well, I never said you were dumb. She's in an old silver Honda at the park across the street. Come alone. Any other scenario and she's dead. I won't wait all night."

Saul squeezed Jayne's hand and bent low to whisper.

"I have to go," he said.

Her eyes opened. He could tell she knew something was wrong, even if she was too drugged to talk. He wished he had words that could bring her comfort, put her world right again. He'd never been good with words but he had other skills. Skills that would keep Jeff Kennedy from ever hurting her again.

"I love you," he said and left the room.

Saul walked into the hospital parking lot. He made a quick call on his cell phone, and with a glance back to ensure no one had followed him, he cut down the street, away from where Kennedy waited. The park had a baseball field, and having played in the Denver Area Law Enforcement Softball League for many years, Saul knew the layout.

It had one main entrance, a road that ended in a parking lot in the middle of the park. The silver Honda would be there, which meant Kennedy would be in the darkness of the bordering trees. Going in from that direction would make Saul an easy target.

Fortunately, he knew a way in from an alley on the east side, behind a long wall of tall shrubs.

Saul moved slowly and quietly through the darkness until he got close enough to see Kennedy in the trees ahead. He was pacing and tapping his pistol against his thigh, his full attention on the road that led up to the parking lot and the car, which waited under the streetlight like a piece of cheese in a mouse trap.

Saul surveyed the area. The trunk of the Honda sat in full light, the hood in shadow.

He moved further back into the trees and circled to the other side of the park. Crouching, he approached the shadowed end of the car, then finished his approach literally crawling on his stomach. From ground level, he assessed the underside of the car and decided too much of the back end was in the light. That ruined his hope of getting under the trunk and trying to communicate with Mrs. Blackstone.

He scooted away from the car and squatted in the darkness.

The speed of Kennedy's pacing increased. He was getting antsy. Starting to wonder if Saul would show. That couldn't be good.

Saul stepped into the light. His pistol was pointed at Kennedy, who had his pistol up before Saul could take a second step.

"Stop right there," Kennedy said. "I can blow the whole thing from here."

Saul stopped, arms still stretched out, pistol aimed at Kennedy's chest.

"Why don't you?" he said.

Kennedy relaxed.

"Don't want things over too fast," he said. "This is way too much fun."

Saul lowered his weapon but kept his arms locked.

"How about you throw me the keys so I can let her go?"

Kennedy walked into the light, a huge grin on his face.

"And how would that benefit me?"

Saul gauged the distance between them.

"You said it's me you want." He took a step forward.

"Stay put," Kennedy said.

Saul was close enough to hear movement in the trunk. There was no sound.

"How do I know you really have a bomb in there? Maybe you're bluffing."

"You know me better than that, Becker." Kennedy reached into his pocket and pulled out a trigger device. "Wireless remote."

Saul raised his arm again, keeping his gun trained on Kennedy's chest.

"That doesn't prove anything," he said. "Looks like a mag light to me."

Kennedy started to breathe heavily.

"The deal is me for her." Saul half-shrugged. "I've got to believe she's in danger before I'll talk about making that happen. Put your gun down and I'll believe the remote trigger is real."

"So you can shoot me?"

"I'm standing right here. If a bomb goes off, it gets me, too."

"Okay." Kennedy came close enough to set his pistol on the trunk. Not so far out of reach he couldn't get to it if he needed to. He raised the hand that held the trigger, his other hand hovered over the pistol. "But do anything stupid…"

Kennedy had only a split second to process the look on Saul's face. All of his smugness was replaced by disbelief as a bullet slammed into his gut. He grabbed his pistol, but it slipped from his grip as he slumped to the ground. His breath whistled and a bloody bubble burst out of his mouth.

Saul kicked the pistol out of reach, bent over, and rummaged through Kennedy's pockets. When he found the key, he turned to the trunk, prayed he was right, and opened it.

The trunk was empty.

An audible sigh of relief created a vacuum, and a tsunami of hate rushed in to fill the void. He could feel his veins pulse as he squatted next to Kennedy and took the trigger out of his hand. It was real, although he'd seen no bomb for it to detonate.

"You love your wireless technology, don't you?" he said. "That's why Mrs. Blackstone didn't answer her phone when I called. You put a transmission blocker on her car. You never had her."

Kennedy opened his mouth a few times but was in no

condition to talk. Saul stood, the light from the parking lot throwing the cloak of his shadow over Kennedy's wound.

He shot him again, in the chest, then bent close. He wanted to watch the life leave Kennedy's eyes, wanted to be absolutely certain that this monster would never hurt anyone again.

His infamous blackened eyes were the last thing Kennedy saw.

Saul leaned against the Honda, next to Kennedy's body, until an SUV came racing up the road. It stopped in the parking lot next to them. Bob Ellington was the first one out. He walked over to Saul and stared at the body for a moment.

"Couldn't wait on us, huh?"

"Nope."

"How'd you get him?"

"There's a back alley he apparently didn't know about."

Ellington looked around the park, taking in every direction.

"Nobody heard or saw anything?" he said.

"Don't think so."

"Looks like good work to me," Ellington said.

"Let's hope the FBI and the police agree."

"Well, he was shot from the front, not the back. He obviously had a weapon and meant to use it. Did he fire any shots?"

"No."

"Want me to fix that?"

"I already have."

CHAPTER 49

SHE FELT SAUL'S HAND and heard his voice, low and steady, telling her she was safe. Words were easy and they couldn't stop her from flinching every time anyone touched her.

When she opened her eyes, Saul brushed his fingers across her brow and sat, very gently, on the mattress beside her.

She asked about the thing she feared most, even with Saul at her side.

"Kennedy?"

The overhead florescent flickered, casting an unnatural glow around the room as it crackled and buzzed.

"Dead," Saul said as he reached past her and turned the light off.

"You're certain?"

"I killed him."

A deep shudder shook her. Saul moved closer and she saw that his face was wet.

"He shot Dean," she said.

"I know."

The thought of her husband brought a reminder that a reckoning was required between her and Saul.

"Will you lie down with me?" she asked, wanting to feel the full length of his body before she made her confession.

He helped her roll to the side, straightened the covers, and crawled in against her back. He placed one arm lightly over her waist.

"Before you left to… you said you loved me?"

"Yes."

"I was afraid I'd dreamed it."

"No dream. I said it. I meant it."

"Saul… I have my memory back."

"That's good, right?"

"No," she said in a whisper. "You love Jayne Doe. I'm not her. I made up that personality as much as I did Cecelia Owens or Anne Thompson. The real me makes Martha look like a pillar of strength."

"None of that matters. I love you."

The declaration felt like salt in her wounds.

"You can't love someone you don't even know."

"I know you."

"You don't, and I'm afraid you won't like me—"

"I know you," he repeated. "And I'm in love with the person who had the courage to make those women up in order to survive."

A nurse opened the door, saw them wrapped together on the bed, and left quietly.

"I've done things," she said when they were alone again. "Things you don't know."

"I know more than you think," he said, "and it doesn't change how I feel about you."

"What do you think you know?"

"I've talked with Tomas Mendez several times."

She didn't know what to say. He did know things, if he'd talked with Tomas. And he still loved her?

"I have something of yours." Saul pulled his arm away from her waist. When his arm came back, he held his palm in front of her face, then opened it. A golden chain with a ruby heart poured down like a waterfall of hope.

A million thoughts exploded through her mind, all at once. Doubts. Hopes. Fears.

Hope won and she folded his fingers back over the necklace, wrapped her hands around his, and tucked it all against her breast.

"Mendez wants to see you," Saul said. "When you've recovered, we can take a trip to the coast. I'll take you home if you want."

She snuggled against him.

"I am home," she said, and felt the warmth of his magnificent smile, even if she couldn't see it.

ACKNOWLEDGEMENTS

There were many people who supported and encouraged me while taking on the task of writing my first novel. Special thanks go to Pat and Veda, who read the earliest pages, assured me the story was worth writing, and then waited impatiently for me to finish. Also, thanks to everyone at The Editorial Department, especially Renni. The book wouldn't be the story it is without her. And finally, I think no author can accomplish such a task as finishing a novel without the love and support of their family. Thanks doesn't even cover what I owe you guys.

www.ingramcontent.com/pod-product-compliance
Lightning Source LLC
Chambersburg PA
CBHW031544240626
47153CB00002B/370